THE WOLF'S MATE

A Grim Hollow Novel

TATI B. ALVAREZ

To Uncle Dan,
I acknowledge you.

AUTHOR'S NOTE

This book contains elements of:

- Death of a loved one (off page)
- Explicit sexual scenes
- Violence
- Strained family relationship
- Torture against FMC
- Fantasy war
- Hospitals and death
- Antagonist hurts family pet (not graphic or
- deadly)

Please make sure you are protecting your mental health. If you need more information send me a message on any of my socials.

Otherwise, happy reading!

Kraken
Lagoon
Nephilim
Land
Dragon's
Keep

Fae Court
an Forest
mon's Clan
Pixie Cove
MESCOS

PROLOGUE

Excerpt From _The Great War_ by the Spiritual Scholars

According to historians of times before, Mescos was once a thriving country full of supernatural creatures and their human companions. In Mescos, humans held their own power, given to them by their god to ensure peace amongst the supernaturals and humans. Humans strengthened their lands and provided immense strength to the supernaturals they mated. Together, their lands, kingdoms, and people thrived.

The time for peace was short-lived, though, as a new danger emerged.

Nephilim, giant winged creatures born from greed and hatred, appeared seemingly overnight. Historians differ in opinion on how these creatures came to be. Some historians argue Nephilim were sent by angry gods, while others say Nephilim traveled from lands far from Mescos. Their origins are still unknown.

The Nephilim brought darkness to the kingdoms. Their leader, Gadreel, led the slaughter of humans to gain their magic. Thousands of humans and supernaturals died in what historians call The Great War. Each human death brought power to the hellish winged creatures.

Knowing they had very little time before the Nephilim became too powerful, the six rulers of Mescos—dragon, pixie, fae, wolf, demon, and kraken—agreed to work together in order to take down the common enemy.

The war between the rulers of Mescos and the Nephilim happened at Dragon's Keep. The rulers of Mescos, their armies, and their human mates fought countless hours against Gadreel's people. Many fell in an attempt to rid Mescos of the vile creatures.

Knowing they were unprepared to slaughter the Nephilim, the Pixie King and his human queen came together, combining their magic as one. Upon seeing this, the other rulers followed suit and, within the mountains east of Dragon's Keep, a magical prison took form.

One by one, Nephilim were captured by the magic and imprisoned within the mountains. Gadreel, knowing his army would not win this war, cursed the rulers of Mescos before he was imprisoned. He damned the kingdoms: in one hundred years, if the rulers did not find their human mates, disaster would fall upon their people, and the Nephilim would rise again.

In his final act of rebellion, Gadreel used the last bit of stolen magic he absorbed from the deaths of humans and destroyed the portal between Mescos and the human world, effectively cutting off access to their human mates.

The leaders of Mescos won that day, but it cost them everything.

Over the next hundred years, the last humans of Mescos

died off. With no connection to the human world, the Nephilim rose again, escaping their prison in the mountains. Now the only hope the six new Kings of Mescos have comes from an unexpected ally known as Ender The Guardian. He alone possesses the power to travel between worlds and bring humans to their supernatural mates.

Little is known about The Guardian.

Today, the safety and future of Mescos hang in the balance. History is being written in real time. These accounts will be updated as necessary.

CHAPTER 1
HETTIE

I shouldn't be here.

When I left my house this morning, kissing my mother and my younger sister goodbye, I promised I'd be home for dinner. My mom smiled, though she wore it like a mask. Call it mom's intuition, but I think she knew something was different this time. Like maybe I wouldn't be coming home this time.

She was right, of course.

"How're you doing back there, honey?" Sister Tammy croons, tapping her fingers against the steering wheel to the beat of whatever Phil Collins song she's listening to.

"I'm fine." I don't mean for my answer to be curt, but I fear if I say more, the tears I've been holding back since this morning will finally spill over.

Crying will not change my mistakes. It also won't take me back to my family. And it definitely won't bring back my father. I'm not even certain I deserve to cry after everything I put them through.

Like I said, I shouldn't be here, but there's no other option. If there were, I wouldn't be making a deal with The

Guardian. We learn at a young age in Grym Hollow that only deeply troubled people seek him out.

I guess that's me. Deeply troubled.

"You know, this is the second person this month I'm taking to The Guardian. Rose Briar was in your place not too long ago. Remember Rose? The poor girl whose fiancé cheated on her with her own sister. Her sister is doing great, by the way. Really enjoying the mom life. But I will say, you young ladies are very brave. Mind if I say a prayer for you?" Sister Tammy launches into a prayer before I can even respond.

Her words are easy to ignore, especially since this isn't the first time I've been the focus of an impromptu prayer from Sister Tammy. She's Grym Hollow's resident nun by day and our taxi service by night. No one in town questions it, so I don't either.

A soft whimper catches my attention, and I look down at the golden retriever at my feet. Grass stares up at me as if asking, *"Are we really doing this?"*

Part of me feels guilty for dragging Grass into my mess, but a selfish part of me is thrilled that he jumped into Sister Tammy's car and refused to budge. He's the one connection I'll have left to my home and to my father. Grass was his dog, and since my father's passing, the dog has taken more interest in me.

Grym Hollow passes in a blur of old, historical buildings dating back to the town founders. The light from the city dims, and soon trees with orange leaves and street-lamps surround us. The chirping of crickets and the occasional hoot from an owl replace the chatter and music of the city.

Sister Tammy turns down her radio and straightens in her seat. Her old sedan comes to a slow roll, but I can't help noticing her grip tightens on the steering wheel, turning her knuckles white.

"There's no convincing you to stay in the car and come back to Grym Hollow? It's the safest place in America, you know. The Guardian can protect you here with his magic. Don't gotta run off. I'm sure your mother and little sister would prefer you with them. Isn't Clarissa's birthday coming up?" Sister Tammy drives the invisible knife deeper into my heart, immobilizing me.

For one second, I allow myself to think about what my life would be like if I stayed. The nights I would spend bouncing between men just to feel an ounce of thrill. Constantly chasing a high that did nothing but hurt my family. Ending up in holding cells until my mom and sister scrounge up enough money to bail me out, knowing this wouldn't be the last time. Knowing every cent should go to my late dad's medical bills.

I wasn't always like this. My father's death affected me more than I cared to admit, and instead of unleashing the pain in a healthy, less destructive way, I did everything and anything I could to run away from it.

I'm so tired of seeing my sister's red-rimmed eyes each time they bail me out. How she hugs me like she might never get the chance to do it again.

I'm tired of listening to my mother cry herself to sleep at night, missing the husband who should have never died. He died because of the stress I constantly put on my family. His heart couldn't take it anymore.

I'm also tired of being the town fuck-up. At least this way, something good will come out of the many mistakes I've made, and maybe my mom will have enough money to give my sister the life and birthday—she deserves.

With the last few dollars I had, I left my sister a necklace. Not the fancy one she has been eyeing, but still a pretty one. A locket with a picture of us from a Christmas party years ago. It's the last thing I was able to do for her, and I hope she understands why I had to leave.

"This is far enough, thank you." I ignore her question and wait until the sedan comes to a complete stop before opening the door. Grass doesn't wait for me to get out. Instead, he uses me as his springboard to jump out of the car and assess the area.

"That's a good dog you got there. I see why you brought him. Must be your guardian angel or something." Sister Tammy laughs, but it seems forced. She's itching to get out of here, just as much as I'm ready to get this over with and start my new life.

"Or something," I say and finally get out of the car. The moment I close the door, Sister Tammy floors it and peels out of the gravel driveway, leaving Grass and me behind.

The Guardian's house is only a small walk up the hill, which allows me some time to mentally prepare to come face-to-face with him again. I've only seen The Guardian once after seeking him out. He's not human, at least not entirely. His skin is an ashy gray, and he has horns protruding from his forehead. He stands a foot taller than a normal man, with muscles that seem carved from stone.

Intimidating in an understatement. The Guardian is completely nightmarish in his solitude and nonhuman-like appearance. And yet, he watches over this town as if he owes us a life debt.

I don't know how he got here, where he came from, or why he is here, and, frankly, I don't care as long as he can help me. I've never claimed to be a good woman, but this is one thing I can do unselfishly for my family.

Next to me, Grass barks, drawing my attention. At first,

I don't see what alerts him. He crouches defensively and growls low, warning me of the dangers ahead. There's only one reason my dog would act like this.

As soon as the thought crosses my mind, a house comes into view. It's nestled between trees, looking out of place in the rather desolate area. The house is a small cottage with a low-pitched gable roof. A covered patio encircles the front of the house, decorated with plants and a cozy seating area.

It's so ordinary; I almost think I'm in the wrong place. There's nothing threatening or life-changing about the house. Yet I can't help but feel that, the moment I step inside, my entire world will change.

Probably because it will, dumbass, I think to myself. Am I doing the right thing? Is my family truly better off without me? Yes. The answer is yes.

That sober thought has me gathering the courage to walk up to the fairytale-looking cottage. Grass whines next to me, and I lean down to pet his head. "It'll be okay." I'm not sure who I'm trying to reassure.

Before I can change my mind, I force myself to knock on the yellow door. I don't have time to gather myself before it swings open. On instinct, both Grass and I take a step back, but that doesn't seem to deter The Guardian.

The man before me is dressed in tailored black slacks and a white buttoned-up shirt. He left the top few unbuttoned, exposing the gray, muscular skin underneath. He shouldn't be attractive because he's not human, and yet, there's something hauntingly beautiful about him. A melancholy kind of beauty.

A certain sadness surrounds him, lurking just underneath the surface. He gives me a pleasant nod, but his eyes look past me as if looking for something—or someone—else.

"Good evening, Ms. Ortega. Blanchette, is it?" He steps out of his house. I peer past him, trying to catch a glimpse inside, but the door closes before I can get a proper look.

"I go by Hettie." Blanchette is a family name—one I despise and got ruthlessly bullied for in junior high. Hettie fits me better, though my family still insists on calling me Blanchette.

I suppose that will not be a problem anymore.

"Hettie, then," he says in a way that tells me he'll never use my preferred name. "Ms. Ortega, do you have the contract I gave you?"

I've only double-checked a thousand times before leaving my house that I have it with me. I spent hours combing through every single detail of the contract, so I know what I'm getting into. I may be reckless, but I'm not stupid.

I dig out the crumpled contract from my bag, handing it over. "I made one change. Grass is coming with me. That's nonnegotiable. I know it says I'll enter alone, or whatever, but I'm not leaving without Grass."

I sound more confident than I feel. I have nothing to barter with him. The Guardian isn't foolish. He knows this too, and yet he nods once, and that's all the confirmation I need. My body sags in relief because, despite the new trajectory of my life, at least I'll have Grass.

"Very well. Besides that, do you have any questions or concerns?" The Guardian asks.

Any sane person would, but I think I've established I'm far from sane. Especially agreeing to something so outlandish and reckless. Who in their right mind would willingly agree to be swept away from the world they know, only to end up in a completely different time and place, about to marry their king?

Someone who is finally doing right by their family.

Someone like me.

I never pictured myself settling down. Not when my life is in constant motion, and stopping leaves me to deal with emotions I'd much rather keep buried. If not, the hurt, embarrassment, and pity would snake their way in, pulling me down until I can't find my way out of the black hole I created.

I'm not thrilled about marrying a stranger—let alone anyone—but the way I see it, this is a mutually beneficial business deal. I get the assurance that my family will be free of my baggage and cared for, and my future husband gets whatever The Guardian promised him.

Still, I've been burned one too many times to fully trust this stranger. "My family will be taken care of? Just as you have listed out in the document?"

"Just as I have listed out. They will receive the financial assistance and resources they need to either improve their home or upgrade if they choose. Your rather extensive list of misdemeanors will no longer be an issue, and your family will no longer be responsible for those fees. Your father's medical bills will be paid in full as well," The Guardian explains. He reminds me of a doctor explaining their patient's prognosis, knowing they'd have to do this again right after.

I don't care how he speaks to me as long as he delivers what we agreed upon.

"How will I know you actually did your part?"

He sighs, but soon his mask of indifference is back in place. "Because, Ms. Ortega, this contract magically binds the signers to their word. Just as you can never leave Mescos, I'll not have peace until my end of the bargain is complete. I'm quite fond of my peace and am unwilling to give that up."

I pause, my body stiffening. I've read the damn contract over and over again and know there's no coming back. I've accepted it, but I still mourn the life I'm leaving. It's strange—perhaps even naïve—to believe him, but something about him makes me feel like I can trust him. Maybe it's his name. The Guardian. He wouldn't have that name if he wasn't in the business of protecting people...would he?

I'm also so damn tired of being lied to, I *want* to believe there are still good people in this world.

"Okay," I finally say, and my acquiescence is enough to get The Guardian walking to the back of his house. I take it as my sign to follow and have to jog to keep up with his long strides. He doesn't slow his pace for me, but he looks over his shoulder to make sure I'm not far away. Grass stays close to me, matching my speed.

"Mescos will be your new home—"

"Yeah, you keep saying that. What is Mescos exactly?" I interrupt, never one to let a question go unasked.

"Another realm. Quite different from this one. Your home will be in the Lycan Forest." The Guardian gives me no further explanation than this. Questions burn on the tip of my tongue, and I nearly ask them, until he stops so suddenly, I almost plow right through him.

At first, nothing remarkable stands out. Small rocks are laid out in a large circle before us. In the center is an archway made of stone; moss and vines cover the pedestals. The Guardian touches the arch, and slowly, a shimmer appears. A creamy-white layer that looks like satin covers the opening of the archway.

"What the fuck is that?"

If the Guardian is upset by my vulgarity, he doesn't

show it. Instead, the giant of a man takes my hand. His grip is surprisingly gentle, and his hands are soft against my own.

"This, Ms. Ortega, is the portal we will use to get to your new home." He starts moving forward. Whether of my own volition or because he's pulling me, I move with him, pulling on Grass's collar so he stays close. "No more dallying. Your alpha is waiting."

My...what?

Before I have the chance to process The Guardian's words, we step through the shimmering veil, and the world around me is no more.

CHAPTER 2
HETTIE

"What the hell was that?" I choke out, falling on my ass in the dirt. The door—or portal, as The Guardian called it—felt like riding a roller coaster in pitch darkness. It wasn't scary as much as it was disorienting and something I would love to never experience again.

Of course, The Guardian looks like he stepped off the fashion runway. He offers me his hand, and I allow him to help me up. Grass barks behind me, letting his displeasure be known.

"Me too, dude," I mumble, shakily getting to my feet with The Guardian's help. Soft fur nuzzles against my leg, and Grass licks me with his slobbery tongue.

Once my world stops spinning, I take in my new surroundings.

We stand on a dirt path in the middle of a woodsy area. Trees the size of three-story buildings loom over the town, providing protection from the sun. All around me are beautifully built cabins, varying in size. The air smells of burning logs, reminding me of cozy nights by the fire. I feel like I've stepped into a Hallmark holiday movie.

Behind us appears to be a market full of women, men, and children weaving in and out of stores. Large dogs, far larger than any dogs I've seen before, walk amongst the crowd. A few people catch my eye, but quickly turn away to whisper something into their friend's ear. I know they are talking about me because they keep looking back.

I fucking hate when people talk about me behind my back. It sets off my rage as if a switch flipped inside me. I must have taken a step toward the gossiping crowd because The Guardian's hand wraps around my forearm.

"I advise you to keep your anger in check. Need I remind you that you are amongst shifters? Wolves, to be exact. You're out of your depths here, Ms. Ortega." He manages to make his firm tone sound gentle.

Wolves? I read and reread the contract at least a million times and could never find out the supernatural entity The Guardian alluded to in the contract. But his alpha comment from earlier now makes sense. And the "dogs" walking around the town...aren't dogs at all. I wait for fear to set in, but my emotions are all over the place right now.

Feeling like a chastised child, I nod once because The Guardian is right. I'm way out of my league here. I'm no stranger to fights, but that was back in Grym Hollow. This is quite literally a completely different world, and no matter how much these people may look like me, they aren't human. Not entirely.

"Come. The packhouse is this way." The Guardian takes off in the direction he points to.

"A packhouse?"

"Yes," The Guardian says, and I wait for him to continue, but he doesn't. This man is obscenely obtuse.

"What's a packhouse?" I try again, keeping my tone light.

"It's a house for the pack."

I fucking lose it.

Or I would if this man didn't scare the living shit out of me. So instead, I silently scream, clutching my bag to my chest and follow after him.

Grass, clearly annoyed with my slow pace, runs up to The Guardian and barks playfully. "Traitor," I whisper, and I swear The Guardian laughs.

We walk in silence the rest of the way to the packhouse, away from the small market. We pass more paved dirt roads that branch off into what look like small neighborhoods with more cabins. Some have laundry hanging from a wire outside, while others have beautiful gardens or a firepit.

It's all so strange and yet...comforting in a weird way.

The Guardian stops abruptly, and Grass does the same. I nearly trip over my dog's tail and curse under my breath.

In front of us stands a large wooden castle. It's the only way I know how to describe it. The house is at least three times wider than the ones we passed, and two, maybe three stories tall. It reminds me of a cozy hotel, the ones run by an elderly couple who feed you stale cookies and burnt coffee.

"This is the packhouse," the Guardian says, and this time, he elaborates. "Think of it as what you would call a city hall. It's also the home of the King Alpha, so it will be your home too."

My jaw drops. "You've got to be joking." Surely he doesn't mean this extravagant house will be where I live.

"No. I hardly ever joke." His serious tone nearly makes me boil over with anxious laughter.

I have only ever lived in one house my entire life. A

shitty two-bedroom home that gets too hot in the summer and too cold in the winter. Clarissa and I shared a room, but it's so small that only one bed fits in there comfortably.

My parents' room is even smaller.

Still, my parents took great pride in that shitty house, doing their best to keep it clean and free of clutter. Even after my father passed, my mother did her best to keep the house running as normal. Because I knew how blessed they felt to even have a home, I never complained about our living conditions. At least not to my family.

But looking at what will be my new house, it now seems...excessive. Does one man really need all this room?

I mutter the question out loud, and The Guardian answers, "He's not the only one who lives here. He has a room for his second-in-command, one for his family, and the employees have staff quarters they are permitted to live in if they so desire. Plus, it's open most days for the pack to come and go as they please."

That makes me feel a little better, but only marginally.

"Lady Blanchette, welcome to Lycan Forest," a deep voice says, and I immediately snap my attention to the front entryway of the house.

A man stands at the top of the stairs, an inviting smile on his face. He looks no older than me and carries himself with a sense of importance. Certain. Collected. The man has dark short-cropped hair, deep umber skin, and eyes that remind me of storm clouds, a beautiful shade with specks of gold.

The man is shirtless, showing off his well-defined muscles, abs that look chiseled from stone. He's also tall. Like *really* tall. His body eclipses the door, and I bet he has to duck his head to get inside.

While I stare at this man like a fucking moron, he

descends the steps of the packhouse. Then, because I apparently live in a Jane Austen novel now, the giant man bows. I'm left to look like a damn idiot. Am I supposed to bow back? Curtsy? High-five?

I settle on a tight smile and the slightest nod, which seems to not offend him.

"Ender, it's a pleasure to finally meet you," the man says to my companion.

"Likewise, Thorne," Ender says, but I'm still stuck on the fact this man—Thorne—called him Ender.

"Your name isn't The Guardian?" My brow furrows, and both men turn to look at me with varying expressions. Thorne grins, and Ender looks bored.

"No. It's more of a title," he gives me a straight answer for once. I take it as a solid win.

Not one to be left out, Grass hurdles himself at Thorne's feet, growling low in the back of his throat. "Grass, stop." I reach for my dog, but Thorne puts his hand up.

"It's fine," he assures and crouches down. Grass barks once, clearly uneasy, but then Thorne reaches out his hand. I'm about to tell him to be careful when he lets out his own low growl.

Grass's body slowly relaxes. The menacing dog from mere seconds ago is now wagging his tail, licking Thorne's outstretched hand. "We're kindred spirits," he says, as if I should understand.

For whatever reason, Ender seems satisfied by their interaction, and even though I hardly trust Ender, I trust Grass. He's always looked out for me and is a good judge of character. So, if he likes this man, then so do I.

"So," I say once Grass stops licking Thorne, "I take it you must be my new husband."

It takes me a moment to realize Thorne is laughing. My face gets hot, warmth rushing into my cheeks.

"I'm sorry, my lady, but I'm afraid I'm already happily mated. I'm simply the greeting party because our King Alpha, your soon-to-be mate, had something come up. But he wanted to make sure someone was here upon your arrival."

"How fucking kind," I mumble under my breath. Good to know my betrothed is an ass who can't even be bothered to show up to greet me himself.

Ender places a hand on my back. It almost feels like he's comforting me until I realize he's pushing me forward, toward the packhouse. "I'm afraid I can't leave until I see your King Alpha. It's part of the contract."

Ender seems put off that he has to stay longer than necessary, but I'm not sure if that is him being rude or just his natural state.

"Of course. He's running late, but we will meet him inside. If you'll follow me."

Thorne doesn't wait for us to respond. He turns on his heels and heads up the entryway.

"Let's go meet your mate, shall we?" Ender offers his arm to me, which I take. Right now, he's the only one keeping me upright.

Silently, we fall in line behind Thorne.

CHAPTER 3
RIP

Today, of all days, my cousin decides to defy my orders.

My patience runs thin. I'm on edge, and the wolves around me notice. Most of them are keeping their distance, not wanting to provoke my anger any more than Tallie already has. She's one of the only people here who can push my boundaries and not end up with a slashed throat.

Though she's testing that theory today.

Especially since I should be meeting the future Luna of our pack right now, but instead I'm waiting for my cousin to be dragged back into my office. Tallie's a fast little thing and pulls out of the guard's grasp. "I don't need to be manhandled, Rip," she growls.

"No, you need to be chained to your house so I don't have to worry about you," I snap.

"I'm not a child!"

"Then stop fucking acting like one." The words come out harsher than I intend, and Tallie bristles, her head bowing slightly in subservience. Guilt washes over me, but only for a moment before I push it aside, filing it away for later.

Tallie doesn't respond, but I didn't expect her to. The few guards around us have the decency to pretend they don't hear the fight between cousins. Still, this moment feels too personal to have my usual guards around me. "Leave us."

None of the alphas hesitate. They bow, showing their respect, before breaking away from us. I don't speak until I hear the alphas' footsteps fade down the hall. "I needed you here today, not gallivanting through the forest with patrol. You could have been hurt by the Nephilim or rogues."

Tallie brushes a stray curl off her forehead, tucking it behind her ear. She wears it down today, her long, dark brown hair falling in bouncy curls. "I was with a bunch of alphas. They wouldn't let me get hurt, and, for the record, I can hold my own in a fight."

Tallie then barrels over, pulling something out from her dress pocket. It takes me a moment to realize it's the leather-bound journal I gifted to her on the Goddess's Moon celebration.

"I went because of this." She shoves the journal in my face, far too close for me to make out. "Oops, sorry."

She's not.

I take the journal from her hands and quickly look over the pages. A drawing of purple flowers takes up the left side of the journal, with arrows showing what each part is. Tallie has a map of Lycan Forest on the other side with red and black X's.

"I've no clue what I'm looking at."

Tallie frowns, clearly unimpressed with my inability to decipher her cryptic message. "I'm keeping track of where we've searched for wolfsbane. The red X's are places we've searched before, but the black X's are places I believe wolfs-bane may be growing."

Now *that* information interests me. Wolfsbane is a healing plant for my people. The search for wolfsbane has been a fruitless effort and continues to be a point of tension in my pack.

"I went with the patrol so I could search here." Tallie points at a black X only a mile away from town, near the stream many of the pack go to when they want to cool down after a hot day.

"Did you find anything?" I attempt to hide the desperation in my voice. Wolfsbane would go a long way to help curing my people.

"No."

The minuscule sliver of hope I allow myself to feel evaporates. I close the journal and hand it back, a heaviness in the pit of my stomach. "Then you risked yourself for nothing."

"Not for nothing, Rip. I—we—had to know. I want to help you search for a cure. You may want to carry the burden of keeping our pack safe alone, but those who care about you won't allow that to happen."

Except it *is* my burden to carry alone. The pack is mine to protect and lead. I accepted that task the moment I became King Alpha. My pack is counting on me, and I refuse to be the alpha who lets his people suffer. We are going through a dangerous time—an ancient curse is coming for my people. How do you fight something you can't see?

Which is why I contacted Ender. It was the last thing I wanted to do. No alpha wants to admit they need help, but my refusal to ask for or accept help has only made things worse. Ender helped the Dragon King, Malix, and I'm counting on him to do the same for me.

"Never mind that, we need to go." I wave off her concerns but make a mental note to look through her journal more extensively at a later time. "Ender is here."

"What?!" Tallie's eyes go comically wide. "That's today?"

"It is, and we are late to meet my wife."

DESPITE KNOWING OF OUR GUESTS' arrival, I'm not prepared to see Ender or the human he's dragged through the portal when I enter the dining room. Tallie trails a few steps behind me, her curiosity palpable. Ender is a symbol of my weakness and inability to protect my pack. I waited for as long as I could, probably longer than I should have, but King Malix was right. I can't protect my pack without his assistance. Not when enemies are closing in.

On my orders, Thorne brought Ender and the human into the dining room. It rarely gets used, save for welcoming new guests. There haven't been any visitors in a while since we closed our borders.

My eyes scan over the poor girl next to Ender. It's the first time I have ever met a human. The last human in our pack died nearly seventy years before I was born. Because of this, I know little about them besides their short life spans and fragility. They're weaker than omegas, the lowest-ranking members of any pack.

The woman before me stands a measly five feet and some inches tall, if that. Long, jet-black hair hangs past her breasts. She's in a tight cotton shirt, the color resembling that of a rose. It does little to hide the curves underneath.

Large breasts and a flat stomach. My guess is she didn't get her body from working out, but rather lack of food. Ender has told me very little about my new mate, but he did mention she is used to going without.

Without what, though? Just food? Judging by the wear and tear on her clothes, I expect it to be a lot more than just nutrition. My wolf growls, unsettled. He doesn't like that his Luna has gone without.

One of her arms is full of black ink, depicting designs ranging from flowers and birds to a serpent wrapped around her shoulder. They tell a story I'm not yet privy to.

My wolf purrs with approval.

I'm still hesitant, though.

Ender extends his gray hand for me to take. It feels like shaking hands with stone, which I suppose isn't far off. "King Alpha Rip," he gestures to the girl, "this is Blanchette, the new Luna of your pack."

Not yet, she isn't. Even as I think it, my wolf growls. He's clearly settled on this stranger, not seeing her as a threat, but I'm not in the business of taking risks these days.

"It's Hettie," the human says, scowling at Ender. Blanchette—or, rather, Hettie—crosses her arms over her chest, pushing up her ample cleavage. She doesn't greet me, and I make no attempt at greeting her either. I'm shit with small talk anyway.

"You have read over the contract then?" Ender asks when I don't immediately respond. My focus remains on the woman at his side.

I offer him a curt nod. I've read and reread the same damn contract every day for the last fortnight, combing through each section until I nearly memorized the points.

Countless late nights with Thorne and Tallie, going over every possible outcome.

I nearly refused Ender's help, but then the first wolf fell to the cursed sickness.

Followed by a dozen more.

It wasn't gradual; it happened so fast.

And more would fall unless I find my human mate. Ender is the only one able to bring humans to Mescos, so, really, there was no choice at all.

And here she is, standing right in front of me, looking both curious and disgusted by my presence. I can work with that.

"Then I need not remind you that her safety is imperative to your future," Ender says.

"I know that," I snap, unable to hold back my ire. "She'll be protected."

"*She* has a fucking name, and *she* doesn't like when you talk about her as if *she* isn't here." Hettie pushes her way past Ender, straight to me. This close, I see fire glowing in her eyes.

My mate has a temper. She's going to be fun to break. And if she's good, maybe I'll put her back together again.

"Is there anything else we need to discuss?" I ask Ender, ignoring the human, which only seems to piss her off more.

Ender sweeps his gaze around the room before landing back on me. "Nothing, Alpha. I will be in touch." With no further goodbyes, Ender takes his leave, opening up a portal with just a flick of his wrist.

Tallie audibly gasps when she sees the portal, something that has been missing from this world for so long to keep our human mates away, thanks to the Nephilim. Ender still possesses the ability to travel between worlds, though no one knows why. He uses it sparingly, though, and has just recently brought humans over with him.

He holds his secrets close, but his involvement is not out of the goodness of his heart. This I know.

The portal closes once Ender is through, leaving Hettie in my care for the first time. I stare down at the human before me. Too small and fragile. She won't be permitted to walk around without protection. I don't fear any of my pack members hurting her, but I can't say the same for the rogues plaguing our land or the Nephilim.

Another item to add to my list. Keep the Luna alive.

Hettie stares at me expectantly, waiting for me to say something. So I do, the first thing that comes to my mind. "You smell like a dog."

That's clearly the wrong fucking thing to say because her brown cheeks grow red. I swear, if she had little fangs, they would be bared right now. The thought is almost amusing.

Though, not to her, because Hettie growls, "You would know that smell, wouldn't you?"

I'm not sure if she's trying to insult me by comparing my dire wolf to a dog, or if I also smell like a dog, but I don't get the chance to ask because a large golden beast rounds the corner and dives straight at me.

CHAPTER 4

HETTIE

Grass barrels across the room, making himself known in the most Grass-like fashion possible. The oversized dog knocks into a chair, tipping it over, and races past me to launch himself at Rip.

Oh my god, I think he's going to maul my not-quite-yet husband. "Grass!" I don't give a shit if Grass hurts Rip, but I don't want this man hurting the only family I have left.

Rip catches him before they topple over, and, much to my dismay, Grass's dramatic leap into Rip's arms wasn't to maul him to death. No, the big baby licks his face, wagging his tail like he does when I offer him an extra treat before bed.

This is twice now that Grass excitedly greeted a stranger. So much for my big protector. "You're a damn teddy bear," I sigh.

To further prove my point, Grass nuzzles his head against Rip.

Great.

Well, at least one of us is happy.

"That's Grass, Hettie's dog companion," Thorne speaks up from behind Rip.

"Grass?" He narrows his eyes. "Why would you name your dog Grass?"

I don't appreciate the judgment I hear in his tone, and I glare. "Because he likes to roll around in grass."

"I see. How...creative," Rip says dismissively. He turns away from me—my damn dog still in his arms. Even from behind, Rip is an intimidating figure. His tight shirt stretches obscenely over his muscles, giving a show of each dip and curve of his body.

I'm unable to control my gaze as it goes straight down to his perfectly rounded ass. I've never considered myself an ass girl, but seeing Rip's has me all but salivating. Rip is what wet dreams are made of.

Too bad he has the personality of a rusty nail.

"I'm going to go show Hettie to our room," Rip says to Thorne and the woman next to Thorne. No one said anything about sharing a fucking room.

"I would rather go to Thorne's room," I mumble under my breath, but before I can say any more, Rip whirls back around, finally letting Grass go.

He closes the distance between us, and I have to tilt my head up to see him properly. His nostrils flare, brown eyes narrowing. There's a slight red flush to his bronze-colored skin, hinting at his barely contained anger.

"Let's make one thing very clear, *human*. You are mine. Whether or not you like it, you belong to me. And no Luna of mine will ever speak of another man's room. Not unless you wish to face the consequences."

Anger coils low in my belly, twisting and churning until nothing but bitterness is left. "I'm yours?" My voice comes out barely above a whisper, soft but not weak.

Many men in my life have thought they owned me. My body. My soul. My heart. Every piece of me has been wrongfully claimed by men who saw me as nothing more than an object. A pretty thing to have on their arm for the night. Coming to Mescos isn't just a fresh start for my family, but it's a fresh start for me too. Rip will not take that away from me.

"I belong to nobody. Even when I become your wife, I don't fucking belong to you. Do you understand me?" I'm chest to chest with Rip, and our size difference has never been more obvious.

If Rip wants to overpower me, there is nothing I can do to stop it. Not only is he the biggest man I've ever seen, but, according to what Ender said, he's also a fucking wolf. I'm just a woman with too much baggage and a loud mouth that has gotten me into many compromising positions.

I half expect him to show his dominance. Men with power don't like to be challenged and are all too willing to put a person in their place; doesn't matter if they are "loved" ones or not. Keeping the power in front of an audience is always most important.

Rip leans closer. So close I can smell his piney scent, reminding me of the trees in my front yard during autumn. My body tenses, waiting for him to react.

"Hettie." I can't decipher his tone. He's not smiling, and yet he sounds amused, which is...not what I'm expecting.

Then he lifts his hand. Flashes of callused hands, drunken nights, and police sirens replay in my mind. My traitorous body flinches, and Rip stills next to me. The room falls into silence; I'm not sure I'm breathing.

After a tense moment, Rip growls, "Why did you flinch?"

Nervous laughter builds inside me, threatening to burst

free, but I tamp it down. I don't answer because I'm not quick enough to come up with a lie. Some secrets are better locked away.

The woman who walked in with Rip steps forward. "Rip, you have a meeting to go to, remember? Let me show Hettie around, okay?"

For a moment, I think Rip will argue. He continues to stare at me as if he can dig inside my soul and extract all my secrets. The thought is terrifying. Finally, he drags his gaze away and nods once.

"Keep her safe," he barks and stomps out of the room, taking the heavy tension with him.

Thorne smiles at me once, bowing slightly, and follows Rip out. He casts one lingering glance over his shoulder to the other woman in the room.

My first meeting with my future husband didn't go well, but I had very little hopes it would. After all, this marriage provides us both with something we want. This isn't a love match, but I don't regret leaving my family for this, knowing they are finally going to be free of burdens.

Free of me.

"I'm Tallie," the woman next to me says. She's a pretty girl, with the most beautiful curly hair that hangs down to the center of her back. Her kind, golden eyes are inviting, and I instantly like her.

"Rip is my cousin. He can be...difficult at times." I can't hide my scoff. Her red lips pull up into a bright smile. "Okay, maybe a lot of the time, but he's honestly not so bad. I promise he has a big heart."

"I'll take your word for it." Though I don't get my hopes up that the big bad wolf is actually gentle and loving.

"So, would you like a tour around Lycan Forest? Or, if

you're tired from your travels, I can show you to your room now, and we can do the tour tomorrow," Tallie offers.

I can't sleep even if I want to. My brain is too wired, with far too many questions begging for answers. What is this place? Are they really wolves? What is my purpose here? What does it mean to marry the King Alpha? The contract wasn't specific, and speaking to Ender is as easy as speaking to a brick wall, so questions are impossible with him.

Ender wasn't very forthcoming with information. The contract was thorough, but it did little to ease my nerves of this unfamiliar world. My place is to marry the King Alpha and help save his kingdom from outside threats.

No idea what said threats are or how me, a fuck-up from Grym Hollow, can help anyone, but Ender stressed that I'm the only one who could.

I don't believe Tallie has the answers, but maybe she can give me some insight into this strange new world. I'd rather not be locked away in some bedroom, waiting for my fate to be sealed.

"I would love a tour. I'll follow your lead," I say.

"This is our main shopping center in town." Tallie gestures to the stores, all clustered together in a semicircle. More cabins line the cobblestone path leading to the town's center with small signs I recognize. Seamstress. Cafe. Grocers. Medicines.

If I didn't walk through a portal this morning, I wouldn't ever think I left Grym Hollow.

"It's not usually this busy. We just have more people here than normal. Many of these people had cabins in different parts of Lycan Forest, but many have moved closer for safety reasons," she explains, justifying the hordes of people coming in and out of stores. Multiple times I had to step out of the way to avoid getting run over by someone not paying attention to where they're going.

"Why are there more people here? Is something going on?" My curiosity gets the best of me.

Tallie stiffens next to me. She seems to mull over my words, like she's not sure the best way to answer. "I can't say much..." she trails off. "Rip will kill me if I do. But I will say that things here aren't good. We are facing new enemies and conflicts we've never encountered before. That's why you are here. To help us."

I'm taken aback by her answer. "Me?" I laugh, but it sounds more panicked than anything. "How the hell am I supposed to help you?" I couldn't help anyone back in Grym Hollow until I left, and I doubt I'll be much help here with literal wolves and monsters.

Tallie just shrugs. "Ender said you would. He was right when King Malix asked for assistance and brought Rose to him. Now he's brought you to us, which means things will get better."

I'm not sure if she says that last part for her benefit or my own. Before I can dive deeper into that, Tallie takes my hand. "Let's keep going. There's a lot more to see." She pulls me into a busy shopping district.

Many people walk in groups. There's very little laughter, just tense whispers and the occasional shout. Many of the shoppers look over their shoulders as if waiting for something to pop out unexpectedly. There's an undercurrent of fear here that I can't shake.

If Tallie notices, she doesn't comment.

"This is shift-change time for the wolves. Morning workers are being replaced by the night workers. That's why you see so much activity right now. Everyone here has a job, usually one they pick for themselves, and they're required to report to their duty when they are able," Tallie says, smiling at an elderly couple walking by her.

Since the start of the tour, I've seen many people of all ages come up and speak to Tallie. Maybe it's because she's the cousin to the King Alpha, but I think she's the type of person others are drawn to because of her friendly disposition. She takes an interest in people, asking them about important happenings in their lives. It appears effortless to her, and I envy her ability to connect with people. It's not something that comes easily to me.

"Why do you call them wolves?" I ask, since this isn't the first time she's referred to her people as such.

"Because that's what we are," she says simply. "Our wolves are our natural form. Who we identify as. These human-like bodies we have are useful in many situations, so that's why you'll see most of us walking around in this form when we're in town."

"So, if you wanted to change into a wolf right now...you could? Does it hurt?" I try to wrap my head around it.

"It hurt the first few times I shifted, but you kinda get used to the pain. Do you want to see?" Tallie grins, all too happy to magically turn into a wolf for my benefit.

"Uhm, maybe next time." I've reached my limit on what I can handle today. The woman in front of me turning into a wolf might just push me over the edge.

Sensing my discomfort, Grass nuzzles my leg. He has stuck by my side since leaving the packhouse, and, despite my cautious attitude toward my new home, Grass is having the time of his life. He loves all the open areas to run. Everyone we pass stares at me with curiosity, but their face transforms to one of wonder when they see Grass next to me.

And apparently everyone is his best friend now because he hasn't growled or barked at anyone. He's gone up to people without fear and instantly rolled over to show his belly. I'm certain Grass has never had this many belly rubs in his life, and he's absolutely loving it.

"Totally understandable. I imagine this is a lot to take in." Tallie reaches out to squeeze my shoulder. Her touch is gentle, making me think of a friend's concern. Maybe Tallie and I could be friends. She'd be my first real one.

"It is." I nod. "Everything is new and overwhelming. Plus, I'm not used to so many people staring at me."

Not even trying to hide their stares, either. It's full-on stop and stare. Even when I catch them, they continue to take me in.

"Ah, yeah, it must be strange. People here aren't used to seeing a human. They know very little about the situation, except that you were brought here for Alpha Rip. You're the talk of the town. But don't worry. Everyone's been instructed to leave you alone and let you get acclimated before they bombard you with questions. Rip didn't want this to be any harder on you than it already has to be."

That is...strangely sweet of him. Maybe he has a sliver of a heart.

The sun is quickly setting, and a new chill stings my skin. I shiver, not prepared for cold weather.

Tallie notices. "Let me show you to your room, so you can get settled tonight." She loops her arm through mine, and I let her lead me back to the packhouse.

"Do you live here too?" I ask.

"No, but I do have a room here if I wanted. I live back in one of the residential areas with my mate."

"You have a mate?"

Tallie is beautiful, but the smile she gives me at the mention of her mate magnifies her beauty tenfold. "I do. You met him, actually. My mate is Thorne."

My jaw drops. "Thorne is your mate? Damn, he's hot." I laugh, then remember I said I wanted to go to his room earlier. "Sorry for what I said—"

Tallie waves off my apology. "No apologies necessary. Rip deserved that for being a jerk. Just don't cast him aside yet. I promise, once he cares about you, he will stop at nothing to make sure you are happy and safe."

Not sure I believe that, I nod at Tallie anyway. She is his cousin, after all, and probably sees a side of Rip that not a lot of other people see. I know very little about him, other than our first impression wasn't great. I have a hard time believing it will get better.

Once inside the packhouse, Tallie leads me up a grand staircase, making me feel like Cinderella. At the top of the stairs, she pulls me to the left, after explaining the right is for guests, and all the rooms are full because of the influx of people in town. "You and Rip are the only ones down this hall. The first door will lead you inside. I'll make sure someone comes by soon and drops off dinner and something for Grass. Do you need anything from me?"

I smile and shake my head, ready for alone time. "I think I'll be fine."

"Good. Well, if you need me, just stop someone in the hall, and they'll come find me," she promises. Doesn't sound like the most effective method, but I nod anyway. "I'll come by in the morning."

Tallie finally lets go of my arm and offers me one last

smile. "I'm excited to have you here in Lycan Forest. I think you'll be good for Rip."

With that, she turns back the way we came, leaving me alone with Grass and my muddled thoughts.

CHAPTER 5
RIP

I don't look back when I leave Hettie in Tallie's capable hands. The meeting could not have gone worse. I thought I had been prepared for the arrival of my human mate, but that couldn't be further from the truth. Her warm, sweet scent filled my senses and awoke a deep, primal part of me.

The elders of Lycan Forest warned me that the draw to a human mate is more powerful than that of an alpha to an omega. It was all-consuming, and the need to mate would be nearly impossible to ignore. Ender had promised he'd find the right human for me, but I didn't believe him until now.

I'd been so close to losing myself, so close to reaching out and touching her...but then she flinched. She fucking flinched away from *me*. It took everything in my power to keep my wolf at bay. He raged inside me, ready to defend the human from whatever demons still plagued her thoughts.

One little human who hasn't even been here a day is

unraveling me piece by piece. I fear what will happen when there's nothing left to unweave.

Thorne walks by my side, dark eyes glancing over at me occasionally, but he keeps his mouth shut. If he senses the unease in my wolf, he wisely keeps it to himself. For now. I know it wasn't his fault that Hettie threatened to go to his room, but I saw nothing but red in that moment. Never have I ever considered hurting my best friend—even when he mated my damn cousin—until that moment.

For now, I push those thoughts to the side. I need my mind clear for the arrival of one of the other kings of Mescos. The only other person who knows what I'm going through and may provide insight on how to save my people. The visit is unexpected and terrible timing, but not one I'm willing to miss.

The alpha outside the meeting room bows at my arrival. "King Alpha Rip, King Malix and Queen Rose are awaiting you. Do you require anything?"

"Tell the kitchen staff to bring out food and mead."

The alpha nods once, opening the door. I sense the Dragon King even before I see him. His presence is strong, and my wolf is on alert. Malix isn't my enemy, but I'm also not keen on having a dragon in Lycan Forest. Especially *this* dragon. Another king on my territory makes me uneasy.

Malix sits at the opposite head of the table with his new wife to his left. This is the first time I've seen Rose. She's a pretty human, petite with deep red, almost brown hair, a stark contrast to her pale complexion. The two of them rise as one, hands clasped tightly together.

If I thought the Dragon King was powerful before, it's nothing compared to the power radiating from him now. Is this what Ender meant when he said Hettie would strengthen me?

"King Alpha." Malix's deep voice thunders in the otherwise silent room. "I would like to introduce you to my wife, Rose Briar."

Rose breaks apart from Malix, coming over to me. Malix tenses, torn between letting Rose go and pulling her back. I don't know the woman, but I doubt she will take kindly to having someone else dictate her moves. Much like Hettie.

"It's nice to meet you, King Alpha." She offers her hand. I take it, only because I'm in the mood to piss off Malix—just a bit. I swear I hear him growl when our hands touch, and the room temperature rises a few degrees.

"It's a pleasure to meet you, Rose. Should I give my condolences for ending up with such a hot-tempered mate?"

"Careful, wolf," Malix warns.

Rose ignores her husband and laughs. "He's not so bad." She smiles, a wistful expression on her face. This human actually loves the dragon. Stranger yet, Malix seems completely enamored with her.

"Where is your mate? I thought Malix mentioned Ender was bringing someone over from Grym Hollow."

Innocent enough question, but still I bristle. I'm not ready to share her with outsiders yet. "She's tired. My cousin, Tallie, is helping her settle in." Not a complete lie. Tallie *is* helping Hettie settle, but that's because I'm not prepared to be around her yet, and our first meeting was less than spectacular. Until she's officially pack, she won't sit in on these meetings.

"Shame. I've never met Hettie, but I've heard her name around town when I lived in Grym Hollow. Maybe next time," Rose says before heading back over to Malix. The two take a seat, and Thorne and I follow. Behind us, the door opens, and two betas walk in carrying trays of buttery biscuits and garlic chicken. My stomach growls, reminding me I haven't eaten today.

We don't speak of Nephilim or curses during dinner. Rose takes over the conversation, filling us in about her life at Grym Hollow. I think of Hettie and what life she might have lived there. Couldn't have been a good one if she made a deal with Ender. Rose left a cheating boyfriend and a sister who betrayed her. What did Hettie leave? More importantly, would we ever get to a place where she would want to tell me? Willingly?

After dinner, dessert is placed in front of us, an iced lemon cake that I take little interest in. I'm eager to get the discussion started. The longer we put this off, the sicker wolves grow with the curse.

Thorne catches my eye from his spot next to me, and I know my second is thinking the same thing. Enough of the pleasantries. I need answers.

"Shall we discuss the reason you're here, then? What updates can you tell me about the Nephilim and Gadreel? Last we met was to warn the leaders of their escape from the mountain." It wasn't all that long ago when Malix summoned all six leaders of Mescos to Kraken's Lagoon. Since then, all of our conversations have been in writing. None of the letters have held any important updates out of fear they could be intercepted.

Malix lets out a deep sigh. For the first time, I see the weight of his kingdom on his shoulder. Like me, we are both young kings, responsible for every life in our kingdom. These are unprecedented times, but it's hard to not feel like I'm failing my people.

"Gadreel and his people attacked Dragon's Keep. They got through our barrier when we were at our weakest. My people fought hard, but it was Rose who saved us." The look he gives his wife makes me feel like I'm intruding on an intimate moment between the couple.

I'm surprised Malix is willing to admit to his weaknesses. Dragons are prideful beings and secretive.

"What do you mean, Rose saved you?" This makes little sense. A mere human against ancient, powerful creatures known as the Nephilim? Giant, human-like creatures with shredded wings, designed to wreak havoc upon the world. Their leader, Gadreel, is more powerful than any of us truly know.

"I restored the barriers," Rose explains.

"Not only that, but she broke the sleeping curse," Malix adds.

"But how?" This time it's Thorne who asks, seemingly just as confused.

"That's the part we can't explain." As soon as Rose says it, both Thorne and my shoulders slump. "Not in any logical way, at least. Ender told me there is magic in Mescos. Magic that humans once possessed. It's there, I feel it, but I didn't really start feeling it until I fell in love with Malix."

Love. How cliché. And utterly useless.

I'm no closer to learning how to save my people than I was at the start of dinner.

"Pardon my bluntness, but love doesn't feel like enough to keep my pack safe. There has to be more to it. We don't have the magical barriers Dragon's Keep has. My people are completely exposed to the Nephilim and rogues—"

"Lycan Forest has rogues? Since when?" Malix tilts his head, mulling over my words.

I bite back my anger, giving him a curt nod. "Since the magic keeping the Nephilim imprisoned started fading."

Malix nods. "That's when we started experiencing changes too. What about the curse? What kind of curse is plaguing your lands? It's going to hit each kingdom differently, but the effect is all the same. Death to our kind."

It's a sensible question from King Malix, one I expected him to ask. Still, I hesitate. Admitting weakness to outsiders sets my people up for attack. I don't believe Malix or his dragons will turn on us, but the thought still lingers. It's not natural for us to seek assistance outside the pack, but with the alarming number of wolves falling each day, I'm backed into a damn corner with no way out.

I catch Thorne's eyes, and he nods once, assuring me he agrees that the only right choice here is to be as transparent as possible.

I still don't fucking like it.

But I tell him anyway.

"My people are losing their connection to their wolves. It starts out as a headache, maybe some night shivers. And then their bodies shut down. I'm watching wolves wither away. Without the connection to their wolves, their bodies cannot sustain them any longer. There's only been a few casualties, but my healers say it will only get worse."

Walking through my infirmary feels a lot like walking through a graveyard. Death clings to every corner. Mourners cry and pray over their loved ones for a cure that seems more impossible by the day.

Neither Malix nor Rose says anything when I finish telling them about the curse. Rose shakes her head, her face a mixture of disbelief and pity. Malix scowls and pulls Rose closer. He visibly relaxes when their shoulders touch. Seeing the change in the Dragon King is shocking. Jealousy rears its ugly head, but I tamp it down. I have no reason to be jealous of another king and their mate.

I've never been interested in taking a mate. I was fine with women warming my bed for a night, maybe two, but I never let it go longer than that. The interest in them left as soon as my needs were filled. As the King Alpha, I know I will have to eventually take a mate, but it wouldn't be for love. It would be for necessity. Kings need heirs.

Images of Hettie's large brown eyes and straight black hair fill my mind. Heat rushes through my body. This damn human has already taken up residency in my head.

I don't like it.

"You should know I received a report from my men that the Nephilim are no longer traveling in a single pack," Malix says, pushing all my thoughts of Hettie to the side. "We lost track of Gadreel and his band of warriors around Demon's Clan, presumably heading toward Pixie Cove."

If Gadreel makes it to Pixie Cove, and they break their way into King Taivan's kingdom, we stand no chance of eliminating them. Pixie Cove harbors most of the magic in Mescos. Access to that type of power for a Nephilim is as good as a death sentence for the rest of our kingdoms.

"But we have identified a horde consisting of ten Nephilim in your area," Malix continues. "They were last seen talking to a group of wolves. Since you mentioned rogues, that makes more sense now."

We have suspected the rogues working with an outside force, but hearing it confirms our biggest fears. The rogues have proved themselves a deadly opponent, led by a wolf who wants nothing more than to bathe in my blood and take my crown. But with the Nephilim in his corner, I fear for the safety and lives of every wolf in my pack.

"The reason I want to meet with you, Rip, is not just to bring harrowing news, but to let you know you have the support of my kingdom. Whatever you need," Malix says, shocking the hell out of me and Thorne.

"King Malix, your offer is very generous, but what is it

you seek in return?" Thorne asks, echoing my question. From my experience, people rarely do shit out of the goodness of their hearts. There's always a price or a demand, and I expect Malix to list his.

But he doesn't.

"I want Mescos free of Nephilim. It doesn't matter that Dragon's Keep is free of Nephilim for now. We won't truly be safe until the Nephilim are killed."

Killed. Not imprisoned like they were so long ago. If there's one thing we've learned from our ancestors is that these creatures don't deserve redemption. Death is the only way out of this.

"You have a lot to think through, and my mate and I have taken up much of your time." Malix stands, helping his wife out of her chair.

Both Thorne and I stand. The meeting provides more insight than I expect, but it doesn't make me feel any better. Instead, I feel a heavy burden settle upon my shoulders, knowing my pack will need to prepare for battle.

Malix shakes hands with Thorne before coming over to me. "For what it's worth, Rip, I don't believe there's a better wolf to lead your pack through this than you. You have my full support. If you need us, all you need to do is call upon us."

We shake hands, something akin to mutual respect passing between us. We understand the burdens and trials that come with the title of kings. That, and the fact we were both young when we had power thrust upon us, expecting to navigate it with little guidance.

Malix steps away, but Rose hangs back. She bites her lip, looking between me and her husband. There's indecision on her face, like she isn't sure she should do what she's thinking. Then, after a moment of hesitation, she approaches me.

My body stiffens, not sure what the human woman plans to say.

"I know it's not my place to speak on your new mate," she starts, "but from someone who was in her place recently, I know what she's going through right now. Changing from our world to Mescos is scary and over-whelming. We left behind so much, so just be patient and kind to her. If you're anything like my husband, I know she's going to love your pack."

The thought of Hettie claiming my pack as her own is equal parts terrifying and dangerously appealing. Her words strike a chord in me, but I'm uncertain I'm ready to explore my relationship with Hettie at the moment. I can't have distractions when I'm trying to keep my people alive. And if I allow myself, Hettie will be a big distraction.

"Little Dragon, we need to go," Malix calls his wife, and she offers him a soft smile. Love and adoration are written plainly on her face, and for just a moment, I allow myself to wonder what that feels like.

"Remember, she's key to your pack's salvation. Don't treat her like an outsider." With that, Rose strolls over to her husband and takes his hand. The power between them is palpable, eclipsing the entire room.

Ender brought them together. Just like he brought Hettie to me. Perhaps I need to put my trust in The Guardian if I want to save my pack.

CHAPTER 6
HETTIE

I sleep like the fucking dead.

I don't remember falling asleep after Tallie showed me to my room. I remember the overwhelming feeling of being a stranger in a new place. I sat on the bed, with Grass jumping up next to me because I just needed a moment to myself. Apparently, that moment turned into crashing the rest of the day.

I wake up disoriented and in an unfamiliar room. This isn't the first time I've woken up in a room that isn't mine, but it is by far the comfiest and cleanest. Grass lays at my feet and doesn't stir when I sit up in bed.

My eyes take a moment to adjust to the dark room. The only light comes from the open curtain, dousing the room in a light glow. It's still dark outside, but the sun is starting to rise.

Two large windows overlook the pine forest, and I can't help but think how beautiful it will be when a thin layer of snow covers the trees. I'm not even certain it snows here, but I secretly hope it does. Grym Hollow gets cold, and sometimes we deal with freezing rain, but never snow.

Besides the bed, there's very little furniture. Two side tables with candles and a dark dresser that looks hand-made are the only pieces adorning the room. It's cozy, but generic, and smells of sandalwood and pine trees.

Although the room is gorgeous, there's very little in the way of personal touches. No photos, a stack of books, or even a spot of dirt. Nothing gives me a glimpse into Rip's life or personality. Not even a family picture.

Because I'm assuming this room is also his, despite his obvious absence. Tallie mentioned Rip and I are the only ones down this hallway. There's a slight dip on the other side of the mattress, outlining what I presume is where Rip's body lies at night.

I'm not sure if I'm relieved or disappointed that he didn't come to bed. Which is fucking crazy because I just met him, and our meeting wasn't ideal. If Rip thought he was getting a docile and even-tempered wife, he's sadly mistaken. After ex-lovers and friends have used you one too many times, you eventually learn how to stand your ground.

I push myself out of bed. Grass raises his head as if asking, *What are you doing?* I'm not exactly sure what I'm doing, but I've never been good at staying in one place for too long. It'll be morning soon, but for now, everyone must still be asleep. Which hopefully means I won't have to face my *mate* yet.

Last night, I dumped my only bag on the floor. I crouch down and rifle through it, finding two pairs of jeans, a bra, some panties, socks, and three shirts. I dig my way to the bottom, grasping for the coat I know is there.

"There you are." My hand grips the coat, and I pull it out. It's more of a cross between a sweater and a coat, one my mom sewed for me a few years ago. She was so proud of it too. She made it in my favorite color, a deep, beautiful red because she knew how badly I wanted the red coat from one of the few clothing shops in Grym Hollow. We couldn't afford it though.

I was moody and stupid back then and made quite the scene that had both me and my mother crying by the end of it. We didn't speak for three days, and on the third day, she came in with this new coat in her hands, saying she made it with love and hoped I liked it.

It's the best gift she ever gave me. And now it's the only memory I have of her.

Tears sting my eyes, but I quickly blink them away. Maybe one day I'll be able to think back to my family without wanting to curl up in a ball and cry myself senseless. Today just won't be that day. I'm sure my mother and sister are going through their own mourning, but in time, they will come to accept and hopefully even thrive in their new life.

I take the coat and a fresh pair of panties into the bathroom. Just like the bedroom, it's far too neat and sterile. Is Rip a clean freak? Because, if he is, this relationship is doomed before it even starts.

There's a small vintage clawfoot tub you might find at an ancient grandma's house, passed down from her mother before her. The toilet is in a semi-private alcove, and exposed pipes run up the walls and through the ceiling. I'm not sure how their plumbing works, but as long as I don't have to piss in an outhouse and bathe in the river, I don't care.

I take care of my business, freshen up, and, for good measure, flick water onto the otherwise pristine mirror.

There. Now it looks like someone uses this room.

When I walk out of the bathroom, putting my coat on,

Grass is waiting for me by the door, doing that thing dogs do when they have to go to the bathroom. He whines and scratches at the door, begging to be let out.

No one told me I had to stay in my room, and even if they did, I'm not starting off my time here as a prisoner locked away in a cage. "Let's go, Grass. No peeing on the floor."

Grass all but barrels past me when I open the door. He bolts down the hallway, nearly knocking into a glass vase full of flowers. "Grass!" I hiss, jogging to follow him down the grand staircase. I half expect to run into someone asking me where I think I'm going in this giant house, but no one's around.

When I finally reach Grass and open the last barrier—the front door—he sprints past me and shoots directly into a grassy area, finally able to relieve himself. Grass is going to love having so much room to run around in and live his best doggy life.

The air is frigid, made worse by the lack of sun. The town is still sleeping, and I'm eager to see it in the light again. Maybe Tallie can take me to the shops so I can build up a warmer wardrobe and make Rip pay for it all. He'll probably ignore me like he did yesterday, which is fine. I don't have to like the man; I just have to marry his ass.

I start to seriously regret not packing heavier clothes when Grass barks, turning my attention to him. He stands deadly still, growling low in his throat. Grass isn't a vicious dog, not by a long shot, but he won't hesitate to defend me when I'm around people he doesn't like. At least that's how he acted in Grym Hollow. Here? He seems to befriend everybody, so I'm not sure how much defending he'll actually do.

Maybe he senses a squirrel. I hope he's just sensing a squirrel.

"Grass? Come here, boy." I whistle, but he ignores me. "Grass!" I call louder, but to no avail. If this dog is seriously going to make me go to him...

Just as the thought crosses my mind, Grass takes off at an alarming speed, heading straight for the woodsy area ahead. "*Dammit!*" I hate running, but there's no way in hell I'm losing Grass—my one connection to home.

"Grass—*fuck!*" My foot slips out from underneath me, and I nearly fall on my ass. The ground is so damn slippery with dew, and I'm not in the proper shoes to go gallivanting through the forest. I use the trees to keep me upright as I chase after Grass.

I'm not a runner. Never claimed to be. I'm hardly athletic. Drinking and smoking don't exactly make me the best candidate to be chasing after this damn dog, but I will not lose him.

Just as I think my lungs will give out and I'll keel over, Grass comes to an abrupt stop a few feet in front of me. He's not acting like his normal self. Grass is a happy dog, but you wouldn't know that by looking at him now. He's crouched low, tail straight up in the air, emitting a deep growl: a warning not to get too close.

"What's wrong, boy? What's going on?" I finally reach him, crouching down to get on his level. I don't fear Grass will hurt me. He's never so much as bitten me, and I've had him since he was a puppy after my father did maintenance on the neighbors' house. There's just something wrong with him, and I don't know what it is. Maybe passing over to Mescos has finally got the better of him.

"Beautiful canine you have there, Red."

I jolt, falling on my ass. The deep baritone voice seemingly comes out of nowhere. Was I followed? Would Rip have people spying on me?

A low chuckle snaps my attention to a figure in front of me. The stranger is partially hidden in shadows and a thicket of trees, nearly blending into their surroundings. They're easy to miss, which explains why I didn't see them before.

"My name's not Red." Out of everything I could have said, that should have landed low on the list. My brain is still frazzled from his damn jump-scare. I take way longer than I like to admit he probably called me "Red" because of my coat. Very clever.

The branches crack as the figure moves toward me. I quickly stand, and Grass moves between my legs, still growling at the stranger and protecting me the only way he knows how.

My breath hitches as a man emerges from the bushes. Deep brown eyes, nearly black, stare back at me, and I can't help feeling like a mouse caught in a trap. The man is large, maybe even more so than Rip. He's only wearing pants, so his muscular, russet-brown skin is on full display. He doesn't seem affected by the chill in the air.

"Hasn't anyone ever told you not to run in the woods at night, Red?" Amusement laces his tone.

"It's technically morning. So, not night," I reply lamely, making the scary man laugh.

"Cheeky. I like you, Red." The stranger steps closer, and I think Grass is going to attack. But when the man looks down, Grass whimpers and moves to hide behind me.

So much for protection.

"So, the rumors are true. You're the new human mate," he says. "My name is Michael. I've been dying to meet you." The man—Michael—looks me over. Not in a way that men at parties look at me when I'm drunk and they're looking for an easy lay.

No, there's something far more sinister in the way he focuses his attention on me.

"I really need to get back. Someone is expecting me, and he'll come looking if I don't show up." It's a lie. No one is waiting for me because no one saw me leave. *Great fucking job, Hettie,* I scold myself. I'm not in Grym Hollow any longer. These aren't people. They're wolves. I've never felt smaller in my life.

"Strange how they let the new Luna walk around with no guards, especially knowing you're human. But then again, Rip has never been the smartest of alphas." Michael's face contorts into a snarl. But just as quickly as his anger comes, a mask of indifference soon takes over.

I have no idea what a damn Luna is, but I don't get the opportunity to ask because Michael says, "Fortunately for you, he won't be your problem for much longer."

Faster than my eyes can follow, Michael snatches my wrist in a punishing grasp. I cry out in pain and try to pull away, but his grip on me tightens.

"Let go of me!" I try to kick, scratch, and twist my way out of his grip, but it's like battling a brick wall. He doesn't budge, and I doubt he even feels my weak attempt at escaping.

Michael just laughs. His eyes, soulless black orbs just moments ago, now shine golden in the moonlight. Terror holds my body captive, and I tense.

"Now why would I give up a human? Don't you know how powerful your kind can be to an alpha?"

Power? Who the fuck has power here? Because it's sure the fuck not me. "I don't know who you think I am, but you have the wrong girl." Maybe this bastard can be reasoned with, since I can't overpower him.

"No, I know exactly who you are, *Hettie*." The color

drains from my face. "You're the pretty human who will help me take back what is mine, and if you're lucky, I might just keep you around to enjoy it."

In the distance, a wolf howls, sounding loud and forlorn. Michael's grip eases on me, but only just. He stops, tilting his head as if he's trying to hear something. Another howl fills the night air.

Are those Rip's people? Do they know I'm gone?

Michael curses under his breath and turns his attention back to me. "I'll see you soon, Little Red. Remember, don't walk in the woods at night. You don't know what monsters walk through here."

Michael lets me go, and I shuffle backward to put distance between us. He winks at me before a loud cracking sound startles me, followed by clothes ripping. Like it's happening in slow motion, Michael's body morphs from that of a man into a monstrous dark gray wolf.

Holy fuck, he just shifted in front of me. Before I can wrap my head around it, Michael—now a wolf—runs back into the woods, disappearing in the shadows.

My body shakes, pure terror and adrenaline working its way through my system. I feel on the verge of a panic attack, and I think Grass senses as much. He's no longer cowering in fear, but he whimpers and licks me to assure us we are okay.

But are we? Or did I just trade one fucked-up situation for another?

"We're okay. We're fine," I say, though I'm not sure who I'm trying to convince.

Just as I say that, a low growl comes from behind us. I whirl around, half expecting to see Michael again, deciding he wants me dead. Golden eyes stare back at me, but unlike Michael, this wolf's fur is midnight-black.

I barely make it two steps away before I hear bones crack and shift. It sounds painful, and I flinch. Seconds later, a very naked—and very pissed—Rip stands in front of me.

I drag my eyes down his body. He's tense, and his muscles are flexed as if expecting a fight. My eyes wander even lower until I see the fucking steel rod between his legs. He's not even hard, but the man is already indecently long and thick.

Has anyone ever been on that thing? And did they receive financial compensation for their broken pussy?

These thoughts are completely inappropriate, and I snap my eyes back to his gaze. His deadly and pissed-off gaze.

I'm so fucking screwed.

CHAPTER 7
RIP

Hettie isn't in our room when I go to check on her in the morning before my duties. I may still be uncertain about the human, but she's still my responsibility to keep safe. She's also not in the dining room or kitchen. None of the guards I pass can tell me where Hettie is. Thorne checks with Tallie, but Tallie hasn't seen her since last night.

How did she get past the two guards stationed outside our room? Why the fuck did no one alert me about her disappearance? I should have better prepared everyone for the human's arrival.

"Where the fuck is she?" I snarl. Anger heats my body, bringing my wolf close to the surface. I've had Hettie for a day, and I've already lost her. Ender is going to be pissed, and my chances of saving my pack will diminish to almost nothing.

"I checked with everyone on duty last night. Only one reported that a civilian saw a woman in red walk through the woods," Thorne says. "Her scent lingers in the house. I think she might have snuck out during shift changes."

I'm already heading toward the front door, with Thorne keeping pace besides me. I smell Grass more than I smell Hettie, which provides me with a faint link to her.

When I reach the front, two alphas stand guard by the front door. "Have you seen her?" my poorly concealed anger slips through in my tone.

The guards share a look with one another, not eager to be the first one to speak. They are wasting my time. Each moment without Hettie puts her in more danger. What kind of King Alpha loses their Luna on the first day?

"Seen who, King Alpha?" one guard inquires, and it's a test of my will not to throttle him where he stands. I almost do, but Thorne places a hand on my shoulder in warning. I can't lose my temper.

"Hettie. Our future Luna," I grit through my teeth.

The man's eyes widen, and something akin to nervousness blooms in his expression. "We've seen no one leave, King Alpha. Shift change happened not too long ago, and, regrettably, the front entrance stood without guards for about five minutes during that switch. Perhaps she left then."

"And why the fuck did you not wait until the next watch came to take your posts?"

"We thought the packhouse was secure, King Alpha. It was no more than a few minutes," he says, like his assurance means anything.

My wolf nearly breaks through the surface. His anger fuels me as I clench my fist. As mad as I am at the alphas guarding the front door, I know deep down they aren't the real ones to blame in this situation.

Without another word, I push past the two guards and head outside. Thorne follows, but I hold up my hand. "Stay here in case she comes back. I need to go find her."

Thorne, my best friend since we were children, eyes me worriedly. He's known me long enough to know I won't change my mind, which is why he relents, nodding. "I'll search for her in town."

I don't engage with him any longer. I've already let too much time pass. As soon as I descend the stairs, my dire wolf rips free of my body. My bones and body reform, and a howl bursts free. It is one of distress, so those on duty know to be vigilant.

My senses are amplified in this form. I rack my brain to remember her scent, since it's mingled with so many others out here. I told her she smelled like a dog, which isn't entirely true. She also smells of honey and a dash of lavender.

I catch the scent of Grass. If the dog is out here, then Hettie shouldn't be too far from him. I saw the way she stared at the giant softie. Losing him would cause her immeasurable pain. I don't mind the dog. He'll make a good companion to Hettie, but not if he leads her into the damn forest.

Because that's where the scent is taking me. Finding her with a mating bond would make this so much easier. I would know how she's feeling. Sense where she's at instead of running blindly through the woods, trying to catch her scent. But I didn't go through with the ceremony yesterday because I didn't want to overwhelm her. That changes today. She can hate me if she must, but I would rather her hatred than her death on my hands.

The dewy ground makes traction difficult. Branches crunch under my paws as I push my legs harder. Soon a soft voice sounds from somewhere ahead, and I know I've found her. Relief doesn't come over me like I thought it would because, mixed with Hettie, another scent comes to the surface. One that makes my hackles rise.

I *know* that scent. I've smelled it before, but the memory is fleeting, and I can't remember where.

When I break through the clearing, Hettie is there, shaking, with her arms wrapped around Grass, who looks equally spooked. The scent here is stronger, and I smell it all over Hettie. *Mine*, my wolf growls, not liking the idea of another person touching her.

Seeing that she is okay flips something inside of me. The anger I've been trying to keep at bay explodes. My dire wolf growls before I shift back. Hettie's eyes go comically wide.

"We're okay. We're fine," Hettie says over and over again. The words barely register. I hear nothing but the sound of my heart drumming in my chest. Hettie slowly backs away from me as I continue to descend on her.

The woman's back hits a tree, and her eyes dart frantically around. She's a doe, cornered by the hunter. I can almost taste her fear, but there's something else there. Something I'm not willing to name yet.

I don't stop moving until our bodies are mere inches apart. I cage her in with my arms and tower over her. She's so damn small, even compared to omegas. Despite the obvious fear in her eyes, she sets her pouty lips in a firm line. "Back up, Rip."

"No." And because I'm a dick, I press closer to her.

Hettie sucks in a breath. She molds her body to the tree, trying but failing to put any distance between us.

"You are not to leave the packhouse alone."

"Yeah, well, that rule might have been helpful an hour ago," she scowls, "and Grass had to pee. No one was around. What the hell would you have me do? Let Grass pee in your bed?"

Hettie's chest heaves, pushing her breasts against my chest. It's a cold morning, and I feel her hardened nipples through the thin fabric. It's very distracting.

"What I expect is for you not to leave the packhouse alone and run out into the damn woods."

"I didn't plan on frolicking through the fucking woods, Rip. Grass was acting crazy, and then someone—"

"Who?" The other familiar scent still lingers.

"I don't know, he called himself Michael and—what the fuck?! Let me down!"

I toss Hettie over my shoulder, and her small fists pound into my back. She squirms, and I'm so tempted to smack her ass, but I don't trust myself to be gentle enough. Not after hearing Michael was here. That's why the scent smelled so familiar. It belonged to the damn leader of the rogues.

How the fuck is he slipping through my guard? Probably the same way Hettie got out of the house with no one seeing her today. I've gotten too lax with our rules and structure. I wanted bodies in these guard roles, but I haven't set the expectations yet, which means the forest is unsafe for the time being. I need to drag Hettie's ass back to the packhouse.

"Grass, come." My command is met by a whimper and then the soft footfalls of Grass walking alongside me. He keeps his head down, sensing my tumultuous mood.

I don't like feeling out of control. Hettie's safety is the most important thing. Not only for her sake, but for the survival of the pack as well. And I've been too distracted by other shit to let that fact fully sink in.

No, it needs to be done. I have to mate with the human.

The thought puts a sour taste in my mouth. It feels a lot like a mating against her will, never mind that is exactly what we both signed up for. King Alphas rarely mate for love. They mate for strength and gain. For the betterment of the pack.

"Put me down!" she shrieks again, pummeling my back with her tiny fists. If there's one thing about this human—she's relentless. She'll need to be for what's coming.

I ignore her protest and carry her the entire way back. She throws curses at me like daggers, hoping they'll cut deep. What she doesn't understand is that her words mean nothing to me. Let her continue her assault. It's worth it if it keeps her safe.

I say nothing to her as I take her back to our room. Curious eyes stare at us, and by this evening, the whole town will know I dragged my human mate kicking and screaming back to my room. Stories of what I do to her will fuel the gossip channels for days.

Let them speak.

I find I no longer care.

CHAPTER 8

HETTIE

"Put me down, you motherfu—*oof!*" The air leaves my lungs as I bounce onto his bed, landing in a heap in the center. That bastard tossed me. *He tossed me!* As if I were nothing more than a sack of potatoes he was discarding.

I grab the closest thing to me, which, unfortunately, is a pillow, and hurl it at his head. He steps to the side, and the pillow hits the wall behind him with a dull thud. It drops pathetically to the ground, only serving to piss me off more.

I lunge for another pillow, but Rip is on top of me in an instant, holding my wrists above my head. My breath comes out in desperate pants as I do everything I can to push the man off me.

"Stop. Struggling," he growls, and I get some satisfaction when my knee catches him between his legs and he grunts.

It's then I realize Rip is still naked, like butt-ass naked. His hardness presses into my thigh, and even through the thin layer of fabric that separates us, I can feel every inch of him. My traitorous body sends heat straight to my core.

I meet his eyes, and his pupils are blown wide with... something. Fuck, lust? Disgust? A mixture of the two? He growls, and my body responds in kind. I don't realize I've stopped fighting him until he slowly, almost reluctantly, lets me go. He backs away and puts as much distance between us as possible.

Through all of this, I didn't make sure Grass was following, but my panic quickly eases when I see him lounging in a doggy bed in the corner. That wasn't there last night, meaning someone brought it up for him today. Grass is sleeping pleasantly, not concerned at all with the giant naked man in the room.

Well, that makes one of us.

"Do you want to tell me why you just dragged me back here like a runaway convict?" I glare, my ire unable to be contained. It's honestly impressive how little we've talked, and yet he's pissed me off both times.

"You are not to leave this house without me, Thorne, or a guard I appoint you." He parrots what he said earlier, and I swear I see the back of my head when I roll my eyes.

Classic fucking alpha males. Always ready to dish out orders with no explanations.

"Who is Michael, and why did he know me?" The man got under my skin. I've run with many crowds before, but Michael's energy...it's different from anything I've ever experienced. It's dangerous.

"Michael knew who you were?" Rip growls, ignoring my question. "How is that even possible?"

"Hell if I know. Who is he?" I will not be ignored for a second time.

"Michael is someone who should have never been able to get past our defenses. He's a threat and won't hesitate to take what he wants." His reply is clipped and gives me little to go on. The lack of information is driving me feral.

"How the fuck do you expect me to be your little queen if you insist on leaving me alone and refuse to answer my questions?" I really want something to throw at him. Like a pan or a shoe. It wouldn't hurt him since he's the fucking Hulk, but it would make me feel better.

Rip presses his lips together in a tight line. He's furious, but so am I. "You'll know what I allow you to know."

The words hit me like a ton of bricks. I blink, trying to process them. Even Rip's eyes widened like he's surprised about what he said. But he's quick to school his features back into an emotionless asshole.

Did I just trade one toxic man for another? A new controlling asshole who feels like keeping me at arm's length until he needs me?

I don't get the chance to retaliate, though, because Tallie rushes into the room, ignoring her cousin's nakedness entirely. "Hettie!" She clutches her chest. "Thank goodness you've been found." She sounds worried, which shocks me. Not even those I considered friends ever worried when I went days, sometimes weeks, without communication.

"Get her ready." Rip's command freezes me in place. "I'll prepare for the ceremony."

"Ceremony? What ceremony?"

I don't expect him to answer, but when he does, my jaw hits the floor. "Our mating ceremony. It's happening tonight."

I STAND in the middle of Tallie's childhood bedroom. A small but tidy bed is pushed up against one wall, with a cute pink chair next to a window. This room also has a fireplace that is currently burning brightly to keep the chill out of this room.

Once Rip left me in the hands of Tallie and her mate, Thorne, the two of them brought me back to Tallie's childhood home. Her mother runs the ceremonies in town, so Tallie explained she's with Rip to prepare for this evening.

I knew today was coming.

I just didn't expect it to come so quickly. Seeing Michael was the catalyst for Rip, but I still don't fully grasp the situation. As soon as we were alone, I attempted to get answers out of Thorne and Tallie. Thorne was apologetic, but said he couldn't tell me anything until I'm pack. Tallie looked like she wanted to say something, but with Thorne there, her hands were tied.

So, in the dark I remain.

"This is definitely your color." Tallie takes a step back, looking over the peach-colored dress she's spent the last thirty minutes tailoring to my body. Thorne nods from his spot on the pink chair. He looks like a giant in a seat made for a gnome, and I fear the chair might break underneath him.

The dress is long-sleeved, protecting my arms from the cold. The skirts flow to the floor, fanning out around me. It's both simple and elegant. Not the type of wedding dress I would pick if this were a marriage I wanted, but it's still pretty.

"What does a mating ceremony entail?" I ask as Tallie fluffs my dress in the back. I doubt the ceremony is the same as a wedding ceremony, so I want to be prepared for what's coming.

"The pack's mistress of ceremonies will tie your hands together. She'll say a few words that tradition calls for, and then she will ask if you accept this mating claim. After you both accept the mating claim, Rip will give you his claiming mark."

Tallie points to a darkened spot on her neck. It looks like a tattoo, but with no real shape or meaning that I can understand. "This is Thorne's mark on me."

"How did you get it?"

"He bit me."

"He *what*?" Surely I misheard. "He *bit* you?"

Tallie laughs and shares a secret glance with Thorne. The two of them radiate love and adoration. He stares at her as if she's the only woman in his universe. Love like that is rare. At the very least, it's not something I have ever experienced. Something a lot like sorrow washes over me.

"It's the best feeling in the world. It's the start of your eternal bond. You can feel the person you mated to in ways you never knew existed. The best way I can describe it is a feeling of completion. Like you found the other part of yourself."

The way Tallie describes it sounds magical. A storybook love, complete with the happily-ever-after. Like this one bite could change everything.

"Is that what you felt about Thorne when you mated him? Or did you mate him out of necessity?" My words are bitter. I don't mean to cause offense, but the picture Tallie is painting isn't one I believe I'm going to share.

A flush creeps over Tallie's cheeks. "We were in love before we mated," she says, almost apologetically. "But it doesn't mean the bond won't still snap into place and you'll feel differently about each other," she rushes, doing her best to console me.

Maybe for people like her and Thorne, who were in love to start with. But for Rip and I? The most I can hope for is a semblance of respect. "Does it hurt?"

Tallie shakes her head. "No, it feels fantastic, actually. But the bit is usually given..." She trails off, looking at Thorne for assistance.

"Given when?" I press, annoyed that they insist on keeping their secrets. I suppose I understand in a way. I'm still an outsider, but I won't be for much longer.

Thorne takes over the question, and his answer immobilizes me. "The bite is usually given during sex. The bite is only half the mating ritual. Sex solidifies the bond."

Pause.

They expect me to fuck Rip? I've barely accepted the fact that I'm to be mated to him for the rest of my life, but I'm not ready for sex. No matter how my body responds to him while he's around.

But what if I don't have a choice in the matter? Would he simply take what I'm not ready to give him? Would Thorne and Tallie stand by and watch while he...

My breath comes faster, and I sway on my feet. I think the room gets hotter, or maybe that's just me. I can't do this. I can't go through with this. I can't, I can't, I can't...

"She's in distress," I hear Tallie say to Thorne, and then she's in front of me, grabbing my arms in a vise-like grip. My feet slip from underneath me, and I realize she's the only thing holding me upright.

"Hettie, I need you to breathe. Can you do that with me? Breathe with me, okay?" She demonstrates breathing in through her nose and out through her mouth. She does this repeatedly until I finally follow suit. The rising panic that threatens to detonate slowly subsides.

"I don't...can't have..." I try to get the words out, but coherent sentences aren't coming.

Tallie understands, though. She nods. "I know, and you won't have to."

"Tallie—" Thorne interjects, but she shoots him a reproachful glare.

"She won't have to," she says more firmly this time. I'm not sure if she's directing that at me or Thorne. "The bite is non-negotiable, but she doesn't have to have sex with Rip. Enough of the bond will be there without it."

Tallie continues to rub my shoulders and whisper soothing words. My anxiety about this situation soon turns into embarrassment. I hate people seeing me like this. It's not the image I want Rip's cousin and second-in-command to have of me, a weak human who is far from home.

"I'm sorry. I...don't know what came over me." I step away from Tallie.

She drops her hands and offers me a reassuring smile that reminds me so much of my sister's that I nearly lose it again.

"The hour grows late, My Star. We need to get our Luna to her ceremony," Thorne says to her.

"Right, of course." Tallie's smile only amplifies her beauty. She is trying to put me at ease, and I appreciate that. "Let's get you to your alpha. He's going to be speechless when he sees you."

CHAPTER 9
RIP

Imelda places the last goblet on the ceremonial altar and steps back. She inspects her work and nods once she's satisfied with what she sees. "This is the best I can do with the time restrictions you've presented me, my boy. I really wish you would hold off just one more night, and I could decorate for this ceremony properly."

Tallie's mother, my aunt Imelda, fixes me with a stern stare only a mother can give. For the past twenty years, Imelda has been the closest thing I've had to a mother. She and Tallie are the only ones I have left.

"We can't wait."

"Not even a day, Rip? Just one day?" she asks. "You are the King Alpha. I've just always pictured planning your ceremony, gathered around all our loved ones. It should be a joyous occasion."

I hate letting down my aunt, but there's no putting this off. Mating ceremonies amongst the pack are a big deal. Celebrations that last well into the night. Typically, there are multiple mated couples at a ceremony, bonding their souls together. As the King Alpha, my ceremony is supposed to be a grand event, lasting all day and all night. Food, music, and lots and lots of sex. Not just from the newly mated couple, but the whole pack. Ceremonies always bring out the animal side of us, and we give into our base instinct.

Normally I would too, but it's just not in the stars for us.

"Michael found her in the woods today," I say.

Aunt Imelda sucks in a deep breath. "Oh my. That poor girl. Is she okay?"

I appreciate her not commenting on my incompetence to keep the human safe. "She's fine. But he knows she's here now, and if he can get through our defenses so easily, I need Hettie to be connected to me. It has to be tonight. To keep her safe."

Aunt Imelda doesn't look pleased. Who would in this situation? She had always hoped to plan a huge ceremony. But she nods all the same. "Thorne and Tallie will be your witnesses, then. Will you be participating in the chase?"

I shake my head. The chase is the most thrilling part of the ceremony. Where one mate stays behind while the other travels deep into the forest. It's a game of cat and mouse that ends in fucking. Hettie is barely a willing participant in this bonding ceremony. I won't subject her to that portion of it.

Even if I want it.

"They're close; I hear them approaching. We best get ready." Imelda grabs the books she needs for tonight.

Not even a full minute later, Tallie emerges from the darkness.

We aren't far from town, maybe half a mile. The ceremony needs to be completed under the moonlight, so we set up a makeshift altar close to Imelda's house. The trees here provide enough privacy. I wanted to be far enough away so no wandering wolf would happen across us, but close enough to reach if a problem arises. I don't need an audience for this. This is duty. Nothing more.

Thorne emerges next, with Hettie by his side. I can't help the growl that leaves my throat when I see him touching her, guiding her through the dark. Rationally, I understand why Thorne needs to have his hand on her, but my wolf wants the other alpha far away from our human.

Mine.

I asked Tallie to help Hettie get ready, and I thought that meant just a simple bath and perhaps warmer clothes. Of course, I should have expected my cousin to do more than I anticipated, just like her mother.

Tallie wears a peach-colored dress. The bodice is cut low, giving me a good glimpse of her full breasts. The dress flows down her body, hugging each curve as if painted on. Her hazel eyes meet mine, and for a second, everything around us drifts away.

I know the effects a human mate can have on a wolf from stories I've heard. How human mates could drive a wolf mad with lust and take away their ability to think straight. Hettie isn't even bonded to me yet, and already I can feel my good sense leaving my body. The possessive part of my nature wants to ruin her. To claim her over and over again in front of anyone who would watch to prove this human is mine.

My mate.

Reminding myself that she's here simply to save my pack stifles those thoughts of claiming. I won't force sex upon her, no matter how badly my body might want it.

Thorne leads Hettie to me, big eyes darting all around as if something will pop out of the dark and harm her. After this morning, those feelings are valid, and I'm brought to shame once again. Hettie deserves to feel safe. As her mate, it's my job to protect her.

What the fuck have I gotten myself into?

Hettie looks at me from under her long lashes. I sense her trepidation, and the need to reach out to assure her she's completely safe is strong. But I also don't want to lie to her. She's not safe. Not as long as she remains here while my pack struggles with a curse and outside forces. Still, I tuck her hand in the crook of my arm, providing the only stability I have.

Thorne moves from the altar and goes to stand next to Tallie. It's still so strange to see him wrap his arm around her. They are newly mated, and although Thorne is my best friend and I would die for him, I also want to hurt him when I see him with Tallie. Maybe that will pass.

"You look beautiful, Hettie," my aunt says before glaring at me. "Doesn't she, Rip?"

Right, I should probably say something instead of standing here like a fucking prick. "You do." Imelda waits for me to say more, but I don't. Not about Hettie at least. "Let's get started."

Hettie bristles beside me, and her hold on my arm gets tighter. I'm not sure if she's aware she's doing that. Imelda starts the ceremony, giving praise to our Moon Goddess and reciting the jargon that has been said at every single mating ceremony since the dawn of time. I only half listen because my focus is on Hettie.

I search her face for regrets. For anything that tells me she doesn't want to be here. Our contract with Ender is binding, so I won't ever be able to let her go back to her home, but I'm also not going to force a woman to mate me if she doesn't want to. I'm not that kind of king. I can't be that type of king. It would make me no better than Michael, using force and power to bend people to his will.

There's trepidation in her expression, yes, but there's something else. Acceptance, maybe? I fear calling it willingness, but it's not sorrow like I thought I would see. This human is...interesting.

"Hettie, take this, darling," Imelda says and hands Hettie a goblet full of murky white liquid. It's not something I've seen before in any of the other rituals.

Before I can ask, Hettie beats me to it. "What is this?" She looks down at the milky substance in her cup and smells it. "It smells like honey."

"Does it? Good, that's what it should smell like," Imelda says proudly. "That, my dear, is an ancient mixture packs would give their humans back when humans were more common amongst our kind. It gives you the ability to allow a mating bond to form. It also prepares your body for your mate."

"Prepares my body? What do you mean?" Hettie furrows her brows and stares at the goblet like it's about to sprout legs and walk away.

Imelda looks at me a second, giving me the option to explain. I sigh. There's no polite way to say this, and I don't have the ability to be tactful right now with my emotions heightened. "Alpha cocks are big," I say, and I swear I hear Thorne snort. "We also knot our mates. Humans can't take that unless they have assistance from the drink."

Hettie's golden-brown face turns ashen. Imelda levels me with a stern glare, and the all-too-familiar feeling of shame washes over me. I scramble to make it right. "I don't expect sex, nor would I ever force you to do something you don't want to do. You only need this drink for the bond to form. Nothing more."

Everyone seems to hold their breath as Hettie looks between me and the drink again. She's clutching it so tightly, her knuckles turn white. Then, as quickly as I blink, the alarm in her face drains away, replaced with a cool mask.

"It's only for the mating bond to stick," I urge.

Hettie pays me little attention, saying, "Bold of you to assume I need assistance taking cock," before downing the contents of the goblet.

I'm fucking speechless. Once again, Hettie surprises me, and I smirk. I hate the fact that she's been on other guys' cocks, even though I shouldn't and have no reason to be, but her confidence is intoxicating.

Imelda is hiding—albeit badly—a smile as she accepts the goblet back from Hettie. The human turns to face me again. "Are you going to bite me now?" She sounds almost bored, and despite my best effort, I let out a growl.

The damn woman smirks.

I picture taking her over my leg and spanking her ass red for her bratty tongue. The thought goes straight to my cock, and I shift uncomfortably.

I don't wait for Imelda to tell me it's time to bite Hettie. I pull the woman close, a small gasp leaving those pouty pink lips. She's breathing hard, clearly not as unaffected as she pretends to be. Her heady scent permeates the air, sending my wolf into a frenzy.

"Mine." My words are more growl than anything. I zone in on her neck. The beautiful, unblemished neck. Hettie tilts her head to the side, offering me up perfect access. I trace a vein protruding in her neck, and she shudders. The sweet smell of her arousal floods my senses.

If I reach between her legs, I know I would find her soaked for me.

I bow my head, scenting her lust, fear, and desperation. It's perfect. My tongue snakes out, needing the taste of her salty skin on it. She shudders in my grasp, and a low chuckle leaves my lips. "So eager."

"Just fucking bite me, Rip—*Oh!*"

My fangs extend, and I bite her neck. She moans, a mixture of pain and pleasure. The sweet taste of her blood fills my mouth, and I growl. My wolf is too close to the surface, and I'm barely in charge of myself. I need to be gentler, need to pull away...but I don't.

I feel the bond start to form. It's not strong, and it won't be unless we have sex. Which seems like a really fucking great thing to do right now. There's no hiding my erection as it presses into Hettie's stomach. She feels it too; I know she does.

It takes everything in my power to force myself away from her and step back. Hettie's eyes are blown wide, and she bites her lip. She whimpers softly, which makes me unreasonably happy. She wants me. Maybe not forever, and maybe not for the entire night. But right now, at this moment, she wants me.

My mate.

And I want to devour her.

CHAPTER 10
HETTIE

He's close. So fucking close. His masculine scent envelops me. I need to pull away, but...I don't. I'm trapped in his heated stare, and I don't want whatever spell we're under to break.

I don't know what possesses me to pull Rip back down, crashing our lips together in a hungry battle for dominance. But the newly formed bond between us has me wanton. Tallie said the feeling is intense. I expected a bad case of lust, not...whatever the fuck this is.

Rip stiffens for a fraction of a second, and then he's there, cupping my face and kissing me like I'm the only woman in his universe. Like if he broke apart from me, he wouldn't ever have this opportunity again.

I feel *everything*. This must be the bond Tallie mentioned. I sense Rip's desire for me. The lust and need he can't control. But I also sense his fear. Fear for the safety of those he loves and fear for not being able to protect me properly.

A needy sound comes out of me that I'll definitely regret later when my body isn't on fire with need. I feel every inch of Rip's body, and his hard cock presses against my stomach. My pussy screams in protest, wanting something we can't have. At least not now. Maybe ever.

Because Rip might be my mate now—whatever that entails—but this isn't a love match. This is a mutually beneficial pairing, and me and my horny vagina need to remember that. No matter how badly I want more than this breathtaking kiss. It's the damn drink that's making me lose my mind to lust. I don't feel in control of my own body or brain. I *feel* him in my head. It's...bizarre.

Once again, Rip is the one to break us apart. I try to hold back my disappointment, but it comes out in the form of a pout, anyway. His face is pure smug male satisfaction, but then he quickly slips back into the mask he's good at wearing. "It's done," he says.

Moments ago, I caught glimpses of Rip. The side he doesn't show to the world. The emotions he fed me suddenly cease, and walls build up around him, not letting anything through. The bond feels...cold. Distant. Desolate.

I expect there to be more to the ceremony. A closing statement, maybe an acknowledgment from Rip, but none of those things happen. Rip nods once to his aunt and reaches for my hand. I try to back away, but he isn't having it. He takes my hand and forces it on his arm, curling his hand over mine.

"I go from being your mate to becoming your prisoner in less than a minute, " I snarl, hoping he can see my reproachful glare.

The side of his mouth quirks up. "You can never make anything easy, can you, Hettie?"

"Where's the fun in that?" I ask with fake sweetness.

"Careful, Dove. Bad girls get spanked."

Heat rushes to my cheeks, and I have to press my thighs

together at the image of Rip bending me over his bed and spanking me. It's equal parts humiliating and sexy. "Don't call me Dove," I murmur, not wanting to give away how much his words affect me.

But does this newfound bond make him feel my emotions? I don't know how to shield them like he does. I should probably add that to my to-do list.

"I think I quite like it, actually. Dove seems fitting."

My scowl only deepens, and Rip stops when he approaches Tallie and Thorne. "You'll handle things tomorrow while Hettie and I are occupied?" he asks.

Occupied? Occupied doing what?

Tallie nods. "Of course. We can handle everything for a day. Oh, and, Hettie, I'll keep Grass with me tonight, if that's alright. He seemed pretty content lounging by the fire."

I forgot Grass stayed behind at Tallie's house. He's loving being the center of attention and spoiled by everyone he passes. I have yet to see another dog here, so I'm thinking Grass might be the only one. And I'm sure he will be more than fine with that.

"Thank you. He's always up early expecting to eat, though."

"So is Thorne." Tallie smiles. Thorne laughs, squeezing her shoulder affectionately.

For a moment, I allow myself to imagine a love so pure and strong, like the one I can see between Thorne and Tallie. I'm not a jealous person, despite how hard my former boyfriends tried to make me, but looking at them, all I can feel is the intense need to have what they have.

"Congratulations. I think you'll make a fine Luna, Hettie." Thorne smiles and leads Tallic away, presumably back home. Imelda isn't far behind them, leaving Rip and me alone.

"That's really all there is to it?" I ask, unable to hide my disappointment. I expected...more.

Rip starts walking, and I'm pulled along with him. "What were you expecting?"

"I..." What was I expecting? Music. Maybe more people in attendance. A slow dance? "I don't know."

"What do humans do for mating?" he sounds genuinely curious.

"Well, we don't mate. We just call it getting married so you can become spouses. There's a big ceremony, an outrageously expensive white dress, and vows from the two getting married. Then afterwards there's a big reception for family and friends to dance, eat, and celebrate."

"Was that what you wanted? A reception? Dancing?"

"I...guess not. It's just different."

Rip stays silent for a long time after, and I think the conversation is over until he says, "Our ceremony wasn't typical. The bonding between the King Alpha and his Luna is usually an all-day celebration. Perhaps more like you were expecting." He pauses but doesn't look at me. "But we don't have the luxury of a grand ceremony. Not with Michael and..."

He trails off, so close to saying more, but leaving me without answers again. "Michael and what? Why couldn't we do the big ceremony? Are you ashamed of me?"

"No." The word comes out harsher than I expect, and I flinch. Rip notices and narrows his eyes. "That is the second time you've flinched around me. Do you want to tell me why?"

"I don't know. Do you want to tell me about Michael and the dangers we are apparently facing?" I shoot back, mostly so I don't have to speak on things I would much rather keep buried. Rip looks like he wants to pry more, but wisely drops it. I'm not naive enough to think it's for good though.

"You'll learn everything you need to know about the pack starting tomorrow, Dove," he says, once again with the stupid nickname.

I don't realize we've made it back to the packhouse until we are walking up the stairs. Two guards open the front door for us, both nodding respectfully at Rip, who acknowledges them with a slight dip of his head. One of the man's eyes goes to my neck and widens when he sees the bite. It must be a sight to see. I feel it throbbing, but it's not really painful anymore.

"Luna," he says in a hasty greeting, bowing formally and pulling the other guard down to join him.

"Erm, you don't have to do that," I say.

"Yes, they do." Rip gives the men a once-over before pulling me through the door, past the confused stares of his men. He walks me up the grand staircase, lit with oil lamps, and leads me to our room.

"Do you think I should put bandages on my neck or—"

"No bandages," he growls. "It's already healing. People need to see my mark on you."

"I think it's grossly unfair that I have to wear your damn mark, but you don't have a mark on your body. Pretty damn sexist, if you ask me."

"I didn't."

"Well, you should."

"Do you want to bite me, Dove?"

Heat pools between my legs at his suggestive words. Despite my annoyance, my body reacts to him on a carnal level. The bond takes my reluctant attraction to him and amplifies everything tenfold.

"I'm just saying I shouldn't be the only one with a mark, like I'm property," I mumble, the bravado from earlier leaving.

The bastard only grins. Seems like the only time he smiles is when he pisses me off. He doesn't reply as he pushes past me to open the door to our room. My body goes stiff as I see him enter. "You're staying in here?"

Rip makes his way to the fireplace, grabbing the stoker that lies against the wall to poke at the already blazing fire. He watches the wood burn for a moment before putting the stoker back.

"It's my room. Where else would I stay, Dove?" he asks like I should have already known that. I just expected him to stay somewhere else like he did last night. The large room suddenly feels too cramped.

Rip then walks into the bathroom, leaving me to my own devices. Today's events hit me all at once, and I bite back a sob. I ignore the prickle of tears stinging my eyes as I find a neatly folded nightgown on the bed. I presume one of Rip's staff members left it for me. I pick up the delicate fabric, the soft silk caressing my skin. It isn't something I would normally wear. It's a little too provocative to wear to bed with a near stranger, but I'll deal.

I listen for any movement that Rip might come out soon, and when I'm certain he won't walk in on me butt-ass naked, I strip. Getting the dress off is no easy task, and I'm certain I hear the undeniable rip of thread. The tulle on the skirt tangles around my legs more than once, and I barely save myself from face-planting.

By the time I get the gown on, I'm panting like I just ran a mile and not simply undressed.

Just as I thought, the gown barely covers my ass, and the neckline is cut low. One wrong move in the middle of the night, and a boob will pop out. The last thing I want to do is give my new mate a show he doesn't deserve. My tits are nice, and it's a privilege to get to see them.

After kicking my clothes out of the way, I climb into bed, facing away from the bathroom door. Thoughts of Michael and my rushed mating ceremony come to mind. Everything is happening so fast, and I'm not even certain I'm safe here like Ender said I would be.

Despite my best efforts, tears run down my cheeks.

I hate crying, but I'm not against it. I firmly believe crying is a show of struggling to win a battle. Where nothing else will purge the emotions swirling and thrashing inside you. But for me personally, I hate crying. It's not cute. It's snotty. And I feel so small.

The door opens behind me, and I hear Rip moving around. Soon the bed dips, and my body immediately tenses. A silly part of me wonders if I stay completely still if he'll notice me. But of course he will. He can sense me now, not to mention I'm a big blob in the middle of his bed.

"Hettie...are you crying?" I can't tell if he sounds horrified or concerned. Probably the former. Who wants a strange woman you just had to mate for life crying in your bed? Sounds like a real downer.

"No." Even as I say it, another tear rolls down my cheek, and I quickly move my hand to wipe it away.

Not quick enough. Rip's arm shoots out and catches my wrist. He is gentle but firm as he rolls me over in bed. My tear-stained cheeks and red-rimmed eyes are a dead give-away to how I'm feeling. For once, I don't see the teasing or apathetic façade Rip usually wears around me. He looks... pained. I can't help but flinch away.

Instantly, Rip drops my hand and pulls back. His pained expression is long gone, and through our bond, I feel his anger get past his defenses. I'm not sure how to react as he storms around the bed and all but drags me up into a sitting position.

"What the hell?!" I gasp, confused and angry by his reaction.

"That's the third time." His jaw is set in a hard line, eyes dark with something I can't quite explain.

"Third time for what?" I swear, if this man plans to spend the rest of my life confusing me, I might just let Michael have me so I can get away from this.

"The third time you've flinched when I touched you. Have I threatened to hurt you?"

"No, but—"

"Have I made any attempt at hurting you?"

"No, but—"

"Do you think I'm going to hurt you?"

"For fuck's sake, Rip—"

"Answer the damn question, Hettie." His voice is unnaturally low. Never once does he take his eyes off me, even when I squirm and try to move away. He keeps me locked into place.

Do I think Rip is going to hurt me? I'm wary around men in general because what woman isn't? I've had my fair share of bad men who left me scarred, not only physically, but mentally as well. So, yeah, maybe I am projecting on Rip.

But do I really think this man is going to hurt me?

"No," I say, surprising myself. "I don't think you'd intentionally hurt me, Rip."

Rip's body relaxes. When he takes my hand again, I don't flinch, not wanting to cause any more problems.

"Then someone else made you fear touch." Silence stretches between us. "Know this, Hettie. I can't promise you much right now, but I can promise you I will never hurt you. You will never know fear when we are alone. I give you my word."

This isn't the first time a man has promised he wouldn't ever hurt me, but it is the first time I believed someone. For all of Rip's faults, I know in this he speaks the truth. "I believe you," I whisper, but the words sound loud in the otherwise quiet room.

Rip holds my attention a moment longer and then nods. Something unspoken passes between us. A small part of the armor we both wear crumbles away. It's not much, but it's a start.

"Good." He abruptly moves back to his side of the bed, leaving me wondering if what just happened between us is something I simply imagined. He slips into the bed next to me, keeping a respectable distance between us. For good measure, though, I construct a mountain of pillows between us.

"Is that necessary?" he asks, deadpan, once I'm finished.

"Very," I hum.

I swear I hear him chuckle, but it's faint. "Sleep well. Tomorrow is going to be a long day."

"What's tomorrow?"

The bed dips again. I feel Rip moving to make himself comfortable. Soon the room is silent once again, and the last thing I hear before sleep overtakes me is, "Answers, Dove. Answers."

CHAPTER 11
RIP

Sleep didn't come easily last night. No one but me has ever slept the entire night in my bed. I prefer to have my own space, even when I entertained previous lovers. It was always in their space or a guest room. Having Hettie so close, her lavender scent all over the pillows and blankets, drove me half mad with lust. My cock doesn't realize that the woman next to us is strictly off-limits.

When dawn finally comes, and the first rays of the morning sun filter through the slightly ajar window, I surrender my battle with sleep and finally get up. Hettie, apparently, didn't have the same problem.

My mate is curled up in her blanket, her thick hair splayed across the pillow. She's out cold and doesn't so much as stir when I get off the bed. In fact, she knocks down the pillow wall between us and moves her body to the center of the bed. Not once waking up.

I let her sleep while I get ready. Today, Hettie gets her answers. She's pack now. She's mine, and she needs to be informed about the curse taking over our pack. Ender is certain she can help, but without the proper knowledge, she wields a dull blade.

I rarely bother with a shirt, but today I look through my meager collection and wonder what her favorite color is. Green? Blue? It's fucking stupid, but I grab the green shirt, thinking Hettie might like it on me best. I pull on my pants just as someone knocks on the door.

A moment later, it opens, and a beta pushes in a cart full of food. The smell of maple syrup hits my senses first, and my stomach growls.

"Do you require anything else, King Alpha?" the beta asks, doing his best not to stare at the woman in my bed. By now, the entire pack knows of Hettie's arrival. Some, if not all, also know I bonded with her last night. We didn't pass many of my people on our way back from the ceremony, but it only takes one look at Hettie's neck to piece together a picture. Word spread quickly after that, I'm sure.

"No, that's all."

The beta nods, and his curiosity gets the best of him. He turns his attention to Hettie. Only her top half is covered by the blanket because she wiggled so much throughout the night. The smooth, golden expanse of her legs is on full display. Her gown is hiked up indecently, showing off more of her thigh than I want this beta to see.

I growl a low warning, and the beta quickly looks away, straightening up. "Leave." My command is harsher than I intend, but it's effective. The beta trips over himself on the way to the door.

Only once he's out and far down the hallway do I approach my sleeping mate. I gently touch my hand to her shoulder, half expecting her to flinch from me like she does when she's awake, but Hettie doesn't. She turns into my hand, rubbing her damn cheek against it. My little dove is *scenting* me.

I'm tempted to stay here for however fucking long Hettie remains asleep...but we don't have the time for such luxuries. "Hettie, it's time to wake up." I gently shake her, but Hettie slaps my hand away.

"Hettie—"

"I heard you," she hisses. Her eyes flutter open, giving me the perfect view of her hazel irises, reminding me of aged tree bark. She purses her red lips in a pout as she pulls the covers up to her chin. "It's early," she mutters.

I nod. "It is."

"Then I'll sleep." She goes to turn away from me, but I stop her before she can, which earns me a name I've never heard before but doesn't sound pleasant.

"You wanted answers. Today is that day, but we have a lot to do. You need to wake up." I feel like a mother trying to rouse their insubordinate teen out of bed. "Breakfast is ready too," I say, hoping food is enough motivation to get her up.

Hettie peers over the blanket at the tray of food and sniffs the air. "Is that pancakes?"

"I believe so, yes." I smelled the syrup earlier, so I'm just assuming. But the kitchen staff is fond of pancakes, so I'm not surprised they're being served to us.

Hettie groans, but the promise of food gets her into a sitting position. She then looks at me expectantly, like I should know what she wants. She gives me an exasperated sigh. "What's the point of having a bond if you don't know I want you to get me pancakes?"

"That's not how the bond works." At least not yet. Right now, I can only sense each other and our emotions. Even that is faint. If we ever solidified the bond with sex, then I could communicate with her through the link only mates have.

"Well, it should," she mutters like a child. "Do you have coffee?"

"What's that?"

A mangled cry leaves her lips, and she simply shakes her head. "A tragedy is what that is, Rip."

She doesn't elaborate, and I don't ask her to. Instead, I move to the cart and carry the tray of food to her, setting it on her lap. Hettie does this weird little shimmy and claps her hands. "Do you always have people bring you food?"

"Yes."

"Damn." She smiles as she digs into her meal. It fills me with immense satisfaction to see my mate stuff her face with a delicious breakfast. I doubt it's something she had regularly back home, though I don't know for sure. She hasn't told me anything about her life before. Perhaps today will change that after I expose our secrets.

"What exactly are we doing today?" Hettie asks between bites of her food.

I grab my tray and sit across from her on the bed. I normally hate eating in bed out of fear I'll leave my bed full of crumbs, but seeing Hettie so comfortable and enjoying her meal, I don't have the heart to move.

"Our first stop will be the infirmary. That's going to answer all of your questions." Or at least it will answer a lot of them. I'm sure more will arise, and I'll deal with those as they come.

"Infirmary? You mean like a hospital?" she wonders, taking a sip of the wild berry juice. She scrunches up her face after the first sip and quickly discards the cup. I don't blame her. The juice is too sweet for my liking.

"I suppose so, yes. I want you to see what threat our pack is facing."

I watch Hettie closely. She seems to consider my words. Questions flash across her face, and I know she wants to ask me more, but she doesn't. Instead, she nods. "I'm ready to see."

Unexplainable pride swells within me. My Luna is ready to meet the rest of our pack. Granted, the meeting will not be a pleasant one because I'm going to expose her to the sickness threatening my pack, but it's necessary. After that, I will show her the better parts of this pack, and maybe—just maybe—she'll fall in love with the people she's meant to lead.

"We will go after you finish breakfast."

Hettie nods, and we eat in companionable silence.

THE AIR IS crisp with the scent of citrusy cleaning soaps. Sickness and death linger in the sterilized space, creating a melancholy atmosphere. Soft cries and weak coughs travel down the hallway, reminding me once again of the troubles my pack face.

The infirmary is our largest building, spanning three stories high with about twenty small rooms per floor. Each room is equipped with their own medical supplies, while the more intensive supplies and medicines remain locked in the medical room on the first floor.

Our pack normally has around five healers and three assistant healers. When more of my pack started to move into town, more healers came with them. Right now, we house close to twenty healers and ten assistants.

I thought it would be enough.

It *had* been enough at the beginning.

But not anymore.

Hettie's head swivels back and forth as we walk down the long, narrow hallway. The curtains for most of the rooms are pulled back, giving us small glimpses inside. Bodies atop cots, some barely breathing while others moan in pain. We pass a room where a mother and a young girl sit around a sickly man. His skin is pulled taut across his pale skin, making him appear skeletal. His wife leans over him, patting his head with a damp cloth. Silent tears run down her cheeks, but she still smiles at their young daughter.

"Is Papa going to die, Mommy?" I hear the small girl ask.

A strangled cry leaves the mother's throat. I recognize her husband. A beta named Grant. He was one of the first to fall to the curse and grows worse every day. It's a miracle he's still with us. He's living on borrowed time, and if nothing can be done soon, he'll be one of the next to die.

The mother—I believe her name is Annelisa—looks up and makes eye contact with me. Her eyes are filled with so much pain and sorrow. "No, sweetie. Papa isn't going to die. Our King Alpha is going to make sure he feels better." The beta holds my gaze, reminding me what happens if I fail. People like Grant will die.

We've watched enough of this poor family's suffering, and I take Hettie's hand, leading her down the hall. More rooms with full beds. More mourning families. Healers race from room to room to check on all their patients. The dark circles under their eyes are more pronounced than they were last week. It'll only get worse as more and more of the infirmary's beds fill up.

"What happened here?" Hettie's voice is barely above a

whisper, but it may as well have been a shout. The death-like halls are unforgiving, and each cough is the sound of a pendulum swinging back and forth. Never knowing when it will all be over.

I lead Hettie down the hall and make a left at the fork. This leads up to a private break room that goes unused. None of the healers have time to use this room anymore. Hettie sits down on a too stiff couch, and I take a seat in the chair in front of her.

The room is cold, much like the rest of the facility, and Hettie trembles, despite her jacket. "There's a blanket next to you." I reach for the quilted blanket. She offers me a smile as I drape it around her. I thought the clothes Tallie chose for Hettie would be enough to keep her warm, but she's going to need something thicker.

"What's happened here, Rip?" she asks again.

I promised her answers. And she's going to get them.

"What did Ender tell you about our pack?"

She shrugs. "Honestly? Not much. Probably so I wouldn't be scared away. I knew I would marry the King Alpha to help his pack. He didn't mention how or why, though."

Sounds like Ender. He can be annoyingly obtuse at the best of times.

"Not too long ago, another human from your world was brought over by Ender to marry the Dragon King Malix. She helped break the dragons out of their sleeping curse and restored the wards around Dragon's Keep that keep the Nephilim out."

"Rose, right?" Hettie questions. "I know of her, but we've never met."

"Yes, perhaps you'll meet her someday."

"I don't really understand who the Nephilim are. I

thought we were dealing with rogues. Are they really your biggest threat, or is it Michael?" I can see her mind working a mile a minute. From her short stay, she has already seen and picked up a lot of conflicting information.

Hettie is smart and intuitive. Those traits will make her a good Luna.

"The Nephilim are creatures of nightmares. Giants with shredded wings and immense power. They are cruelty and darkness personified. Their leader, Gadreel, wants to remake Mescos in his image by annihilating everything and everyone in his path." The way Malix described these horrendous beasts, I know my pack won't be able to fight them on our own. Hence the need for his help when the time comes.

I dive into the brief history of the Great War, when the rulers of Mescos came together to imprison the Nephilim. The curse Gadreel cast upon the rulers that in one hundred years, if the kings of Mescos do not find their mate, they will fall to the Nephilim's curse. It's all a lot to take in, and I expect Hettie to stop me. I wouldn't blame her if she said the story overwhelmed her.

But she doesn't.

She listens and nods. She doesn't flinch or appear scared, like I thought she would. She looks...like the pack Luna.

Pride and something else I'm not ready to admit swell in my chest. Her calming presence takes away a little of the stress, which is more than anyone else has done.

"So, these sick people...it's because of the curse," she says slowly. "What exactly is the curse that makes your pack so sick?"

"Our."

"Hmm?"

"Our," I repeat. "Our pack, Dove." Her lips quirk up in a phantom smile. It soon falls as I go on. "The curse is making our wolf go dormant."

Hettie's brow furrows. "What do you mean?"

"Every wolf is born with two souls inside their body. That of a human and the other of a wolf. We are one and have always been one. The curse is taking our wolf from us, leaving us shadows of what we once were. Our bodies can't handle the loss of our wolf. We grow sick and eventually..."

"Die," she whispers what I cannot. "But..." She pauses, trying to formulate her thoughts. "I don't understand how Michael fits into this."

"Michael." I can't keep the growl out of my voice. The rogue is worse than the dirt beneath my feet. When the day finally comes, I will gladly tear his head from his body. Like I should have done long ago. "He has been my enemy since my ascension to king. He wanted to be King Alpha, so we fought for the title. When I bested him, I made my first foolish mistake as king. I let him live." It's a condensed version of the truth, but enough for now.

"You showed mercy," Hettie says, reaching out to put her hand on my thigh. Neither one of us move. My mate is touching me, and my wolf fucking loves it. As if sensing my wayward thoughts, Hettie blushes and pulls back. "So, he's the leader of the rogues?"

I nod. "He's the reason we can't make our sick wolves better."

"So, there's a cure?" Hettie perks up, hope blazing behind her eyes.

I hate to be the one to extinguish her flame, but she needs to know everything. "Yes, but the only known cure is in Michael's possession, and we believe he is working with the Nephilim, but we aren't sure why."

"What is the cure?"

"I can show you."

There's no hesitancy in her gaze or voice as she reaches for my hand again. It's a soft touch. A whisper of a touch. I feel it all the same. Like fire coursing through my veins. The same fire is within her.

Hettie squeezes my hand. "Show me."

CHAPTER 12

HETTIE

Rip leads me out of the infirmary, but not before I pass through the rooms of sick and crying family members. My heart breaks a little, picturing the small girl next to her father's bedside, crying into his chest. Pain and loss radiate from the building; I feel suffocated by it all.

And this is what Rip has been dealing with the entire time? Alone, at that. I at least had a family, broken as it was, but a family for support, nonetheless.

No one should have to carry this burden alone.

I know the pain of losing a loved one. The hopelessness that eats away at you until nothing remains but a shell of your former self. Life eventually goes on, and you are expected to adapt, but mentally you are still reliving the day that changed your life forever.

I couldn't save my father, but maybe I can save someone else's. And, if I'm lucky, maybe it will ease some of the guilt that plagues me each day.

Rip's hold on my hand is firm but gentle. Curious eyes follow us as we walk through dirt paths. A few people stop to show their respect for Rip, and no matter how busy he appears, he makes sure to take the time to greet everyone.

It's...unexpected.

Soon the infirmary is a speck behind me, and we arrive in a residential neighborhood. I frown, looking at the rows of weathered but well taken care of homes. My confusion only grows as Rip pulls me closer and leads us toward one of the houses.

"The cure is in here?" Then, because I watch too many crime documentaries: "Or did you come here to kill me so no one will notice?" I'm joking. Mostly.

For the first time since I've met Rip, the man barks out a real, genuine laugh. Which does little to disprove my murder theory, but makes me oddly proud that I'm able to make him laugh.

"No, Dove, I don't plan on killing you. The cure, or what we hope to be the cure, is in here." Rip and I reach the door, and instead of knocking, he walks in like he owns the house. Maybe he does.

The house is one large room, though I suspect it had once been an actual home with different rooms. The wooden walls are dull and lifeless. The smell of burning incense fills the room, almost overpowering the rotting wood smell. Almost.

There's a single threadbare couch pushed against one wall, and two large desks spanning most of the room. Each desk is piled high with both broken and non-broken pencils. Papers are scattered across the surface and underneath the desk. Different plants and vials take up the rest of the space, but nothing else stands out.

"The curse hit us unexpectedly, and we hadn't prepared a space for mass production of wolfsbane," Rip explains the hasty made lab. "All of the healers' space had been taken up with sick wolves. Out of sheer necessity, I put together a place for the strongest healers to work together in hopes their combined knowledge would help produce a cure. So far, we haven't gotten far."

We aren't alone in this rotting cottage. Four other people are bent over a desk, all staring at a strange purple bud and talking at once. Lost in their own discussion, the team doesn't realize we've walked in until Rip clears his throat.

All four heads pop up at once. It's a motley crew composed of three women and a man. The group ranges from someone around my age to the oldest woman, who could be their great grandmother.

They all realize at the same time who stands before them, and a chorus of "Hi, King Alpha," greets us. The youngest man stares at our clasped hands. I don't realize I'm still holding Rip's hand, but now that I'm aware, I should probably take my hand back. And I would, but...my hand in his feels nice. Rip makes no move to pull away either.

Rip greets them, stopping at the oldest woman. "Lucielle, this is my mate, Hettie."

Lucielle's eyes widen. The woman makes her way over to me and bows her head. "It's a pleasure to meet you, Luna."

That title and bowing are going to take a while to get used to, but I return the gesture. No one gasps or seems offended by my action, so I take it as a good sign.

"Lucielle's mate was one of the first victims of the curse. She's been the lead healer in our search for a cure," Rip says.

At the mention of her fallen mate, Lucielle winces. I know that pain. It cuts deep and fast, even when you think you can handle it. She wears the grief, even now.

"I wish I could have met him," I say gently. I don't apologize because I heard so many apologies when my father died, and it didn't matter how many times people said it. It would not bring back my father, and it's not like they caused his death.

"Thank you. He was a good alpha. Worked in Alpha Rip's guard team."

"He was one of the best alphas on my team. His service will be remembered," Rip assures. Unlike other people in powerful positions, he doesn't sound like he's rehearsed these lines a hundred times. They feel genuine. True.

Rip cares for the pack he leads. And damn if that doesn't make me warm all over.

"Did you need something, King Alpha?" Lucielle asks after a moment, snapping me back to the present. We were here for a reason. And it's not for me to develop a damn crush on my mate.

"I want you to show your Luna the cure." Rip gestures to the messy desks. "Or what we have of it."

"Not much, unfortunately. Please come, Luna." Lucielle gestures me forward, and I follow. I try to drop my hand away from Rip, but he holds tight and squeezes gently until I lace our fingers back together.

So, I guess we hold hands now. Cute.

Lucielle brings me to the only clean part of the desk. There's a rack of small vials off to one side and purple petals scattered in the center. "These are wolfsbane petals. Are you familiar with wolfsbane, Luna?" When I shake my head, she continues, "It's both death and life. Too much will kill even the strongest of alphas. But the perfect amount? That can wake the dormant wolf."

"Has this been tested? Is the sickness contagious?" As soon as the question is out, I immediately blush. What a fucking stupid thing to ask. Of course it has been tested, or else they wouldn't know it could cure their sickness.

"Only once," Rip speaks up. "From what we've gathered, you can't contract the sickness. It's random and strikes deadly. But typically, it strikes adults. So far most of the alphas in our pack have been hit with it.

"But," he continues, blowing out a deep breath, "a couple of weeks ago, a child fell ill. The first one. Our stash of wolfsbane is limited. You're looking at what's left."

"But these are only a few petals." Horror seizes me at the thought of all the sick bodies back in the infirmary. I'm looking at the flower that could save them, but isn't enough to save them all.

"We had more, but we used most of our stash on the pup. Within a few days, she was completely healed, but it took up almost everything we had," Lucielle explains. "Michael and his rogues have cut off our access to wolfsbane."

"We can only assume they are working with the Nephilim," Rip interjects. "I don't understand his angle. Michael isn't stupid. He should know that whatever the Nephilim promised him, they don't intend to keep it."

Michael hadn't seemed completely sane when he ambushed me in the forest, but from our brief interaction, I know the man is smart. Smarter than he let others believe. And he said he wanted me, but for what reason?

"King Alpha, we have been unsuccessful at growing wolfsbane. Our last few batches have died before they've bloomed. We were going to discard the remains—"

"No, keep them," Rip interrupts.

"Keep them?" Lucielle pursed her lips. "But they are useless."

"Perhaps. But I want nothing thrown out. We keep

everything. I won't risk the chance of accidentally tossing a key ingredient away."

Lucielle doesn't look convinced that anything they save will be beneficial, but I see Rip's logic. There's no harm in keeping something that may be deemed useless. It would be devastating to realize that the ingredient you threw away was needed in the end.

"Of course, King Alpha." Lucielle nods. "Is there anything else we can help you with?"

Rip shakes his head. "No, but please note your Luna has access to this room. If she wishes, she will come for updates when I can't."

I snap my head in his direction, unsure if I heard him correctly. "Really?" I can't keep the skepticism out of my voice. "You'd let me come here without you?" I don't know why the words shock me as much as they do. Maybe a part of me thought I would be little more than a decorative piece in this relationship. I never believed I would actually be a partner in this pack. Only an outsider.

Rip narrows his eyes at me, sending a mixture of fear and arousal through me. How can this man elicit two vastly different emotions? I want to simultaneously run away from him, but also feel his hard body against mine. These are not the thoughts I should have right now.

Rip pulls me out of the makeshift lab. Our hands are still firmly clasped together when he shuts the door behind me. I still know very little about shifters and their world, but I know they have superior hearing, judging from my few interactions. This is only an illusion of privacy. The four people inside can probably hear us if they care enough to pay attention.

"I want to make one thing very clear, Hettie," Rip says,

voice low. In the early afternoon glow, he looks like a ravenous god, beautiful and strong, with his eyes set on me.

"You are my Luna. Not my employee or a mere human. You're my mate, and with that comes certain privileges. You're to help me take care of our pack. You are smart, charismatic, and kind, when you want to be." He smirks.

"You were doing great until the last part." I glare, though I sound slightly breathless. His words hit me. Rip has known me a grand total of a couple of days and is already placing trust in me. He sees me as capable and not less than.

The breeze picks up around us, and goosebumps form on my arms. My nipples harden, easily noticeable through my thin top. I'm not sure who thought this outfit would be warm, but it's definitely not. My hair, which I attempted to tie back in a bun, comes loose and a strand of it blows into my eyes. Rip reaches out and gently tucks it behind my ear.

The gesture is far more intimate than it should be.

And I don't flinch.

Our eyes meet, and the bond sparks to life, begging me to move closer. To press my body against this man I barely know but am drawn to. How much of this is the mate bond, and how much of it is my need to have him close?

Rip also appears to be fighting a silent battle. Slowly, far too slowly, he drops his hand back down to his side. When he speaks again, his voice drops an octave. "You're here to save us, Hettie. What you want, you'll get. You're my partner. My Luna. I will not stand in your way. Do you understand, Dove?"

"Yes, Alpha." The words tumble out of me before I realize what I'm saying. Rip sucks in a breath as he takes a step forward. There's something feral in the way he looks at me, something I know I should feel scared about, but heat pools between my thighs instead.

"Say it again," he growls. His hand reaches up, but this time it circles my neck. It's the first time I don't flinch away from a male's touch. A needy sound leaves me involuntarily. How did things change so drastically, so fast? His thumb brushes my bottom lip. "Again, Dove."

The command in his voice weakens my resolve. "Yes, Alpha," I say automatically, and his hold on me tightens.

"I like it when you call me Alpha," he says as if the hand on my neck and thumb on my lip isn't a dead giveaway. I can't help but feel smug knowing that, as crazy as he is driving me, I'm doing the same to him.

Because I'm feeling particularly bratty, I lean into his touch, nearly choking myself. It only makes this exchange hotter because I love a good hand necklace in bed. Rip's nostrils flare, and I swear he's seconds away from snapping. Do I want that?

"Only good boys get called Alpha." The flash of anger and desire that flashes across his features leaves me feeling victorious as I step out of his grip and turn my back on him. It takes everything in my power not to turn my head to see his expression. The overwhelming feeling of lust coming from the bond tells me all I need to know.

"Let's go, Alpha. I'm sure there's more you need to show me." I keep walking, and for a long time, I don't hear Rip follow me. I think I may have taken it a step too far when I hear the crunch of grass behind and the heat from Rip's body as he catches up.

"Just remember, Dove. Naughty girls get punished," he says.

This time I'm the one left stunned, mouth slightly ajar.

"Come," he calls again, and I find myself following orders for once.

CHAPTER 13
RIP

A glass of red wine sits untouched in front of Hettie on the dining room table. She's more enamored with the small tray of biscuits and fruits. She catches me staring and raises her brow as she bites down on a grape. Some of the juice rolls down her chin, and I watch as it disappears. I'm tempted to lick up the juices myself.

"What?" Hettie mumbles in between bites. "If you wanted some, you should have said something." She keeps the bowl of fruit close to her, protecting it like a mother bird would protect her nest.

"Not a fan of wine?" I ask.

"Hmm? Oh, no, not really. Never liked the taste of wine. I like beer though." Hettie scoots the glass over to me. "You can have it. Just not the food."

I'm reminded again of how thin Hettie is. I will gladly keep bringing out food if she so desires. But this small moment reminds me that I still know virtually nothing about my mate. I'm a greedy bastard, and I want to know everything. It's about time she spills her secrets.

Starting with why she's here.

"Hettie, why did you make the deal with Ender to become my wife?" I ask the burning question on my mind. Really, I want to know just how bad things were that made her want to leave her world entirely.

"Ah, fuck," Hettie mumbles under her breath, leaning back in her chair. She doesn't seem surprised that I asked the question, but she also doesn't look eager to share. "Does it matter?" she asks after a pregnant pause.

"I would argue it matters the most. I made the deal with Ender to strengthen my pack against rogues and Nephilim. I gain so much by you being here, but I can't figure out what you gain." *Tell me,* I want to say. My wolf begs me to say, but I once promised her that I wouldn't make her do anything she doesn't want to do. That includes now.

Hettie clenches her jaw, tightening her hold on the bowl of fruit. The confident woman from seconds ago is gone. All I see now is a fearful, lost girl, unsure how to proceed.

"You can talk to me, Dove." My voice is gentle. A light purr rumbles through my throat, and Hettie's shoulders slouch.

"You're going to regret taking me as your wife if I told you." She seems genuinely worried about my opinion of her. My wolf stirs inside me, needing to comfort his mate.

"I highly doubt that. You don't become the King Alpha without blood on your hands. Whatever you have to tell me, there will be no judgment on my end." Because, at the end of the day, Hettie is a survivor. Or she wouldn't be sitting in front of me now.

"My father died," she says so gently that I can barely

hear her. "He was in and out of hospitals for the last few months of his life, and it's my fault."

"Why do you say that?"

"Because," she sighs and crosses her arms over her chest, "I was constantly putting so much stress on the family. I was never satisfied or appreciated the life they worked so hard to give my sister and me." She sniffles, and I see the first tear run down her cheek.

There's more to the story, I know there is, but I'm not going to push her. I'll let her talk to me on her own terms. Instead, I don't even think. I act on instinct and push out of my chair to move in front of her.

"Rip?" The fear in her voice breaks my fucking heart.

She thinks I'm going to leave, but I don't. I crouch down in front of her so I can be at eye-level. I feel her confusion and distress through our bond as if her pain is my own.

I can't fucking stand her tears. Her pain is palpable, and I feel hopeless. I do the only thing I can and pull her in for a hug. I give her the opportunity to pull away from me, but she doesn't. Hettie leans into my touch, crying into my shoulder.

"You don't need to tell me. Not until you're ready, Dove. Patience isn't a virtue I possess, but for you? I can be."

"I'm sorry," she says even though she has nothing to apologize for. Hettie slowly peels herself away from me, wiping her eyes. She laughs humorlessly. "God, I'm pathetic. Now you know you mated a fuck-up."

Her poor attempt at humor has me growling. "You are far from pathetic. You made mistakes, but your mistakes didn't kill your father, Hettie. It was simply his time. But," I sigh, running a hand through my hair, "I know what it feels like to let down a parent."

"You do?" she asks curiously, her head tilting to the side.

I'm asking her to share something difficult; it seems only fair I should do the same. "Yes. I was too late to help my own father. He died in a fight. The fight for King Alpha against Michael."

Hettie's eyes widen. "Wait...Michael killed your father? I thought you were the one to fight him. Is that why he's not part of your pack?"

It's been years since I've relived my father's death. Years since I've watched my mom follow my father in death shortly after. She couldn't live in a world without him, so she left it. It happened so long ago, but it still stings like it was yesterday. Grief never leaves you, just lurks in the corner and appears when you least expect it.

"I did fight him, but the truth is more complicated than that," I sigh. "My father reigned as the King Alpha for decades. I was expected to take up the position once my father decided to retire. However, Michael was my father's second at the time. He was a bastard back then too, but a good strategist. Being second was never good enough for Michael, so he challenged my father for the throne.

"When they were set to fight, his advisors suggested I fight in his place. But I didn't feel prepared. I was barely older than a pup, still trying to find my footing. My father saw the fear in my eyes and denied their suggestions. He said this was his fight alone."

Guilt slices through me and cuts deep, even so many years later.

"Oh, Rip..." Hettie reaches out for me, taking my hand in hers. It's so small compared to mine. She's cold to the touch, but that doesn't seem to bother her right now. "You can't blame yourself for that. You were young."

If only it were that simple. I don't know if I'll ever forgive myself for letting my father fight, knowing he was an older alpha going against an alpha in his prime. For being scared when I should have been brave.

"The fight lasted ten minutes. In the end, my father fell to Michael. That should have been enough to make him king, but I couldn't let my father's death go without trying to avenge him. So, I fought Michael, something I should have done in the first place."

"And you won," Hettie murmurs.

"I won. But I didn't kill Michael...clearly. I didn't want my first act as king to be sentencing someone to death, so I banished him. Over the years, more wolves left the pack to join Michael because they didn't like my leadership." I should have killed him. Had every reason to kill him, but I couldn't bring myself to do it back then. It's still the biggest mistake I've made as King Alpha.

This feels a lot like a turning point for both of us. Understanding colors the bond. Understanding of our trauma and for one another. The feeling is different but... right.

"I guess we are both fucked up then, huh? Perfect pairing." Hettie grins, defusing the tension growing between us.

"You think we're perfect, Dove?" I smirk. Getting back into a teasing mood is much easier than all the heavy shit we just let out.

Hettie rolls her eyes. "Of course you would think like that." She tries to feign anger, but her smile gives her away. "Now go back to your chair so I can get back to my food."

And just like that, the conversation is over. She gave me far more than I expected, and I'm starting to see my Luna in a new light. And she's stronger than she gives herself credit for.

a new light. And she's stronger than she gives herself credit for.

CHAPTER 14

HETTIE

Over the next week, Rip and I share no more moments like the one we had outside the makeshift lab, which I've now dubbed The House of Wolfsbane, or HW for short. We also haven't poured our hearts out to one another again. Part of me feels bad for not going into further detail about my life before Mescos and the reasons I sought out Ender, but I'm not ready.

I know telling Rip about my past will feel like a weight lifted off my shoulders. He won't judge me; there was only concern and understanding in his eyes the other night. Learning about his parents put a lot of things in perspective for me too. Like why Rip is the way he is. Why he cares so much about his pack and keeping everyone safe. He doesn't want to fail again.

Rip and I spend most of our days together, except for when he has patrol, or something else important comes up. Then Tallie and Thorne are with me. But every night, I go to sleep next to him and wake up next to him—albeit grumpily because mornings suck.

109

It's…comforting.

Lycan Forest, although not home, has started to feel familiar. The pain of leaving home is still there, but it's no longer sharp and all-consuming. I'll never stop missing my sister and mother, but the pain, in time, should become more manageable. I wonder what their life is like now? If Ender kept his part of the bargain, which I have to believe he did, are they upgrading the house? Buying a new one? Maybe going on a vacation?

Most of my time now is spent learning about the pack, like the procedures and laws Rip has put into place. I hesitate to learn about the way he leads his people, because I'm not sure I'm the leader they deserve. The more I learn about the pack and the operations, the more I appreciate Rip and his ability to lead a pack of this size.

Everyone in the pack contributes, whether it's running patrols, working at the packhouse, or running one of the businesses in town. My favorite is working with Tallie in the nursery with the pups—children of the pack. They range in age from infants to talkative preteens, and I steal away to the nursery whenever I have some downtime.

Which, surprisingly, isn't much. Rip has stayed true to his word about making me an equal partner. I have attended one meeting he conducted with his pack council. Most of the information involved things I had little knowledge about, like territory borders and correspondence with other kingdoms. When the topic changed to Nephilim and Michael, the room grew tense.

The forest and borders have been quiet. I thought this was good news, but Rip looked stressed. His body grew rigid, and he drummed his fingers against the hard wood of the table. Each tap filled the room with apprehension.

We left that meeting with a heavy feeling of uneasiness.

I try not to dwell on that feeling for too long. When I wake up the next day, I'm surprised to find Rip still snoring softly next to me. He had gone on patrol last night to amp up security since Michael was able to sneak in so easily. With the vast number of sick wolves, we have very few wolves to spare, so Rip has been working overtime. I had fallen asleep alone, which I told myself was fine. I pretended like I didn't miss him.

I felt him come to bed last night, but I was too tired and groggy to greet him properly. His warm body kept the chill away, and for the last few nights, I have woken up with my head on his chest and his arm curled around my waist. Our bodies seem to gravitate toward one another in the middle of the night. Today is no different. So much for the pillow wall I tried to construct.

I don't want to wake him, so I carefully shimmy out of his grasp. He stirs the moment my feet hit the floor, and I pause, hoping if I stay silent and still, he won't wake up. The steady rise and fall of his chest give me the confidence to move again. I go to the bathroom to take care of my needs. Warm, steamy water awaits in a basin for me, and I use it to wash my face and brush my teeth.

When I'm positive I no longer have morning breath, I tiptoe back out of the bathroom in search of clothes. I accidentally trip over Grass in the process. He's taken over quite the pillow fort at the end of the bed.

"Shit, sorry, buddy," I whisper.

Grass just huffs and goes back to bed.

Tallie supplied me with a stash of outfits, all of which are still lying in a neat pile on the floor. I'm not the tidiest of people, and if Rip notices, he doesn't seem to care.

I search the pile until I find wool leggings in a light brown color and a matching hoodie. This damn cold weather is going to take a long time to get used to. Tallie even said they are expecting snow.

I turn my head once, making sure Rip is still asleep before I strip down where I stand. The cold air hits my naked body, and I shiver. My nipples pebble to painful points. I bend down, searching for panties, and find a cute cotton pair. I pull those on, quickly followed by my leggings. They are a little loose, but not to the point they threaten to fall down when I walk. I don't bother with a bra; instead, I pull the large hoodie over my head and wrap myself in its warm embrace.

Finally feeling I won't freeze to death, I turn around and stop dead in my tracks.

Rip sits at the edge of the bed, his gaze burning into mine. I hadn't even heard him move. Something in his expression tells me I just gave this man a free show. Maybe it's the way his dark eyes scan my body, feeling as if they are undressing me all over again. Or the slight bulge pressing against his sleep pants.

A cock has never made my mouth water—I would never give a man that much power. Their inflated egos need no more praise. But Rip's? Fuck, I can't stop wondering what it would feel like with my lips wrapped around his length.

"How long have you been awake?" I try to make my voice sound casual, but there's a slight breathiness to my tone.

"Long enough," he says in that low, gruff morning voice that makes me nearly have to change my panties.

"How much did you see?"

"Not nearly enough, Dove." His lips twitch up to a predatory smirk. His stare pins me in place, caught between fleeing and saying fuck it. One taste of him couldn't hurt... could it? He is my mate, after all, so it seems only natural.

"Your scent is fucking intoxicating when you're turned on," he growls, licking his lips as if he can taste me. Part of me feels embarrassed about him smelling my arousal—I didn't even know shifters could do that. Still, the other part of me relishes the attention, needing more of it.

"And how do you know I'm turned on?" We're playing with fire. One stray ember will set us ablaze, but I don't think I care.

"Because." Rip is up, crossing the room in three powerful strides. He presses against me and forces me to move until my back hits the wall. He leans so close, ducking his head. His nose brushes against my cheek, and I feel something wet on my neck where his bite is. Was that his tongue?

My body acts of its own accord, arching into him. The impressive erection presses into my hip, pinning me in place.

"Because," he starts again, hot breath against my neck, "your scent consumes me. It blooms around you, begging me to touch you. Is that what you want, Dove? To be touched?"

My panties are soaked. His nostrils flare, and I know he's picking up my arousal again. "Yes." The answer comes out as a surprise, but once out, I don't dare take it back.

Something changed between us over the last couple of days. A sort of understanding for each other's pasts, and part of me is desperate to explore this growing tension. Even though I swore I wouldn't fall into the bed of any eligible man showing me an ounce of kindness.

But this is Rip. This is different.

Rip's lips press against the mark he placed on my neck. It's mostly healed now, outlining where his teeth sank into my flesh, creating a scar. He brings his hand up to cup my breasts above my shirt, and I let out a breathy moan. "Is that what you want, Hettie? For me to fuck you? To finish my claim on you?"

"Fuck yes."

He chuckles deeply. "Needy thing, aren't you?"

He doesn't know half of it.

I don't want to fight this anymore. I don't care to think of all the reasons this could be a stupid-ass decision; I just want to feel. "Rip, please—"

His lips crash against mine in a claiming kiss, stealing the breath from my lungs. His hand reaches up to bracket my neck, pulling me closer. I give in to his demands, a strangled gasp leaving my lips.

His tongue pries my lips open, forcing his way inside. This kiss is different from our mating ceremony kiss. For one, there isn't an audience—not counting Grass—which Rip uses to his advantage. He rough thumb runs over my nipple, and my body arches closer.

The need to have him closer is almost painful. Wetness pools between my thighs, and my clit throbs, begging to be touched.

It's both too much and not enough.

My hands rest on his chest, feeling the hard muscles I want to trace with my tongue. Taste the saltiness of his skin and feel him tense underneath me.

Would he fuck me hard? Or take his time and draw out my orgasm?

Either way, I want to find out.

"Hettie," Rip pants. His lips brush against mine. I whimper at the lost contact, and he presses another panty-melting kiss to my swollen lips.

My mind is a cloud of lust, need, and desperation.

Talking is an effort, but I need him to stop holding back and ruin me. Fuck the aftermath; I need him *now*.

"Rip, please—"

That's all I manage to get out before there is a loud knock on the door, followed by a sweet feminine voice. "Hettie? Rip? You two in there? I'm coming in."

Tallie bursts through the door, a wide smile on her face. Her eyes sweep the room until they land on us and widen. "Oh."

Rip curses under his breath and pushes me behind him. My face flames red as I desperately try to get myself together. Was my whole boob out? What did she see? Fuck, how am I going to answer her questions that she'll surely ask now about my relationship with her cousin when I can barely answer them for myself?

"Yesterday we planned on going to the nursery together, but if you two are busy..." Tallie breaks off with a laugh that she tries to hide with a cough.

"Give us a moment, Tallie. Hettie will be down in a minute," Rip says, though he doesn't sound happy about it.

"Of course. I'll wait for our Luna downstairs."

I wait until I hear the door shut behind her before peering around Rip to make sure the coast is clear. "Holy fuck." Tallie is a splash of cold water, awakening me from my horny state. "I need to go."

"Hettie—" Rip reaches out for me, but I sidestep his grip.

"Just give me a moment, and we can go." I plaster a smile on, even as I feel Rip's walls slowly rebuild. Disappointment mars his features, but he nods regardless.

Like the chicken shit I am, I hurry to the bathroom and shut the door, putting distance between us. I need to breathe. To think.

What the fuck am I doing?

CHAPTER 15

RIP

My wolf is unsettled. If I'm being honest, he's been unsettled since the moment Hettie arrived at our doorstep. It only increased during our mating ceremony. The hold this human has over me is both complicated and frustrating. I can't turn my mind off. Can't stop thinking about her.

The need to finish our bond is so fucking strong and painful.

And my resolve is growing weaker.

Hettie is afraid though. Afraid to give in to me. That much was proven by this morning and her mad dash to get away from me when Tallie caught us in our bedroom. I can't help but wonder what would have happened if we were never caught. How far would it have gone?

I know Hettie wants me. The truth is in her body language and the way her desire scents the air each time I'm near. But I will not take a woman who isn't completely willing.

If my Dove wants me, she's going to approach me first.

I've been a patient man up until this point. I can wait a little longer. I need her to be completely ready for me.

Because she is going to want me. That much is inevitable. She just needs to stop fighting it.

Hettie and Tallie walk ahead of Thorne and me, heading to the nursery. Grass trots between the two women, happy as can be. The nursery is my cousin's favorite job in the pack, besides planning ceremonies, and Hettie has accompanied her as often as time will allow.

They don't need Thorne and me trailing behind them, but I'm not eager to let her out of my sight. Even if that means I'll play babysitter to a group of overactive pups. I would be lying if I said seeing her caring for the pups didn't make me think of her belly swollen with mine.

Stepping into the nursery, laughter, crying, and the faint smell of urine assault my senses. "If you two are staying, you better make yourself useful," Tallie says, tying her hair up into a messy bun.

"It's hot when you threaten me." Thorne winks at my cousin and narrowly misses my punch to the arm. Just because I gave them my blessing to mate doesn't mean I want to hear them flirt.

Thorne just laughs at my reaction and follows Tallie to the toddler room. Grass goes with her, and instantly the small children flock to Grass, who preens at all the attention. Hettie stays with the babies, picking up a crying little boy. I watch her as she gently bounces the boy in her arms, cooing at him until he calms down.

"You're a natural," I say, startling her.

"Oh, it's just because I'm an older sister." She shrugs off my words. "My sister and I have a fourteen-year age difference, and I helped my mom a lot when my sister was a baby."

This is the first glimpse I get of her family. She hasn't offered much, and I'm not one to pry, but I find myself doing just that. "I bet you were a good older sister."

"I wasn't." Her words come out soft, and she looks down at the sleeping babe in her arms. "Leaving was the best thing I ever did for them."

"That can't be true," I say, even though I have no way to back my statement up. All I know is it brought her to Ender, which in turn brought her to me.

"You don't know the type of person I was...am. Like I said the last time, if you knew, you wouldn't look twice at me."

"Why don't you tell me what type of woman you think you are, Dove, and I'll tell you the woman I see."

Hettie scowls. "Don't pretend like you know everything about me." She turns from me, placing the sleeping baby into his crib once again before whirling back on me. The fire in her gaze ignites something inside me, and I smirk.

My human has found her claws.

She ignores me as she goes from crib to crib, checking on the other sleeping babies. There's only four today, mostly the children of beta or alpha mothers. Omega mothers have a harder time separating themselves from their children because of their natural biology to care for their young.

"Are you just going to stand there like a fucking creep and stare at me?" she asks, finally taking a seat on the wooden rocking chair.

"Such language around children," I chide.

Hettie rolls her eyes. "They can't talk. Plus, they're sleeping." She waits for me to respond, and when I don't, she groans. "Fine, stare at me. I don't care."

Something tells me she cares a lot, but I have played

with her enough. I let the conversation drop as I take a seat in the only other chair available. It's an atrocious combination of pink and throw-up green that is better suited for a child than my large body. It sags under my weight, threatening to break if I make a wrong move.

Hettie snorts. "You look ridiculous."

I probably do, but I still frown. "Is this your attempt at asking me to sit with you? You just have to ask nicely, Dove."

"First, I'm not a fucking dove. And, second, first come, first serve. Your big ass gets the small chair." Her sinful lips, the very ones I kissed earlier today, quirk up into a flirty smile.

"You've been checking out my ass, mate?"

"You are literally impossible to talk to." From seemingly nowhere, Hettie produces a small pillow and chucks it at my head. It hits my forehead before falling on the floor with a dull thud.

Hettie brings her hand up to stifle her giggle.

"You're going to pay for that, Dove."

She doesn't have the chance to respond. In seconds, I'm out of my chair and snatching her up. "Hey!" she protests as I crush her body against mine.

"If I didn't know any better, I'd think you like picking fights with me."

"Of course you would, you freak." She thrashes against me, but not really attempting to move out of my grip. She does it because she thinks she has to and not because she wants to.

She's enjoying this all too much.

"Are you going to fight with me every day, mate?"

My little Dove stares at me defiantly. Her nostrils flare,

and her breaths come quicker. The smell of lavender blooms around her, intoxicating me.

"Maybe."

"I sure hope so."

Hettie and I are locked in a silent battle, but she is gravely mistaken if she believes I'll fold. I don't know what prompts me to get under her skin every chance I get, but she calls to me like a flame to a moth. I know getting too close will burn me, but I don't think I mind.

Barking from the next room makes Hettie's head snap around. "Grass?" she calls, stepping away from me.

Grass barges into the room, barking at the top of his lungs. The sleeping pups toss and turn in their cribs before cries fill the air. "Grass!" Hettie yells again, running after her dog.

Grass thrashes against the door, pawing at it with a low growl. I haven't ever seen her dog act this way. He's usually belly up, hoping for a belly rub. But this is...fear?

I tense. "Do not open that door," I bark, but to no avail.

Hettie opens the door before I get my full command out, and Grass makes a beeline out. Hettie rushes after, chasing the damn dog. Has she learned nothing from the last time she attempted to chase Grass? Last time it led her straight to Michael.

A sick feeling has my stomach in knots. *Something is wrong.* The thought appears suddenly, just as Thorne bursts through the playroom door, eyes alert. The playroom is the only room in the cabin with windows looking out into town, so I know what he's going to say even before he says it.

"The rogues are attacking."

CHAPTER 16
HETTIE

Grass rushes out of the nursery, and I react on instinct. "Grass!" This is eerily familiar. Me chasing after Grass, and him ignoring me. I didn't like how it ended up the last time, and I doubt I'll like it now.

At first glance, nothing seems strange besides the human woman running after her very loud and poorly trained dog. When Grass comes to an immediate stop, I sigh in relief and finally catch up with him. "You've got to stop doing that, boy. What the hell are you on?"

Grass whimpers and doesn't calm down. He clearly wants me to see something, but I don't know what I should look for. "I really wish you could talk," I mumble.

That's when I hear it. The sound of screams and howls coming from the town's square. Wolves the size of lions attack the unsuspecting shoppers. These wolves aren't pack—why else would they be attacking us? They have to be rogues. Not just a few, but dozens.

It's violent. It's scary. And reminds me of my mortality.

My suspicions are confirmed when Thorne and Rip run my way. Thorne shifts; his body tears itself apart and rebuilds in less than seconds. A large brown wolf stands where Thorne once stood. He howls, and Rip sprints past him. "Go!" he tells his second, and Thorne doesn't hesitate as he rushes into battle.

"Hettie, let's go." Rip grabs my arm and pulls me to him.

"What are you doing?" Panic fills me as we move farther away from the battle happening below.

"Getting you to safety. Grass, come."

Grass listens to the alpha command and follows at my heels.

"No, Rip, you can't—"

"Let me do this, Hettie! Don't argue for once."

I dig my heels into the ground, trying to stop. "I'm okay, Rip. They need you. Don't you hear them screaming?"

"Listen—"

"No, you listen!" I shoot back, stunning both Rip and Grass. I take the opportunity to wiggle out of his grasp. "I'm fine. But those people aren't. Help them, Rip. You're their King Alpha."

"And you're their Luna. You need to be safe," he grits through his teeth.

"No, I'm their Luna. I need to help my people. This is my pack too, is it not? That's what you tell me. I will not go hide."

"You will die if you attempt to join the battle, Hettie. You understand that, don't you?" Rip looks ready to drag me back, but I'm not letting him. No matter how he feels.

"You fight the battle, then. I'm going back to the nursery. The pups need me."

I can see him battle with himself. I almost believe he

won't let me go, and I'm prepared to plead my case again until he growls, "Stay here one minute." Rip doesn't wait for me to respond. He rushes away, and suddenly I feel exposed out here in the open.

Rip comes back a moment later carrying an...ax? "What the hell is that?" I gesture to the massive sharp tool in his hand.

To my surprise—and horror—Rip hands it over to me. "Protection. You know how to use it?"

"I feel like it's self-explanatory?" I test the weapon out in my hands. It's heavy as hell, and I wish I didn't skip all those arms days at the gym. Still, I can at least raise it.

Rip nods in approval. "Straight back to the nursery. I'll make sure your path is clear. Don't leave Tallie."

"I won't," I promise, and this is a promise I intend to keep.

"Be fucking careful," Rip insists once again before he shifts in front of me; his clothes shred and falls to the floor. His black wolf stares at me, urging me to follow.

So I do.

None of the rogues have made it this far yet, so Rip only passes wolves running into the action. I run the last few feet to the nursery, awkwardly carrying the ax next to me. "Go! I'm fine!" I shout and pry open the nursery door.

"Hettie! Thank goddess you're okay!" Tallie cries as soon as she sees me. A group of crying kids cling to her legs, scared out of their mind. "Is that an ax?" she asks, looking down at the weapon in my hands.

"Yeah, Rip gave it to me." I wave it off. "Do we have someplace safe to take the pups?" Being out in the open like this feels too vulnerable, especially with how many windows there are in the other room. If we are lucky, the attack won't extend this far, but I'm not counting on that.

"Yes, every building here has a safe room. Locks from the inside." Tallie detaches the crying kids from her legs before moving toward a crib. She pushes it out of the way and tears down a random curtain I believed to be covering a window.

A door hides behind the curtain, and Tallie pulls hard to get it open. "Hurry! We need to get them all inside."

We start with the most vulnerable, packing all the babies into one crib and pushing it inside. The kids who clung to Tallie moments ago all run inside. Grass goes with them and allows the kids to hold and cry into his fur. He's keeping a few of the older kids calm, which I'm thankful for.

"Is that all of them?" I ask, frantically looking around the room for another head to pop up.

"Yeah, I think so—*Hettie, look out!*" Tallie screams.

Her warning comes too late. The window behind me shatters, raining down hundreds of small shards of glass. The look of absolute fear from Tallie spurns me into action. "Don't come out until Rip or Thorne comes back."

"Hettie!" I cut off her cries, shutting the door to the safe room. I hear the audible lock and say a quick prayer of thanks that Tallie didn't risk the children by opening the door again. An unsettling laugh emits from somewhere behind me, and I grasp the ax tightly in my hands. It suddenly feels so much smaller.

"Hettie..." A low male purr sends shivers down my back. Not how Rip's voice does. This is mocking and lacks all friendliness. I know who it is before I even turn around.

"Michael." I try to keep the tremble out of my voice, but my shaking body betrays me. I turn to see a man clad in shadows. Bright yellow wolf eyes stare at me through the darkness. I've never claimed to be a brave person, and right now, it takes everything in me not to turn around and bang on the door, begging Tallie to let me in. My chance of hiding is gone.

"Hettie." Michael's voice is deeper than I remember. He emerges slowly from the darkness, completely nude. Scars decorate his body from past altercations. Jagged pink marks line his chest and stomach. It only serves to make him more terrifying. "Pleasure to see you again."

"What do you want?"

Michael steps closer, and I instantly raise my ax. The rogue just chuckles. "Don't hurt yourself, Red. The tool is bigger than you." Michael eyes me, stalking his prey to intimidate me. He uses the same nickname he called me back in the woods when I wore the red coat my mother made for me.

I've been around men like Michael before. Scary men. Men who take what they want regardless of who it hurts. Michael is the same. He may be the leader of his little band of rogues, but I bet none of them respect him like our pack respects Rip.

"Why are you here? Why are you attacking my pack?" I press, trying to keep him talking. If he's talking, he's not actively trying to hurt me.

"Your pack? That fool has already mated you?" Michael sounds annoyed, like that fact just caused him a lot of inconvenience. "My, how quickly you've made yourself at home here, Red. Tell me, has your mate shown you what is happening to his people? How sick they're getting under his rule?"

Boiling anger overflows, all thoughts of fear forgotten. "His rule? You are the one hiding the wolfsbane from us. You're the one working with the Nephilim against your own kind. This is your doing, Michael. And for what?"

Something flashes in the rogue's eye. The smallest glimmer of true anger. It's there and gone in a blink before Michael puts back on his mask of indifference. His unsettling smile does little to extinguish the mounting panic I feel.

Where's Rip? Is he okay? Is our pack okay? If Michael kills me, will Tallie and the children be next?

If Michael's going to kill me, he would have done it back in the woods with no one around. No, he needs me for something.

I step forward, mustering up the little courage I have. The ax glistens in the dim light, feeling like a safety net in my hands. "What do you want?"

"The same thing I wanted when I first met you. I want you."

"Then why don't you just take me? You don't have to attack my entire pack. You had the chance to have me in the woods, but you let me get away. If anyone is inept at their job, it's you, Michael."

Michael's face contorts in a sneer. "Careful, Red," he warns. "Let's make something very clear. If it was as easy as taking you for myself, I would. Let's make no mistake there. But that's not how things work. I need you to come to me freely."

Now it's my turn to laugh. "Freely? You must be ten kinds of delusional if you ever think I would willingly come with you."

Faster than my eyes can track, Michael closes the distance between us. His large hand wraps around my throat as he pushes me back against the wall *hard*. Pain blooms in my head, and my vision goes blurry.

"I'm many things, Red. Delusional is not one of them.

But until you agree to come with me, your people will suffer."

"Rip will beat you," I gasp through his hold.

"Will he?" His hold on my neck tightens, effectively cutting off my air. I struggle against him, but Michael is strong. Far too strong, and the harder I try to get away from him, the harder his grip becomes. I no longer have the best hold on my ax, and I try to move my hand in a way that doesn't alert Michael.

"Because he seems far too distracted with his new Luna. Oh, and I hear he's down many wolves to the curse, yes? Pity. For him, not me, because it was too easy to get past his sloppy defenses, even without the help of our new Nephilim friends," he says.

This is the first time I've heard Michael admit his involvement with the Nephilim. I don't know what this means for Rip or our pack, but it's nothing good. I just need to survive long enough to let Rip know.

A howl in the distance momentarily distracts Michael. It's all I need to grab my ax and bring it down hard upon him. My aiming is terrible because the thing is so damn heavy, and I only snag his arm. Blood blooms from the shallow surface wound. "You little bitch," he growls and stumbles back.

I don't stop. I bring the ax down again harder, and this time, it slices deep into his side. More blood spurts from the opening, but the fucker won't go down. I try again, hoping to hit something that will incapacitate him, or worse, but Michael expects my move. He reaches his hand up, stopping my assault before it can cause any more damage.

"You're going to pay for that, Red," Michael hisses, throwing my ax across the room. I cry out, but he uses that moment to backhand me across the face. Pain bursts through my cheek, and my vision gets hazy. This isn't the first time a man has hit me, but it is the hardest.

"This could have been a lot easier, Red." He shakes his head, like he's disappointed in me.

"Go to hell," I growl. He approaches me again, but I spit in his direction, catching him in the eye. I'm not surprised to see red since my mouth tastes of copper.

Michael forces me back against the wall, and my head hits the surface. Not hard, but enough for it to hurt. A cold fear comes over me, and I wonder if he's going to kill me. Poor Tallie. She's never going to forgive herself. And Rip...

Then the howling from earlier grows louder, and I wonder if someone is coming. Rip? Thorne?

Michael curses under his breath and stops, as if listening for something, before turning his attention back to me, teeth bared. "We're done here for now. Enjoy cleaning up the mess my rogues caused. Hope you have extra beds for all those who were bit today."

Before I get the chance to ask him why, Michael shifts. His wolf is twice the size of me, and he snaps his canines in my direction. I scream, true fear radiating from me now that I'm without my weapon.

But he doesn't stay for long. Michael huffs once more before leaping out the broken window and running off into the chaos. More howls sound in the distance, and a few wolves run by, following Michael back into the dark forest.

I give myself a minute to catch my breath. The pain in the back of my skull is throbbing, and I would kill for some pain medication right now. A small pool of blood from Michael's wound darkens the hardwood floors. My shirt is a mess, but I try to ignore that another person's blood is on me. I might actually throw up if I think about it too hard.

I make my way across the room on unsteady feet to grab

the bloodied ax. As I lean down to pick it up, the door to the nursery bursts off its hinges and falls to the floor with a loud bang. Two large wolves rush in, bloodied and growling.

And despite my best efforts, I scream.

CHAPTER 17

RIP

We were ambushed. Rogues, more than I have ever seen in the past, flood our town, taking advantage of my unsuspecting pack. We've had rogue attacks, but never within our town, where omegas and children walk freely.

They are supposed to feel safe here.

I was supposed to keep them safe.

Thorne, along with a few other alphas from my guard, were on the scene first, keeping the rogues back to give the omegas and their children time to flee. Any rogue unfortunate enough to cross my path met the same end. For far too long, I took rogue after rogue down, hearing my brothers do the same.

By the end, blood coats my fur, but most of it is not my own.

Throughout all this, I have yet to find Michael. But I know he's here, leading the attack. He wouldn't be one to hide in the forest while his people did his dirty work.

But where the fuck is he?

I'm on edge. Distracted. My wolf grows more feral the

longer I'm away from Hettie. If we had completed the bond, I would be able to sense her right now. To know she's okay. Because she has to be okay. I refuse to think any other way. My Dove is strong. Stronger than even she gives herself credit for.

Amidst the battle, a howl reverberates around us, picked up by a few other wolves. None of them are mine. It's a signal. The moment that thought crosses my head, the rogues who have not fallen start to retreat. What the fuck? One moment they are attempting to rip my pack to shreds, and the next they tuck tail and disappear through the forest.

From the corner of my eye, I see a flash of dark gray fur sprint past me. I growl, turning around so fast, I kick up dirt and pebbles. The large wolf howls, joining the others in the forest. This wolf is bigger than the others, and I know instantly who it is.

Michael.

Leaving from the direction of the nursery. Among the chaos, he's eluded me.

Without thinking, I sprint toward the small cabin a few yards ahead. I push my legs faster than they have ever carried me, feeling the strain almost immediately. A dire wolf reaches my side, running next to me. I don't need to look over to know Thorne is trailing me. His mate—my cousin—is also in the nursery.

If he touched Hettie or Tallie...

I burst through the front door of the nursery, ignoring the way it broke off the hinges and fell to the ground. I scan the room, and the smell of blood is overwhelming. Pools of crimson splatter the floor, and the worst nightmares plague my mind.

Hettie dead with her throat ripped out.

Hettie in pieces.

Hettie and Tallie all bloodied and bruised with fear forever etched on their faces.

The loud, ear-piercing scream pulls me out of the darkness and toward the adjoining room. That's when I see her. My Dove, soaked with blood and looking like the Goddess of Death. Her hair is a wild, matted mess, and her eyes dart back and forth in a frenzy. She clutches the bloody ax tightly, putting it between her and me.

I shift, but Hettie doesn't recognize me yet. She's in survival mode. Her brain isn't allowing her to think rationally. "Hettie..." I try to keep my voice soft and gentle, even though inside I'm screaming. I want her in my arms. I want to look over her body and make sure no harm has come to her.

More importantly, I want to kill Michael. Like I should have done a long time ago.

"Here." Thorne tosses me a pair of pants that I quickly put on. I don't know where he got them, but I also don't care. Hettie doesn't need a naked man coming at her.

"Get back!" she screams, swinging the ax hard enough to scare me. In other circumstances, I'd be proud of Hettie for standing her ground. Now, though? I'm doing everything in my power to keep myself in check and not spook her further.

"Dove, it's okay. You're safe, Hettie. They're gone. You did it, mate. You protected your pack." Pride swells deep in my chest. My mate, the pack's Luna, protected those who couldn't protect themselves.

Maybe she is the salvation we'll need to win this war.

"Rip?" Slowly Hettie puts down the ax, letting it drop with a dull thud.

"It's me." The words are barely out of my mouth before

she flings herself at me. Instinctually, my arms go around her, holding her close. I expect to hear sobs, now that the adrenaline from the fight has worn off. To finally allow herself to give in to the fear. I hold her tight, wishing I could take those feelings away.

But Hettie doesn't cry.

She clings to me, grounding herself back into reality, but sheds no tears for whatever horrific ordeal she has just faced.

"I need to check you for injuries," I say gently yet firmly. I hold her at arm's length, eyes scanning over her body. There's so much blood. There's an angry red mark in the shape of a hand on the left side of her face.

"Was that Michael's doing?" My voice is dangerously low. Molten hot fury courses through me at the thought of someone else touching my mate. Hurting her.

Hettie must see the rising anger because she reaches out to grab my face. "Alpha, I'm okay. I'm fine," she assures me, or tries to.

I come undone.

We move as one, drawn to each other by an invisible string. I don't know who initiated the kiss, but soon our lips are crashing together, desperate for the other. I pry her lips apart with my tongue, and she gives in to me, moaning when our tongues touch. I kiss her to know she's there. I kiss her to know she's okay.

I kiss her because I need her.

This isn't enough. Not nearly enough. Too many clothes in the way. I ache for her in a way I've never felt before. She came into my life and stole the very heart from my chest.

But all too soon, she's pulling away from me, lips swollen from our kiss. "Tallie. The pups."

I take a moment to understand what she is saying, and then her meaning is clear. "Where?"

"In the safe room, over there." She points to a wall where two cribs have been pushed apart.

Thorne, no longer in his wolf form, bangs on the door. "Tallie! Open up. It's over." There's a panic in his voice I know all too well.

Time passes slowly as we are helpless to do anything but stand and watch. Clicking sounds from within, and then the door opens with a groan. We let out a collective sigh of relief, and Thorne pulls the door open the rest of the way. Scared cries of the pups greet us, but crying means they are alive.

That Tallie and Hettie saved them.

"Hettie? Hettie!" Tallie tumbles out, pushing past Thorne. The moment their eyes meet, my cousin bursts into tears and sprints over to her Luna.

"She needs a healer, Rip! Why are you just standing there?" she cries, ignoring the blood as she wraps her arms around my mate.

Hettie holds her. She needs this as much as Tallie does. "I'm okay. I promise," she whispers repeatedly. My mate just went through a traumatic experience, and yet she's the one comforting Tallie.

I give the women a moment of privacy as I turn toward my second. "Their parents should be on their way. Will you make sure every pup gets home? If their parents are injured, we'll deal with that." I don't know how many of my pack are injured or if we lost any wolves. The aftermath of today's battle will be my problem after I learn exactly what happened here. Why Michael risked his people to find Hettie but not take her.

"Tallie," I call, and my cousin reluctantly pulls away from Hettie. "Will you assist Thorne with the pups?"

"We'll talk later," Hettie promises, giving Tallie's shoulder an encouraging squeeze. "Take Grass with you. He'll keep them calm until an adult can pick up their child."

"Promise me you're okay?" Tallie looks over the blood coating her body. It's hard to imagine that Hettie sustained little to no injury while her body is painted in red.

"I'm okay. I'll tell you all about it later," she promises.

Thorne gently pulls Tallie to him and whispers something in her ear. Tallie nods once before retreating into the safe room to help corral the scared pups until their parents can reach them. Already I hear a few wolves running our way, desperate to make sure their pups are safe.

And they are. Because of my cousin and the pack Luna.

"You did great, Hettie. Thank you for protecting my mate. I owe you my life," Thorne says to Hettie, reverence and respect shining in his eyes.

My girl blushes. "She's my friend. I protect my friends."

"Hettie." At the sound of her name, she looks up at me through dark lashes. She sways on her feet, and in an instant I'm by her side. "You need to sit."

Hettie doesn't argue with me, which only proves how shaken she really is. I take her back to the other room, careful of the broken glass as I navigate her to the small couch. It sags under our weight, and we sink into the cushions.

"We need to talk about what happened." The last thing I want to do is push her, but with Michael on the loose, we no longer have the luxury of time. "I wouldn't ask you about it right now if it wasn't important, Dove."

"I know." Her voice is so small. Hettie's larger-than-life

personality pales to a dying ember. I hate seeing her like this. Hate knowing she was scared and alone.

"Michael came here. He's working with the Nephilim, Rip. He admitted it to me. He...told me he hopes we have extra beds for those bitten. What does he mean by that? What happens when a rogue bites one of our pack members?"

"I don't know," I admit. "This is the first major attack on our lands. Usually we can contain it before they reach the city. My guards have been bit, I'm certain, but nothing has happened to them."

Yet, I think but don't voice.

"Michael implied something bad is going to happen. But I couldn't get any more out of him. He got so close to me, and I just reacted. That ax you gave me? I brought it down on him. I wanted to kill him, Rip. I never had this feeling of bloodlust before, but I wanted him dead. I wasn't strong enough, though, and he—" She gestures to the mark on her face, and newfound anger flares to life. I suspected that was Michael's doing, but hearing it confirmed intensifies the hatred I have for the rogue bastard.

Michael will die.

And soon.

"I'm so sorry, Rip. This is all my fault." Then Hettie shatters my heart into a million small shards. The dam holding back her emotions finally breaks. She puts her head in her hands and cries. "I was brought here to help, but I'm only making things worse. Ender was wrong. I don't belong here."

"That's bullshit, and you know it—"

"It's not!" she cries, looking up at me with tear-stained eyes. "Michael told me he came here for me. Told me this wouldn't stop until I came to him willingly. I don't know why he wants me, but he does. If I stay here, more people will get hurt. Or worse. I can't, Rip. Don't you get it? I came here to get away from people I've hurt. I can't fucking do it again. I refuse!"

Hettie breaks down, curling into herself. Her shoulders shake with her sobs, and I can't take it. "Hettie." I lose all pretenses of control and drag her over to me. She puts up a weak fight, but I cage my arms around her as soon as she's in my lap.

"I need you to understand something, Dove, and then we will never have this fucking conversation again. This isn't your fault."

Hettie opens her mouth to argue, but I'm faster. I clamp my hand over her lips, and she lets out a strangled cry. My mate attempts to bite me in hopes I'll let go. Jokes on her though, because I fucking love it.

"If you want something to bite, Dove, I'll give you my neck later. Mark it up as you see fit."

She glares up at me, but her scent gives her lust away. She likes the thought of that.

"I don't give a shit what Michael said," I continue while I have her attention. "None of this is your fault. And don't for a second think I'm going to let you sacrifice yourself for this pack. Michael's a liar. Once he has you, there's no stopping him from killing every one of us for you to watch.

"What's going to happen is we're going to rid our pack of this disease and the rogues. We will also take care of the Nephilim. I don't have the answers about how we're going to do that, but I know we will find a solution together. Because we are going to survive this shit and come out on top. Do you understand me, mate?"

I let my hand fall away from her mouth, giving her voice back. There's a new hardness in her expression that wasn't there moments ago. "I understand, Alpha. Together."

At this moment, I feel like I can take on a herd of Nephilim and rogues. I lean down and press a firm kiss to her lips. "Good," I say once I pull away. "Now let me clean you up."

"Shouldn't we check on the pack first?" she asks.

"No. Let me take care of you." The need to clean her up and make sure there's no other injuries on her she's trying to hide from me is strong. "Thorne and Tallie will check in on the pack. We will join them later."

"But—"

"Argue with me, and I swear I'll spank that ass and drag you back to our room anyway," I growl. "Now let's go."

"Spanking sounds fine with me, actually."

"Hettie," I groan, picturing her over my knee, ass bared. My cock hardens at the thought of her red cheeks and the moans she'd make.

"Fine," she sighs dramatically, taking hold of my hand. It feels like the most natural thing in the world. "Let's go so you can see that I'm fine, and we can get back to our pack— *Rip!* I can walk; put me the fuck down!"

There is no way I would allow Hettie to walk back to the packhouse while she's unsteady on her feet. This also gives me an excuse to touch her, which I'm not passing up, even as she protests most of the way back. She gives up trying to argue with me about halfway home and falls into a pout instead. It's damn cute.

Once back in our room, I sit her on the bed. "Strip," I call over my shoulder, heading to the bathroom for some necessities. I hear her grumble about "stubborn alphas," which I ignore and grab a towel, wetting it with warm water, and a salve for her cheek.

When I come back into the room, Hettie is naked in my —our—bed. Her beautiful body is on display for me, but I don't allow myself to drink her in. It would be too easy to give in to temptation, but I brought her here for a reason. My eyes scan her body for injuries. I find none but a red mark on her cheek and dried blood on the top of her head. Blood coats her arms, but none of it belongs to her. Only Michael.

Pride swells in my chest at the fight my mate put up. I lean down and work in silence, cleaning Michael's blood off her. The once white towel is now stained pink. I drop it to the ground and reach for the salve. "Does your face sting?"

"A little," she admits. "My head too."

"I'll make tea for your headache soon, but this should help your cheek." I dip into the salve, bring my hand to her face and gently rub it on her. Our eyes are locked in an intense stare, drawing me closer to her.

Hettie's breath hitches before biting down on her lip. She's only a hair's breadth away from me now. I could kiss her. I want to kiss her, but before I get the opportunity, Hettie clears her throat and breaks the silence.

"Am I healed, Dr. Rip?" she asks, trying to lighten the mood with humor. Just like she did this morning before things could go any further. She's scared of something; I just don't know what.

Reluctantly, I pull back. "You are. I'm proud of you, Hettie. What you did today was amazing. Our pack will remember this."

The smile that lights up her features isn't one I've seen before. Her eyes shine with unshed tears, and I wonder if she's ever heard those words before.

"Thank you." Hettie pushes herself off the bed. "Give me five minutes to get ready. I want to check on everyone and help Tallie get the pups back to their families."

As much as I want to stay in this room and have my Dove to myself, I can't. Our duty is to our pack, and the pack deserves to see their Luna.

CHAPTER 18

HETTIE

The infirmary is just as sterile as the last time I was here. It's cold, and death lingers in the air. The sound of sickness is everywhere. In every cough. In every moan. In every cry. I hate it. It seeps deep into my bones, making each step feel heavier than the last. I'm transported back to the hospital my father stayed at for his final days.

Rip squeezes my arm, and I tilt my head up to get a good look at him. He pulls me closer, offering me silent comfort. He must have picked up my emotions from the bond. After telling him a little about my father, Rip knows better than anyone how uneasy I am around medical facilities. But this is a necessity.

Since the attack two days ago, he hasn't slept much. Neither have I. He's been busy dealing with his patrol, making sure that what happened two days ago doesn't happen again. It's more difficult than ever because we have fewer wolves daily. I wish I could help more, but I feel limited in what I can do.

I'm not a wolf. I don't have the abilities that come with being a wolf shifter. I'm just a human.

Rip thinks I'm capable of more. Ender too, or else he wouldn't have brought me here, but I'm still figuring out how I fit in here.

"Are you okay?" Rip spares me a quick glance. He's distracted, has been for the last few days, but he's not forgotten to check in on me. It feels…nice.

"I'm fine." It's not a lie, exactly, but it's not fully the truth. I'm still shaken up from the attack and Michael's ominous words. But right now, we have other things to worry about. A sick feeling stirs in the pit of my stomach at what the doctors might inform us today.

Rip and I aren't alone. Thorne's there too, and, by my request, so is Tallie. Call it trauma bonding, but the last two days, we've been inseparable. She keeps me calm, and I think I do the same for her, especially when both Thorne and Rip are otherwise occupied. Which has been a lot in the last forty-eight hours.

Lucielle, the lead healer in charge of creating a cure, is also with us. She wears her white lab coat like armor, wrapping her arms around herself. I remember Rip explaining that her husband was one of the first to die from the curse. Being back at the place where the love of your life took their last breath is the worst feeling.

Her ivory-colored skin is even paler than the last time I met her. She looks like a ghost wandering these halls. Perhaps she is. Too many memories linger here, and not good ones. Despite the heartache she is forced to endure again, she keeps her head high as we walk into the only available room left at the infirmary, which happened to be a breakroom for the healers.

An older man awaits us, though I don't catch his name

when Rip introduces the beta as a healer. The beta's glasses are slightly askew and sit low on his nose. Dark circles lie underneath his eyes, and he runs his hand through hair that needs a good washing. This beta requested his King Alpha and Luna, but that's all any of us knows.

"I'm afraid I have some damning news, King Alpha." His grave tone gives way to my earlier fears, and I reach for Rip just as he threads his fingers through mine. It's a new development between us, reaching out for each other during trying times. He grounds me in a way no one else has before, and I hope I can do the same.

"Out with it, then. What is it, beta?" Rip's agitation simmers through, but he is doing his best to hold it back.

"We had hoped the injured wolves from the attack would show progress. Unfortunately, none of them have healed. With injuries like theirs, they should have left the day they were admitted," he says.

"So why haven't they left yet?" Rip asks what we all want to know.

"We believe, and maybe Healer Lucielle can help confirm this, the bites from the rogues caused the curse to set in on these wolves. This is a new and very concerning development."

Everyone stiffens at the news. It's like a punch to the gut. Fighting rogues now would be nearly impossible. Lucielle doesn't look surprised though, just sad. "I feared this would be the next natural progression. If you can bring me to a patient, I can start my assessment."

"Do you need anything from me, Lucielle?" Rip asks as I squeeze his hand gently.

The beta woman sighs and shakes her head. "Prayers, King Alpha. I need your prayers."

SWEAT POURS FROM MY FACE. I shrug off my coat, letting it fall to the ground. The cool air provides me an instant reprieve, and I bring the ax down on the marked target again. It's off by a quarter of an inch, and I groan. That's the closest I've made it, but the weight of the ax is throwing me off.

"That's not bad," Rip says, checking my mark. Effortlessly, he pulls out my ax from the wood, handing it back to me like it weighs little more than a feather. To him, it probably does. But I feel like my arms are about to fall off when he hands it over.

We've been at this for over an hour now, though I swear it feels like weeks. "I better have the strongest fucking arms after this," I mutter, groaning as I heave the ax over my shoulder.

Rip smirks. "You'll be a fierce warrior."

Not yet, but Rip is determined I become one. After hearing the news about our wolves yesterday at the infirmary, he got it into his mind that I need to become a damn Olympic lumberjack and insisted I learn how to use this weapon. I argued for a lighter weapon, like a dagger or a gun, but they had none—so I'm stuck with this hefty thing. The last two days have been ax training sessions, which have left my body sore in places I didn't even know could get sore.

"Try again." Rip points to the red X he painted on a tree trunk. "Right in the center."

"I'll ax you right in the center," I mutter.

"What was that, Dove?"

"Nothing, Alpha," I say sweetly—too sweetly.

Rip just smirks and gestures for me to go on. "This will be the last one. Then you can rest," he promises.

Despite the way my arms scream in protest, I raise them above my head. I keep the red X in my line of vision, focusing all my attention on it. And then I bring the ax down hard, splintering the wood in the very center of the X.

I beam up at Rip, who returns the bright smile. Something akin to pride shines in his eyes, and I soak in the delight. "Good job, Hettie. If your target remains in a seated position, you'll for sure hit them every time."

My smile instantly vanishes, along with the fuzzy thoughts of my husband. "Asshole. I was actually starting to like you there for a minute."

"Well, let me make it up to you," Rip suggests.

"And how do you plan on doing that?" I raise my brow, crossing my arms over my chest. It only pushes up my boobs, and I see the moment Rip notices this as well. He takes in his fill and lets me know he's looking too.

Finally, the man seems to remember the boobs are attached to a person and lifts his head to meet my gaze. "Have dinner with me tonight."

I roll my eyes. "We have dinner together every night."

"No," he says. "We have dinner together with Thorn, Tallie, my Aunt Imelda, and sometimes others. I want you to myself tonight."

Well, that is different. He's right, though. It's never just the two of us. We always have others around us for dinner, and I've never complained. But...if this whole marriage thing is going to work, we need time just for us that doesn't involve lying in the same bed together.

The answer is easy. "Yes, Rip. I would love to have dinner with you tonight."

The boyish grin that spreads across his face has me

giggling. *Giggling.* Like a damn school girl who just spoke to her first crush. "Happiness looks good on you, Rip," I beam once I'm able to control myself.

"Something else will look good on me too." Just like that, the boyish grin is gone, replaced by a seductive smirk that has my panties flooded. He stares at me like he's undressing me with his eyes. Normally this makes me uncomfortable, but with Rip? I feel desired.

Suddenly Rip's gaze snaps away from me, and he straightens his posture, becoming a stoic alpha once again. My brow furrows, and I turn to see what caught his attention.

Standing a few feet away from me is a woman who looks to be around my age. She's tan, with beautiful chocolate-brown hair that hangs down her back in natural curls. Despite the crisp air, the woman only wears a thin dress. On her hip is a child who can't be any older than two years old, snuggling into his mother happily.

"King Alpha Rip. Queen Luna Hettie," she greets both of us, bowing her head in respect. Rip mimics her motions, and I stand there like a moron. This is the first time I've heard someone call me a queen, and it feels...right.

"Omega Isla," Rip greets. "Is everything okay?"

"Yes, King Alpha. I'm sorry for bothering you, but I actually came here to speak to your mate," she admits, turning her attention to me. My heart starts to pound loudly against my chest, but Rip reaches for me. His touch alone provides me with strength and stability.

Isla's eyes turn glossy as a few tears roll down her cheeks. "I didn't get the opportunity to thank you for protecting my son during the attack. Because of you and your bravery, Desmond is unharmed. I can't thank you enough for keeping my son safe."

Desmond pokes his head up to peer around his mother. He holds a chubby hand up and waves before burrowing his head back into the crook of his mother's neck. Isla holds him tighter, leaning down to place a kiss on the top of his head.

I don't realize I'm crying until Rip wipes away a stray tear. I glance up to see nothing but pride and admiration in my mate's eyes. "I'm so proud of you," he mouths, and it takes everything in me to hold back the dam of tears threatening to spill over. Mescos has turned me into a damn crier.

No one has ever been proud of me in my life. Granted, I've never given a person reason to be proud of me, but my goal in coming to Mescos was to start over. It's such an immense honor and confidence boost to have someone believe in you. It's a feeling I could easily get addicted to.

I take a deep breath, hoping my voice is steady as I speak to Isla. "I'm glad Desmond is okay. You don't need to thank me. He's pack, and I will always protect the pups in our pack." As I say the words, I realize how much I mean them. This pack is my family now. I'm here to protect them, and that's exactly what I want to do.

Isla catches me off guard and hugs me. I tense but then snake my arms around her. We share this moment together. Woman to woman. Using the hug to convey everything our words cannot.

When she pulls away, Isla is still crying, but she beams at me. "I wanted to make sure I thanked you in person. I'll leave you two to enjoy the rest of your evening."

Isla says goodbye to Rip before leaving us alone. My eyes lock with his, and he pulls me in for a kiss. One I easily surrender to. "My Luna," he purrs into the kiss.

And for the first time, I feel like one.

CHAPTER 19
RIP

There are many productive ways I should be spending my time, especially knowing my pack isn't safe from Michael. I pride myself on the safety of my pack, but these last few weeks, I've felt little more than a failure. A King Alpha who cannot protect his pack is no alpha at all. Giving in to failure is exactly what Michael wants, though, and I refuse to submit to a traitor who goes against their own kind.

I could also spend my time finding wolfsbane to help cure the wolves withering away in the infirmary. My team of healers has been working around the clock to find something to ease the pain of the cursed wolves. There may not be another cure besides wolfsbane, but that doesn't stop Lucielle from trying.

I should be with her now.

But no.

Instead, I'm pacing back and forth in the courtyard, dressed in a suit I've never touched before, waiting to have dinner with my wife. Conflicting feelings war inside me. On one hand, I shouldn't allow myself the luxury of a date when my pack is suffering. But on the other hand, I need to strengthen the bond with my Luna. Rose and Malix said love is the only way to come out victorious in this war.

I don't know if what I feel for Hettie is love, but it's... something. Fragile. Breakable. Explosive. I don't know what to think about my feelings toward my wife, but I know she's mine.

"Where are they?" My voice comes out as a sneer. From my peripheral vision, I see Thorne smirk. He stands on guard just a few feet away from me. I have him here to calm me, but it's not working. Unfortunately, Thorne is in my line of fire.

"They should be here soon. Perhaps a drink of champagne will ease your nerves."

"Perhaps not," I hiss. If Thorne takes my attitude personally, he doesn't show it. He knows me well enough to know I'm not angry at him. I'm not truly angry at all, but rather restless. I don't think that will go away until I see Hettie.

As if thinking her name brings her into existence, I feel her near. Our bond is weak, but it's enough to know she's made it back inside the packhouse. The soft smile on Thorne's lips tells me he senses Tallie. Under normal circumstances, I would make fun of his obsession with his mate. That was before I had one of my own. I get it now. Maybe not on the same level as Thorne and Tallie because they fell deeply in love before mating, but the things I feel for Hettie...it makes me absolutely feral.

The smell of Hettie perfumes the air, lavender reminding me of a spring day, so out of place in our wintery weather. I turn in time to see Tallie walk through the glass doors. She gives me a wink before stepping out of the way, exposing my wife.

Our eyes meet, and time stops.

Hettie wears a floor-length red gown. The billowy sleeves are sheer, cuffing at her wrists. The bodice of the dress hugs her curves perfectly and flares out around her hips. Tallie piled Hettie's raven-colored hair into a low bun; a few dark strands frame her face. A peach blush tints her cheeks, and her lips remind me of ripe strawberries.

She is a portrait come to life, a beauty only an artist can capture. I want to fall on my knees and worship every inch of her body.

"Your Luna is ready for you." Tallie smiles, taking Thorne's hand. "We'll take care of everything tonight. You enjoy one another."

I nod, my words not yet coming to me. All I know is that I need the pair of them gone.

Hettie and I remain locked in a stare, neither of us speaking, as my best friend and cousin take their leave. Then it's just the two of us.

"You look beautiful, Dove."

My words seem to catch her off guard, and her blush deepens. She runs a hand down the silk of her dress. "It's not too much?"

"It's perfect. You're perfect."

Like a plant to sunlight, we gravitate toward each other. I take her hand, leading her toward the table set up for us by the kitchen staff. The garden is covered in a thin layer of snow. No flowers bloom, and no tree holds any leaves. Even in death, the scene is beautiful, knowing that, in a few short months, the area will come alive once again.

A burning fire warms the air around the table. I watch Hettie as she sits, wondering if she's cold. She doesn't shiver, but I ask anyway. "Are you cold?"

"Surprisingly, no. Your cousin's room was sweltering hot. It actually feels wonderful out here," she assures.

I take my seat across from her. A mixture of cheese, meats, and bread sits in the center for us to graze from. Despite not eating since this morning, I don't find myself particularly hungry, but I still grab a piece of bread, giving my hands and mouth something to do.

I'm rusty at this whole wooing thing. I've never had to seduce a woman before or try hard to get one to flirt with me. I took the ones who threw themselves at me to bed. We'd have a fun night, but that's all. It ended quickly. Small talk, compliments, and getting to know another person on a deeper level has never been my strong suit.

If Hettie feels awkward, she doesn't show it. Her eyes sparkle as she takes in the setup. "A charcuterie board? I've always wanted to learn how to make one of these." She reaches for a bit of everything, not shy about taking food.

Good. There's no reason to be.

"How are you adjusting to your life here?" This is probably a question I should have asked long ago, but I'm not sure I was ready for the answer then. I'm still not completely ready to hear the answer now because, if she says she hates it here, then I can't keep her here against her will. I can't send her back to her world, but I'd figure something out.

"I didn't think I would like it here." I appreciate the honesty, but I still tense, hoping her mind has changed. "But I...I don't know. I just feel like I'm supposed to be here? Tallie has been amazing, and I love helping her out at the nursery, and then there's you..."

She trails off, biting her lower lip. Hettie averts her gaze from me, and I've never wanted to reach across the table and bracket her neck more than I do now. Then she couldn't escape my gaze. But I'm not a beast, at least not entirely. "Look at me, Hettie. Not at the ground. Me."

There's a slight hesitation before she obeys, meeting my gaze once again. "What about me?" I ask, needing to hear what she thinks about me. If she's affected as much as I am.

"You're...you. And I'm...me. And we're..."

"Eloquently put, mate. But I need you to be more specific."

Hettie groans. "Don't make me say it."

"You sound like I'm torturing you," I say, deadpan, "when all I want to know is what you think about when you think of me."

"That's the thing, Rip. I can't *stop* thinking about you. You aren't the type of man I'm used to." Another sliver of her past, but not one that satisfies my need to know everything about her.

"What type of men are you used to, Dove?" My mind takes me back to the few times she's flinched when I've moved my hand toward her face. That is an indicator of the type of men she is accustomed to. Weak men who need to prove their dominance over people physically smaller than they are.

Men like Michael.

"It's mostly my fault. I always put myself into these situations, even knowing what might happen. My actions hurt many people, both emotionally and financially. It's why I made the deal with Ender."

I wait in anticipation, wondering if this is the moment she will finally trust me enough to open up to me fully. She knows about my parents and life before her, but much of her life is still so unknown to me. Before I can ask her more about it, though, a beta brings out our dinner. Pork roast with a medley of vegetables. Despite not being hungry only moments before, my mouth waters.

When the beta leaves, I ask, "You made the deal with Ender to escape these men?"

Hettie pushes the diced carrots around on her plate, separating them from the rest of the veggies. I make a mental note that my mate isn't a fan of carrots, filing it away for later.

"Yes...and no," she says slowly. "My fucked-up obsession with bad men was a major reason, but I can't blame all my actions on them. They were my actions. I so badly wanted to feel important and accepted by these idiots who did stupid shit. Petty theft. Got involved with drugs, nothing hardcore, just enough to land me in jail for a night or two until my mom could scrounge up enough money to bail me out.

"We were so deeply in debt because of me. My father was the main breadwinner of the family, and when he died...we all struggled. My mother most of all. I tried to help with the bills, but I couldn't keep a job and fucked up the small income I had."

Hettie goes silent. She blinks rapidly, holding back tears. Her small body trembles, and I feel her fear through the bond. Fear of the past? Or fear of telling me? I'm not certain, but I don't push her to say more. I don't fill the silence with useless talk either. I let her words sit between us until she's ready to continue.

"So, I made a deal with Ender," she says after a pregnant pause. "That I would come here and marry the King Alpha, and he will make sure my mother and sister are taken care of. I don't know if he held up his end of the bargain—"

"He did."

Hettie snaps her head up. Her expression is a mixture of hope and relief. "He did? How do you know? Have you talked to him?"

"I haven't talked to him," I admit, and her body deflates. But I quickly add, "He's bound by his word. All Guardians are, or were. Ender is the last one, I think. If your contract stated he'd take care of your family, then he has. Your sister and mother are living the life you have always wanted them to have."

This time, tears fall down her cheeks, but there's no sadness in her eyes. Only relief and something that resembles acceptance. Acceptance of her mistakes. Acceptance of the future she provided for them but will not be part of. It was a selfless act and one her family might never truly understand.

But I do.

"I know why Ender chose you for me."

Hettie tilts her head and scrunches up her nose in a way that's both adorable and funny. "Why?"

My finger curls, gesturing for her to come to me. Hettie just stares, and I think she's going to ignore my wish until I hear her chair rubbing against the concrete. There's no hesitation as she draws near and promptly sits her pretty ass down on my lap. I hadn't expected her to actually comply, but this woman is full of surprises.

This close, I can properly admire every curve of her body. The way her pouty lips look painted in red. The smell of lavender that is distinctly her. The same smell all over my sheets. My clothes. My skin. It drives me fucking wild, and she doesn't even know the effect she has on me. If she did, she wouldn't be sitting on my lap right now. Not when I want to ruin her from the inside out.

"Do I have to ask again, Alpha?" the seductress purrs, eliciting a growl from deep within my chest.

My body responds to her, and I'm helpless to stop it. I bring my hand up to tangle in her hair, grabbing hold and giving it the smallest of tugs. Hettie bites her lip as her desire permeates the air. "He chose you because you are a true Luna. Because you understand what sacrifice is. You put others before yourself to a detriment, I might add. You're strong, Hettie. No one else deserves the title but you."

"Careful, Alpha," she says breathlessly, "it almost sounds as if you like me."

"And if I do?" I draw her closer until our chests touch and I feel her heart beating against mine. "Would that be so bad, Dove?"

"Only if you come to realize you don't care for me." Her voice is so small, reminding me of a scared doe. I don't know the other men who came before me, but they all deserve to have their hearts ripped from their chest. I'd do it. If she wanted me to. Present them on a platter for her.

Because somehow Hettie has wound her way around my heart and squeezes it tight. There are a million reasons we shouldn't take this any further. It's too dangerous. I'll get distracted. Hettie could get hurt...

But none of them stop me as I press my lips against her shoulder. It's a soft touch, barely there at all. Still, I feel Hettie shiver under my touch. "A man who doesn't care for you is a fool, Dove, and I've never been a foolish man. Stubborn and impatient? Plenty of times. But never foolish.

"Kiss me, Rip."

The words are the permission I need to stop fighting the urge to make her mine that has only grown stronger since our mating ceremony. My lips are on her, and I devour my mate. She tastes of champagne, and I lick away every drop. Hettie moans, and I think that sound will be my undoing.

I break apart from her abruptly.

"Rip—?" she cries, clearly confused by my sudden change.

I sweep my hand across the table of our plates, glasses, and utensils. It all clatters to the floor, making a mess I'll feel bad about later. There's nothing more appetizing to me at this moment than the woman rubbing herself against me.

I lay Hettie down on top of it, my eyes roaming over the expanse of her body. "You make me a starving man, Hettie. I almost think you enjoy teasing your alpha."

"Rip," she whines. "Just fucking kiss me."

And so I do.

I claim her lips, prying them apart with my tongue. She opens beautifully for me, a sigh of pleasure leaving her lips. She's laid out for me like a feast I'm dying to devour. I've been patient. I've made sure she's comfortable. All the while, my wolf howls and rages for me to take her. She's mine and needs to be claimed as mine.

"Rip," she pleads, bunching up my shirt in her small hands. She's so tiny and delicate, but it's all a mirage. My mate is steel and unbreakable.

I slide my hand up the outside of her dress until I feel the curve of her full breast. I hesitate only a second, allowing her time to stop me if she wishes, but Hettie leans into my touch.

"Eager girl," I laugh, taunting her. Before she responds, I squeeze her breast, running my thumb over her taut nipple through the fabric.

Her desire fills the air, and Hettie hooks a leg around me, pulling me closer. I know she feels just how hard I am for her. There's no missing the erection behind my pants. I need her. I want her. But I don't give a shit about my pleasure. I just want Hettie to come undone by my touch. It's about time my wife orgasms with my name on her lips.

"Rip," she moans again. I enjoy seeing her worked up, rubbing that sweet pussy all over my hardening cock.

"What do you want, Hettie? I need you to be very clear in your needs, mate." I tease her nipple again. I want to rip the damn dress off her, but I'm certain my cousin would skin me alive if I ruined the gown she spent all day finding for Hettie.

"You," she whimpers. "I need you to make me feel wanted."

"You need your alpha to play with that pretty pussy you keep grinding all over me? Tell me, mate, are you wet for me?" I already know the answer. I can smell the sweet scent of her desire, but still. I want to hear it from her lips.

"Fuck yes. Are you going to do something about it, Alpha? Or am I going to have to take care of myself?" She juts her bottom lip out, doing her best to look annoyed, but the flush to her cheeks and the lust in her eyes tell me a different story.

"You aren't touching that pussy, Dove. If you want to cum, you ask your alpha. Let me hear you say you want that."

"Are you fucking serious right now?" she growls. "Just fuck—*what the fuck, Rip?*" she screams, her voice going breathy as I bring my hand down to slap her pussy. My mate is too bratty for her own good. Lucky for her, I enjoy taming brats.

"Ask me, Hettie. Ask me to let you cum," I say, voice even as I stare upon her frustrated face.

"You dick—fine!" she hisses as I slap her pussy again.

Her legs quiver, and she lets out a delicious moan. "Alpha, will you make me cum?" she asks with forced patience.

We will work on her tone. "Good girl. All you have to do is ask."

She curses my name under her breath.

I kneel by the table, moving Hettie to the edge. Her dress is already bunched up, but I push it up more, exposing her smooth, brown thighs. Her legs open for me, but one article of clothing still remains between us. I make quick work of her panties, tugging them down her legs and pocketing them. A reminder of tonight.

When the cold breeze of the winter's night hits her bare pussy, Hettie shivers and tries to close her legs. Though I'm not sure if it's from the chill in the air or her own insecurities. Either way, I place my hands on her thighs, keeping her spread for me.

"Unless you want this to end, you'll keep your legs open for me. Understand?"

"Yes, Alpha."

Yes, Alpha. The sweetest fucking words I've ever heard.

Her pussy is so fucking wet, and she smells fucking delicious. I yank her closer, and she lets out a mix of a gasp and a moan. I press my fingers harder into her thighs, making sure she knows to keep them open as I lean forward.

The first lick of her seam has us both moaning. "You taste so fucking good, Hettie. So sweet, like candy. Did you know that?"

"N-no," she whimpers.

"You're my dessert, Dove."

And then I start to eat her out in earnest. I can't stop. I can't slow down. I wanted to take this slow. Play with her and slowly coax her to orgasm, but I'm too impatient right now. My tongue darts inside of her, her cream so sweet on my tongue.

She moans my name or screams. I'm not really sure. I can't concentrate on anything other than devouring her pussy.

My tongue sweeps over her clit, eliciting a loud, sensual moan. She reaches for me, tugging on my hair. It adds the perfect amount of pain, making me growl. I suck the sensitive bundle of nerves into my mouth, pressing a finger inside her.

She clenches around the digit. She's so fucking tight. I want to sheath my cock deep inside of her, inch by inch. Feel her stretch and tighten around me. It'll be fucking heaven.

"Fuck," she pants, grinding down on my face.

I laugh softly. "Ride my face, mate."

This is a command she doesn't fight me on. Her hips work against my tongue. I add a second finger, moving it in and out in rhythmic timing. It's not enough, not nearly enough, but it'll do for now.

"Alpha!" Hettie screams as her orgasm takes her over. Her body spasms, and her legs tighten around my head. I taste her satisfaction, groaning with each swipe of my tongue. I don't let up, not until she collapses back on the table.

"Fuck." Her breaths come out in labored pants. "Give me a minute, and then I want to please you."

There is nothing I want to see more than her lips wrapped around my cock, but tonight isn't about me. It's about her, and the way her eyelids droop, I know she's tired from today's events and her orgasm.

"Not tonight, Dove."

"But—"

I kiss away her protest, letting Hettie taste her cream on my lips. She moans softly, wrapping her arms around my neck. "Not tonight," I repeat against her lips. "You'll take my cock soon, but right now I'm taking you to bed."

Hettie looks ready to protest further, but then thinks better of it because she acquiesces. She rests her head against my chest, and I ignore the mess we've made of dinner. I will apologize to the staff later, but I don't regret a single second of tonight.

"You're a good alpha." Hettie's words are hardly audible, but I hear them. Pride swells in my chest along with something else I can't fully describe. Adoration? Hope?

By the time I carry my mate upstairs and to our bed, she's fast asleep.

HETTIE

Three days have passed since Rip laid me out on the dinner table and feasted upon my pussy like his fucking life depended on it. Three days of the scene playing over and over in my head rent-free. The phantom touch of his lips, his tongue, forever etched in my brain. This man sank his claws into me, and I loved every second.

I expected things to become awkward between us. That maybe Rip would regret what we did, and I would have to pretend to be completely unaffected by it all. However, he didn't shy away from me in the days that followed. In fact, he kisses me good morning, and it feels like the most natural thing in the world.

But there hasn't been any repeat of our dinner date, much to my dismay. Rip has been pulled in every direction, and it's wearing on him, even if he won't admit it. I feel his exhaustion in our bond and the way he carries himself. We only see each other at night and in the mornings right before he leaves on patrols or for meetings.

When he left this morning, Rip promised he'd see me

this afternoon. Then he kissed me goodbye, leaving me alone with Grass. A familiar feeling took residence inside me. Loneliness, which made little sense. Tallie or Thorne, sometimes both, were with me during the day. I enjoyed their company, especially Tallie's. She's Rip's opposite in every way, but she shares the same stubbornness as her cousin.

A stubbornness I miss when Rip isn't around. Being the King Alpha's mate demands sacrifice, or so I've been told, but I'm selfishly missing the time he spends away because I want him to spend his time with me.

And I think he wants that too, if the soft caresses and lingering looks are any indication.

I think I'm falling for him, and I don't know how to stop. I'm not even sure I want to.

Grass licks my toes, pulling me away from thoughts of Rip. He whines, ready to start our day. He's pissed at me for taking him away from his new best friend, Tallie, so I'm certain he's also eager to get back to her.

Traitor.

But a damn cute one.

I stumble out of bed, dressing in jeans, warm boots, and a warm coat. Snow falls in abundance in Lycan Forest, and the chill seeps deep within my bones. I thought I would love snow, and, admittedly, it is beautiful, but the cold is painful. The shifters never seem bothered by the cold since some are perfectly content to walk barefoot or shirtless. I can barely walk out of the packhouse without covering my face for too long.

I told Tallie we would meet at the packhouse to walk over to the House of Wolfsbane together. I haven't looked over the healer's progress, but I want to hear any new information they may have uncovered. Only two more wolves have fallen ill from the curse, but more will follow. I'm here to help with a cure, so I need to be actively trying to do so.

I don't want to know what happens if I fail the pack. Every death will be my fault. Every cursed wolf will be because of me. I left Grym Hollow because I'm a fuck-up, but I refuse to be the same person here. I'm their damn Luna.

Grass barrels past me as soon as I get the door opened. He barks once, his tail wagging excitedly as he dashes down the hall. He pauses at the top of the stairs, waiting for me, but the moment I reach him, he all but rolls down the grand staircase.

Getting out of the packhouse takes longer than I would have liked since Grass insists on stopping to let everyone he crosses pet him. They all indulge him, and despite my eagerness to get to the lab, I can't help but smile. I love how much Grass has thrived here, making my decision to bring him along the right one.

When Grass suddenly bolts off toward the entrance, I know Tallie is here. I hurry and go to greet my friend. She's brought Thorne with her today, and I feel a stab of loneliness in my chest. Possibly jealousy too. I don't want Thorne; I want Rip here with me. Seeing them together reminds me I'm without him.

"Good morning, Hettie." Tallie gives me a big hug once she untangles herself from Grass, who has moved on to accost Thorne. Tallie wears similar jeans as me with a long-sleeved black shirt. I envy her ability to face the cold. Her hair is done, beautiful curls bouncing as she walks. She is sunshine, and I can't help but smile at her radiance.

"Rip wanted Thorne to join us today, and, well, I didn't fight him on that." She almost looks apologetic, but not quite.

"Good thing I like the both of you." I smile, and she loops her arm through mine.

"Ready to go?" I nod, and Tallie leads us outside, Thorne and Grass following closely behind us.

The moment we are out the door, I'm miserable. The frigid air nips at my skin, making my face sting. "Are your winters normally like this?"

"Oh, no," Tallie assures, and I let out a sigh of relief until she says, "They are much worse."

"Wonderful. Can't fucking wait," I say, deadpan.

"What was the weather like where you came from?" Thorne asks from behind us. He's busy making sure Grass doesn't get lost in the snow, which I'm thankful for.

"Warm, mostly. Grym Hollow doesn't really have extreme weather. Our winter is chilly, but nowhere near this. I've never seen snow in real life until I came here," I admit.

"Really?" Tallie asks incredulously. "You probably know this by now, but shifters run hot. So snow is the best time for us." She then goes on a spiel about snow and why the shifters love it so much.

Admittedly, I tune her out. Not because I'm not interested in what she has to say, but the whistling wind keeps distracting me. "Ugh, how do you deal with this?" I interrupt her. "The wind is so loud."

Tallie looks back at Thorne, confusion etched across her brows. "The wind? No, it's not. It's quiet out here today."

I scoff. "Very funny. How can you not hear it? It's like a loud bell in my ear that won't go away." I don't notice that they stop walking until I look back. Now it's my turn to be confused. "What's going on?"

Instead of answering my question, Tallie asks one of her own, "What does the wind sound like?"

Both she and Thorne are looking at me like I sprouted another head. I don't know what game they're playing, but I'll bite. "It sounds like a low whistle mixed with a soft howl. I'm not sure if that makes sense."

"What direction do you hear it coming from?" Tallie asks.

I shrug. "I don't know. I guess where the wind is blowing from? So, this way." I point to the left of me, and they share another knowing glance at each other.

Now it's pissing me off.

Before I can say anything, Tallie says, "No, Hettie. The wind is coming from the east. You just pointed south."

"O...kay? And?" I'm clearly missing something. "Do you want to tell me what you're thinking, or are we just going to continue to play the 'Let's Confuse Hettie' game?"

"I'll tell you, but first, can you lead us in the direction you hear the sound?" Tallie lets go of Thorne's hand to move closer to me. "I know this makes little sense, but just trust me."

Tallie has never given me a reason not to trust her, so I nod. I'm not sure what she's getting at, but clearly she thinks it's important enough to follow through.

I tune out everyone else around me and listen to my surroundings. The faint crunch of snow from eager feet. Soft chatter carrying from town. Then, finally, the low whistle starts again. Fainter than before, but my body moves of its own accord.

Tallie says something behind me, and Grass barks once, but I'm already walking away from them. I'm a slave to my body as it pulls me farther and farther away from them.

"Hettie!" Tallie calls, but I'm unable to reply. Unable to do anything but follow the sound that holds me prisoner.

Snow crunches behind me, so I know they aren't far

behind. None of them stop me, and I'm not sure if they could. Invisible hands wrap around me and refuse to let go. The sensation is almost painful, but each step closer to the mysterious sound eases that tightness coiling in my body.

A tree branch scratches my cheek as I pass through a densely wooded part of the forest. The snow isn't as thick here since the trees provide a semblance of coverage. Doesn't make it any less cold though, and I pull my coat tighter around me. The whistling is getting louder, but I'm not sure how far into the woods I'll have to go. Thorne is here with me, so I know I'm not defenseless if Michael is scouting this place, but it still fills me with unease.

I wind my way through trees until the whistling turns into a low hum. Like someone is leaning over and purring in my ear. My body shivers and not from the cold. All at once, the sounds stop, and I'm left in front of what looks like a bear's den.

Fuck, I hope no damn bears live here.

"The sound stopped here." I gesture to the small cave in front of me. "How far away did we travel from town?"

"Not that far. Maybe a mile. We shouldn't stay here long, though." Thorne approaches the opening of the cave. "Luna, stay back with Tallie. I'm going to check this out. I've never seen it before," he admits, scratching his head.

Thorne disappears inside the maybe-bear cave, but he doesn't go alone. Grass runs after Thorne, and I whirl on Tallie. "What just happened? What do you think is in there?"

Tallie's attention is on the cave, waiting for her mate to reemerge. "It's an old legend of our people," she says, like that explains everything.

I wait for her to say more, but when she doesn't, I groan. "Tallie, please, focus. What is going on?"

Finally, Tallie turns her gaze to me. A look of wonder and curiosity plays across her expression. "There's an old story of our people. A legend, really, of chosen ones coming to the pack's aid during times of dire need. These people are called to what they seek by hearing a whistling sound. It is said the ones with the gift provided their packs with resources and guidance that others couldn't. Not even the King Alpha.

"But there have only been rumors of these people in our history. Most were labeled as resourceful, and a few were even considered witches, but none of them were ever proved to be touched by our Goddess."

I hear her words, but they are slow to register. Legends? Witches? Goddesses? I feel like I have been thrown into a fantasy movie and suddenly became the main character. It's honestly not so far from the truth.

"What are you saying? That I'm hearing shit because some Goddess decided to bless me?" It seems outrageous and inconceivable. I'm a human from Grym Hollow. A woman who screwed up more times than I can count. I'm not worthy of whatever Tallie is talking about. Someone like Tallie or Thorne would fit the legends better. Nothing about me is remarkable enough to warrant such a gift.

Tallie opens her mouth to speak, but a bark from behind us makes us turn to see Thorne and Grass walking out of the tunnel. Thorne's eyes are wide, mouth slightly agape, as his eyes find me.

"What is it?" I think the worst. Dead packmate? A rogue? Something else?

"Oh my goddess," Tallie gasps, and my eyes drop to Thorne's hands.

I didn't notice it at first, but it's clear as day now. He's holding two medium-sized bundles of purple flowers. "Are those—?"

"Wolfsbane." Thorne grins. "Yes, Luna, these are wolfsbane. Enough to save a few of our wolves."

"Goddess blessed!" Tallie beams, throwing her arms around me, nearly knocking me on my ass. "You really are a true Luna! We have to go now and tell Rip!"

There's so much more I want to say and ask, but before I can, Tallie grabs my hands and pulls me along. All the way back to the packhouse.

All the way back to Rip.

CHAPTER 21

RIP

"They're getting closer, my King. Just yesterday we had a spotting of another Nephilim. That's four, maybe five so far. And if they are truly working with the rogues, it won't be long until another attack on our town," an alpha by the name of Remy says.

"It might be time to call in the dragons, sir," a female alpha suggests.

I know they're right, but I fucking hate that it's come to this. I trust Malix and his dragons, but I'm uneasy with strangers in our village. I don't believe Malix would ever betray me, but there is that small inkling of doubt I can't simply ignore.

"Stay on alert. Summoning the dragons is our last choice. For now, we keep patrolling and taking down rogues as we see them." My decision isn't popular. I can see the barely concealed anger in all of my guards' faces. But I fear calling the dragons will only worsen our situation before they get here, and I can't spare many more—or any —wolves.

"King Alpha, if I may—" Remy starts but doesn't get to

finish. The door to my study slams open, and Tallie stands there, eyes wide and hair a mess.

Instantly, I'm out of my chair. My stomach drops as I think the worst has happened. Where's Hettie? Is she okay? Did Michael attack? As soon as the fear comes, it leaves the moment I see Hettie come up behind Tallie with Thorne at her heels.

"Alpha, you're going to want to hear this," Thorne says. Tallie isn't one to interrupt, and if Thorne didn't stop her, I know whatever it is must be important.

"Leave us," I tell the room of mostly alphas. Immediately, the guards stand and file out. A few linger in hopes to hear what news the Luna, my cousin, and my second have brought, but Thorne growls. It effectively gets the stragglers to leave.

"What is going on?" The words are barely out of my mouth before Thorne tosses something on the table.

It takes my brain a moment to register what I'm seeing.

Flowers.

Purple flowers.

"Wolfsbane?" Incredulity laces my words. It should have been impossible to find wolfsbane. My men have scoured the entire forest, hoping to find the plant. Tallie has made maps hoping to discover something we've missed, but each search has proven fruitless.

Michael has blocked our access to their main growing ground of wolfsbane. The only way the wolfsbane in Thorne's hand could have been procured is if someone went into Michael's territory, risking their own life. The blooming excitement I felt only moments ago extinguishes, replaced with anger.

"Where was this found? Who journeyed past our protective borders into Michael's rogue lands?"

"No one," Tallie says, bouncing on the balls of her feet. She's like a mouse who finally found her cheese. She flashes me a toothy smile. "Hettie found it and—"

"You let my mate put herself in danger?" I growl, my attention flickering to Hettie, standing behind Tallie with Grass at her feet. I catch the eye roll Hettie gives me, completely diminishing the danger she was in.

"Rip, listen," Thorne urges. "You know we would never do anything to put Hettie in danger. You need to listen to what happened."

My instinct is to snap at him. Berate Thorne for going along with whatever plan they concocted, but when it comes to Hettie, I can't trust my rational thinking because it doesn't exist.

So, I take a deep breath, trying to calm the raging fire within me, and nod once at Tallie to continue.

"Hettie led us straight to the wolfsbane. She asked us why the wind was so loud, but neither Thorne nor I could hear anything, so I asked Hettie to follow the sound. She followed the call and led us straight to a cave with wolfs-bane," Tallie says.

"In a place we've never seen before," Thorne adds.

"Because we were never meant to find it. It was always meant to be Hettie! That's why Ender brought her to you. She hears the call. Who knows what else this could mean for us," Tallie exclaims.

Hettie shifts, clearly uncomfortable with my cousin's praise.

"Is that true, mate?" I ask, my voice gentle, full of awe. The woman—no, the Luna of our legends—standing in front of me can save our pack from this curse. There's not nearly enough wolfsbane to cure every cursed wolf, but it's a start. One that will only continue to grow as Hettie is called to the cure.

"I mean, yeah?" She shrugs. "I don't really understand it. I did little besides getting lucky and lead Thorne and Tallie to a cave that just so happened to have wolfsbane."

"Not true, Luna. Do you know how many times I've led guards past that hidden cave, searching for any signs of wolfsbane?" Thorne asks. Hettie just shrugs. "More times than I can count. That's how many. In none of those trips did we ever discover what you found, and we've searched that area inside and out."

"So, what? The wolfsbane just magically appeared?" Hettie asks in disbelief. "That's not how things work."

"Maybe not back in Grym Hollow, but here, magic thrives." I gently push past my cousin, who happily steps aside and into Thorne's arms. Hettie tracks me with her eyes, dipping her head back once I'm in front of her.

She's so damn short. So fucking breakable. But the power this woman holds makes her appear larger than life.

And she's all mine.

"You found wolfsbane because it wanted you to find it," I say, admiration lacing my words.

"You speak of it like it's a living entity." She blushes.

"Isn't it, though? You live in a world of supernatural beings. Of magic and curses. Everything here is alive in some way, and you are the person it calls to. That's your magic."

Hettie doesn't look fully convinced, but I don't need her to be. I'll make sure she understands how truly important her role is here. "You are the thing of legends, Hettie. I now understand why Michael and the Nephilim would want you."

"Why?" She sucks in a breath as I press closer, not

caring that we aren't alone. Tallie giggles softly, and Thorne whispers something to her, but I ignore them.

"Because you have the power to sway a war in your favor. You just don't realize it yet."

Hettie's lips form a cute O, but I don't give her a chance to respond. My lips are on hers, kissing her deeply. I try to convey my gratitude this way because words will not suffice.

Hettie's body melds to mine. I feel every curve and slope of her body, wishing we were alone. With great reluctance, I break the kiss, and Hettie whimpers. "Not fair," she murmurs.

A low laugh emanates from my chest. "So needy, Dove."

Hettie just shrugs, not ashamed of her need. Good. Maybe it makes me a cocky bastard, but I love how she wants me and isn't afraid to admit it.

"Rip," Thorne's voice breaks through the lust fog in my brain. I reluctantly tear my gaze away from Hettie, though I nearly lose all sense of control when she takes my hand.

Fuck, this feels so right.

"Tallie and I will take this to Lucielle, so she can create the tonics. Do you want me to tell her how we found it if she asks?" he inquires.

"Yes," I say immediately. "They should know who is responsible for their healing."

"But..." Hettie cuts in, all heads swiveling in her direction. "What if this was a one-time thing, and I can't do it again?"

Tallie shakes her head, adamant in her belief in her Luna. It makes me love my cousin a little more. "You will. This wasn't a fluke. You will be called to find more soon. We just need to be patient."

Hettie looks ready to argue but changes her mind and

nods. "Okay...if you believe this can happen again, I don't see the need to keep it from people like Lucielle."

"Do you want to join us?" Tallie asks with a knowing smile. "Or do you have...other matters to attend to?"

"I'm afraid we will both be extremely busy." I smirk, squeezing Hettie's hand. I have a lot of thanking to do with Hettie, but I need her alone.

Tallie hugs Hettie, and Thorne nods in my direction before they take their leave.

And finally, I'm blissfully and completely alone with my girl.

CHAPTER 22

HETTIE

I thoroughly enjoy how Rip shows his gratitude. His tongue is quickly becoming the best part about him, not that I will admit that to him. His damn ego is big enough with each orgasm he draws from me. It racks through my body, and when I finally reach my peak, I see stars.

Fucking stars, because my mate knows how to make me scream his name over and over again.

He hasn't let me take care of him yet, though. I don't understand why because I know he must be in pain with blue balls. I want to reciprocate, but Rip continually pushes me away. I would almost be insulted if it weren't for the mind-blowing orgasms he gives. Fuck, can that man eat pussy like it's going out of style.

But it's the same treatment every night for the past three nights. He leaves me feeling weightless and satisfied, before locking himself in that bathroom. When he comes out, he looks composed, minus the glazed-over look in his eyes. Part of me wonders if he thinks he'll lose control over his wolf if he allows me to reciprocate. I never have the opportunity to ask why he's hidden from me the last few nights because he wraps me in his arms and promptly falls asleep. And in the morning, he's gone, leaving only a note with a promise to see me later.

This morning starts no differently. I wake up to an empty bed—empty other than Grass, who has taken to Rip's side of the bed when he leaves. Damn spoiled dog. Grass huffs as I push myself up, having the audacity to glare at me for jostling the bed and waking him.

"Sorry, Oh Great King." I roll my eyes, but he's a dog so he doesn't reply.

I take care of my morning needs, changing into something I hope will keep me warm in the dropping temperatures. I rouse Grass out of bed—he isn't thrilled about it— and open my door, expecting to see Thorne waiting for me.

Except Thorne isn't here today. Neither is Tallie. Another guard, one I have only seen in passing, stands there. She gives me a curt smile. "Are you ready, Luna?"

"Yes, but where's Thorne?"

"Alpha Thorne is in a meeting, filling in for the King Alpha," she says like she just didn't make the situation more confusing.

Where the fuck is Rip then?

"Will you take me to Thorne, please?"

"Yes, Luna. I'm instructed to take you to him."

Well, that's good at least. The woman then takes off toward the pack meeting rooms, somewhere I rarely go. Grass trots behind me, taking in everything like he hasn't seen it a dozen times before.

My confusion only mounts when my temporary escort leads me to a closed door, knocking once. From inside, papers rustle and muffled voices speak, but I can't make out any of them.

After what feels like a century but is probably only thirty seconds later, the door opens, and Thorne's serene face greets me. He nods at the woman. "Thank you, Alpha Layla. You're free to go back to your duties."

Without another word, the woman—Layla—leaves. She clearly doesn't want to prolong the inevitable.

Once she rounds the corner, leaving me alone with Thorne, I ask, "Where's Rip?"

"He's...indisposed at the moment. He wanted me to let you know he's fine but won't be back for the next couple of days."

Thorne isn't lying to me as much as he's withholding the truth. "Yeah, that's not going to cut it. Where is Rip? And why couldn't he tell me himself?" Just when I thought we were making progress too. Why the hell would he just leave?

"I really can't say more than that—"

"Thorne, just tell her," a familiar voice abruptly cuts Thorne off. Tallie pushes her way past her mate. If Thorne truly wanted to stop her, he could, but he seems almost relieved that Tallie is defying him.

"Where's Rip?" I parrot, sounding like a broken record, except I don't care—I want answers.

"Rip is at a cabin not far from here. But he's going to remain there for a couple days," Tallie says.

"Why? Did something happen?"

Tallie and Thorne share a glance, communicating without their voices. It's both amazing to see and annoying as fuck because I don't know what's passing between them. It would be incredibly convenient if Rip and I could do the same.

"Let me tell her. Just go back in, and I'll be there in a minute," Tallie finally says to Thorne.

"Are you taking her to him?"

"If she wants to, but that's her choice. We will not make it for her."

My anxiety only continues to mount. I hate that they're talking about me like I'm not there. Where the fuck is Rip?

Thorne hesitates, but only for a moment. "Very well. Take Layla with you, so you aren't walking back alone." He then leans down and presses a kiss to her lips, soft but loving. I can't help but feel like I shouldn't be witnessing such an intimate moment.

When they finally break apart, Tallie loops her arm through mine. "I'm not sure how much you know about wolf shifter biology, so this might not make sense to you. Rip is away because he didn't want you to feel obligated to...uhm, join in."

"Join in? On what?" She isn't making any sense, and frankly, I'm tired of beating around the bush. "Tallie, I need you just to tell me. I can't make a decision until I know what is going on."

"I know," she sighs. "And I encouraged him to tell you himself, but Rip can be an idiot, as most men are."

I nod in agreement because she's not wrong there.

"Rip is going through his rut right now." She looks over my face, waiting for a reaction.

My face must turn four shades of red because Tallie giggles. "I take it you know what that is?"

"I mean, I've read about it in books...but I don't know if it's the same thing." She doesn't speak, expecting me to go on. "It's where...it involves sex?" I squeak out, feeling like a damn virgin who just saw her first penis.

Pathetic.

"That is the simplistic nature of it, yes." She nods. "A rut is the male equivalent of a female's heat. The carnal desire and need to mate is at an all-time high. Sex and claiming go hand in hand. Most males will fill that need by mating with their partner, but some use Rut Escorts."

"What's a Rut Escort?" I could guess, but I want to hear it confirmed.

"Wolves who will help the males get through their rut. We also have Heat Escorts too. But Rip isn't with a Rut Escort," she says quickly before my mind can think of my mate fucking someone else. Jealousy flares to life, so potent, I almost choke on it.

No one touches Rip.

No one.

He's mine.

"He's alone," Tallie continues. "I told him he needed to tell you, but he didn't want you to feel obligated to..."

"Let him fuck me?" I ask.

"Well, to put it bluntly, yeah." Tallie shrugs. "But it's more than just sex if it's your mate. The connection you share with that person is intense. Your mind is consumed with the other, and only the feel of flesh against flesh will satisfy you."

Part of me understands why Rip wouldn't want to tell me. I appreciate his decision to not make me feel obligated, but by not telling me, he took away my choice.

Something about taking this step with Rip seems final. Like there's no turning back after this. Do I want that? Does he? I could remain by his side as his Luna, but never his lover. Never his true mate.

But...

I could also *have* him. All of him. In ways no one else has.

My mind has been made up for some time now, but I've

been too nervous to admit it to myself. I want Rip. Truly want him. And I think he wants me too.

Honestly, there's only one way to figure that out.

"Take me to him, Tallie."

A slow, knowing smile spreads across her red lips. "As you wish, Luna."

I SENSE Rip's heightened emotions before I see him. Tallie leads me to a private cabin not far from town. She wound her way down the wooded path, leading us past the residential homes, to a few private and well-spaced-out cabins.

Tallie refers to them as "Mating Cottages," spaces set aside for mates or wolves with their hired escort to escape for much-needed privacy. Apparently, wolves can get loud and aggressive during their rut, and this adds an extra layer of protection if they choose it.

"Are you certain you'll be okay?" Tallie asks as if I'm going into battle rather than about to face my extremely horny husband.

The thought of him in the cottage, hard and feral over me, makes me press my legs together. There is an underlying current of fear, but mostly I feel like, if I don't see Rip, I won't be able to get him out of my system.

"I'll be fine. Will you keep Grass for me?" I love my dog, but if I'm about to get completely dominated by my ravenous mate, there's no way in hell I want Grass to witness that.

"Of course," she promises. "But remember, if you change your mind, you'll need to run like hell. Call for a guard because Rip won't be entirely in control of his body or actions."

"Got it. If I change my mind, run away from my mate who enjoys chasing me," I mumble. "I'll be fine, Tallie. I want to do this." Very badly, but I'm not going to tell his cousin that.

Tallie gives me a knowing smile. "Alright, then. Don't say I didn't warn you." With that, she calls for Grass, who frolics over to her. Then they leave together. I wait until they are little more than silhouettes in the distance before I force my legs to carry me forward.

Fear and excitement churn low in my belly. If I can sense him, then Rip knows I'm here too. There's a thud and something that sounds like a grunt, then nothing at all. Taking a deep breath, I grab the doorknob and turn.

The cabin is dark. The embers are all that remain of a once-burning fire. There's little furniture in the main room, just a large couch and a coffee table that has seen better days. A small kitchenette sits over on the left with a bowl of fruit on the counter. There's also a hallway between the kitchen and main room leading down to what I can only assume is the bedroom and bathroom.

I take a step into the cool room, shutting the door behind me. Wood creaking snaps my attention to the darkened hallway. I feel the eyes of a predator on me, waiting for the moment I let my guard down.

"Rip?" My voice comes out breathier than I anticipate, and I'm greeted with a low warning growl.

"You shouldn't be here, Dove." Rip's voice reverberates around me, sending shivers down my back. I shouldn't feel this aroused, but I can't help it. Not when I know my husband is barely containing himself.

"You don't get to make that decision for me," I retort, receiving a deep laugh in response.

"Do you lack self-preservation? I'm more wolf than human, mate. And if you stay here a minute longer, I can't be held responsible for my actions." Another out. A smart woman would take it.

But a needy, horny woman who wants nothing more than to be ravished by her mate stays and plays the eager prey.

"Neither can I, Alpha. Are you going to come out and play?" I'm taunting his wolf, wanting him to show his claws and teeth.

I get my wish.

Faster than I can track, a blur of darkness rushes at me. I fly back, hitting the wall with a hard thud, but Rip cushions my head with his hand. The air is knocked from my lungs, and a hand brackets my neck. Rip hovers over me, but I barely recognize him.

His pupils are blown wide, with a ring of gold around his irises. He's shirtless, and his pants are unbuttoned. Like he was in the middle of something, but I interrupted him. Though it's dark, there's no mistaking the bulge in his pants, outlining his perfect cock.

My mouth waters, and I moan.

The crazed look in his eyes only heightens as he smirks. "Wanton thing, aren't you?"

"Rip—"

"No," he snarls. "Alpha. Call me by my fucking title. Let me hear it out of those pouty lips."

I swallow audibly, understanding what Tallie and Thorne meant when they said Rip wasn't himself. This man before me is crass, dominant, overbearing, and undeniably sexy.

Wetness pools between my legs.

"Alpha," I start again. "Let me take care of you."

"Show me how you'll service your alpha then," he hisses.

I should feel put off by his dickish behavior, but it only turns me on more. Probably because it's Rip and not some other man I met on the streets who is as cruel as his words. Rip cares for me, even in this state. He's rough, but there's still a part of him holding back. Allowing me to decide to stay or go.

I sink to the floor, on my knees.

Rip doesn't stop me this time, like he's done every other time. He's finally giving in, no longer able to hide his rut from me. The hunger in his eyes only intensifies.

I finish the work of pulling down his pants, freeing him from the confines of the material. His thickness pops out. I've seen him nude before, but never this close and never in this position.

Rip takes my hesitancy as not wanting to continue, and he tenses, pulling back. "Hettie, you don't—"

"Stop making my damn decisions for me, Alpha, and get back here so I can suck your cock."

Heat flares in his eyes, and he moves forward again. He strokes my cheek before bunching up my hair in his fist, keeping it out of my face.

"Mouth, mate," he orders, and I'm helpless to obey. I open for him, parting my lips. With his free hand, he grabs his shaft and guides his cock to my lips. I moan, eagerly flicking my tongue out to catch the bead of pre-cum pooling at his tip.

"Fuck," Rip groans. There's something exceptionally sexy when he moans for me. Heat rushes through my body, and I fucking love the way it makes me feel.

He's by far the largest man I've ever taken to bed, not that he has had much competition. The men I've slept with acted like dicks to compensate for what they clearly didn't have.

I try to relax my jaw, breathing through my nose. He's only halfway down, but I am already full. I gag around his length and reach up to wrap my hand around the base of his cock.

"That's my good girl. Relax, mate. Let me take over." He's barely hanging on by a thread, the last of his restraints unraveling. Still, I obey, because I *trust* him, and let him take the lead.

Rips thrusts his hips. Nothing about him is gentle or sweet at this moment. No, he fucks my face, using my mouth for his own pleasure. It's embarrassing and humiliating, but I can't get enough of it. Tears pool in my eyes from his roughness. Already, I can taste his desire, knowing he won't last much longer.

"You going to swallow for me, pet? Milk me for every last drop?" His filthy words go straight to my clit. The friction of my pants rubbing against me provides little relief. If I had been thinking ahead, I would have stripped down.

But this pleasure is about him. He's made it about me night after night. I can take a few moments of sexual frustration.

A growl erupts through Rip's body, and he roars into the dimly lit room. His movements become frantic, and I'm helpless to do anything other than take it.

"Fuck!" That is the only warning before a hot, salty liquid pools in my mouth faster than I can swallow it down.

His come spills from my lips, down my chin. I can only imagine what I look like to him right now. A needy woman with her mate's cum obscenely dripping down her body.

I swear Rip is thinking the same thing because he's slow to pull out of my mouth. "You on your knees with my cock in your mouth is a pretty picture, Hettie. One I wish to capture again."

When he finally leaves my mouth, I feel strangely empty. Though I can breathe much better, so that's the tradeoff, I suppose.

Looking at Rip, I can tell that fucking my mouth didn't even take the edge off. His pupils are still dilated, and his cock is still hard.

"This is just the start, Hettie. You wanted to join me on my rut, so that slutty mouth and pretty pussy are mine. Now strip."

"Yes, Alpha." The words leave my lips before I can fully register them. My body is working on autopilot as I strip for him, ready to take whatever my mate gives me.

CHAPTER 23
RIP

I am a man undone.

With a goddess at my feet, I know nothing else but pleasure.

Hettie isn't supposed to be here. She was never meant to see me like this: feral with slipping control. If I had known she'd be here, I would have prepared her for my unleashing.

It's too late now. She's here, in the thick of it, and I can't let her go.

Hettie's chest rises and falls, my cum still dripping down her chin. It's filthy, and I can't help but want to paint her with my release. Claiming her over and over again, so there's no mistake who she belongs to.

Who *I* belong to.

This woman will be both the death and rebirth of me. I just know it.

"Rip." The neediness in her voice has the hair on the back of my neck standing up. My cock throbs, still as hard as before. Her mouth helped ease some of the pain that comes with my rut, but still didn't completely satisfy it.

I need more, and I plan on taking everything she offers.

"Take me," she pleads, looking up at me with those damn honey-colored eyes.

The tortured expression on my face morphs into one of wicked delight. I reach down, scooping Hettie up in my arms. Her scent erupts around me. Her desire is so thick and sweet. If I reach my hand between her thighs, I know she would be dripping for me.

I say nothing as I briskly whisk her away, back down the dark hallway to the cozy bedroom. It's plain, with nothing more than a bed, but it's all I need. When I toss her on the bed, Hettie bounces once. The next second, I'm on her again.

I press Hettie down on the mattress. She moans softly, her body arching toward mine. She trembles under my touch, and I kiss down her body. I taste the saltiness and faint floral flavor of her skin. She smells so fucking good. I groan, unable to contain myself. Kissing down to her breast, I pull her hard nipple into my mouth.

"Oh god, yes," my mate moans, letting her head fall back, exposing her slim neck. How I crave to sink my teeth into my mark on her neck, completing the mating ritual at last. Because that's what is going to happen after this. There's no turning back, and I won't let her shy away from me. She wants this—and me—as much as I want her.

I move to tease her other nipple, my hand snaking down between her legs. I rest my hand atop her mound, covering her completely. "This pussy is mine," I growl.

"Prove it, Alpha," my sassy mate pants. "Prove my pussy is yours."

She's baiting me, that little brat. And I fucking love it.

My thumb finds her clit, and I stroke her using small,

circular motions. "This pussy became mine the moment we mated."

Before she can reply, I lean down, running my tongue along her pussy lips. She's completely drenched for me. Her honey coats my tongue, and I swallow. "Fucking beautiful. You're primed to take me, aren't you mate?"

"Yes, fuck, Alpha. Stop playing with me. I need you inside of me. Please."

I enjoy hearing her beg, and if this was any other time, I might prolong her pleasure for no other reason than to get her completely worked up. And partially for my sick amusement.

But this isn't any other time, and I'm doing everything in my power now to rut against her repeatedly until I satisfy my need to dominate. To knot my mate until we are both screaming from satisfaction.

"You've never taken a wolf's cock before, Dove. I'm about to ruin you."

"Do it. Ruin me. I want it."

If I were a good man, I would take this time and remind her about knotting, but I'm barely a man at all right now. My hard cock leaks on Hettie's stomach, but she doesn't seem to mind.

She reaches out, wrapping her hand around my shaft. My entire body is on fire. I'm the one about to dominate my mate, but there is no question who's in charge. This woman will have me worshiping at her feet soon.

And I'd gladly do it.

Hettie leads me to her entrance and runs my tip along her folds. We groan in unison as her wetness slicks my cock. She then lines me up with her entrance, and all rational thinking is gone.

I grab Hettie's hips, pulling her closer. I slowly guide my

way inside her, watching her pussy lips stretch obscenely around my cock. Hettie is so damn tight, but I know she can take me. Her body is primed for this. Not everyone can take an alpha's cock, but Hettie can. She will.

I watch her expression closely as I slide the last few inches inside of her. She cries out for me when I'm fully seated, legs trembling from the intrusion. I clamp my hands around her thighs, keeping her open. "You were made for my cock, Dove. See how well you take me?"

"You're...so big," she pants out, biting her lower lip.

I lean down and suck her lip into my mouth. That drags a long moan from her, and she relaxes underneath me.

Our combined scent wraps around us, reminding me of home. I don't know when Hettie became the object of all my desires and the most important person in my life, but somewhere between meeting her and now, the shift took place.

"You can take it, mate," I say at last, and she doesn't argue. She just looks at me with something akin to admiration and passion. A look a woman would give to her lover.

I move my hips, testing out how she feels. When Hettie meets my thrust with her own, the last of my restraint snaps, and I start to fuck her in earnest.

She is temptation personified, and I'm her willing subject.

I have often thought about what it would be like to truly have Hettie, but the daydream does not accurately represent the reality. Hettie squeezes my cock perfectly and takes down every inch like she is made for me.

She *is* made for me.

The room fills with the lewd sound of our fucking. My heavy balls slapping against her ass with each thrust. I'm already so fucking close, I'm not going to last much longer.

"I'm about to claim you, Hettie. Tell me yes," I say, not slowing my movement down. I'm dangerously close to succumbing to the pleasure, but I hold off. Only barely. Already I can feel my knot trying to form inside her. I didn't have the time to educate her on the mating rituals of wolves, but she is about to get a crash course now.

"Yes. God, yes, Rip," she cries, digging her nails into my shoulders. Her legs move to wrap around me, pulling me in even deeper.

It's too much.

It's not enough.

I don't think; I just react. My lips find the soft flesh of her neck, kissing and teasing her. This is where I marked her during our mating ceremony. The outline of my teeth forever etched into her neck. I need to feel that again. My canines extend, and before I can think properly, I bite down hard on her neck.

She screams. Or I scream. I don't fucking know. I don't know where she starts and I end. The bond that has been hiding in reserve for so long roars to life. Hettie's feelings and emotions mix with my own until she's imprinted herself upon my soul, our mind link finally snapping in place.

Meaning Ender found my true mate and brought her to me.

"*Come for me, mate,*" I say through the newly formed bond. I sense her surprise immediately.

"*Rip? Is that you?*"

"*Yes, love. Our mate bond is complete. I can tease you whenever I want now.*"

"*Fuck...*"

My movements grow frantic. Her blood coats my lips,

and I lick them and her wound clean. Her legs tighten around me, which sends me over the edge.

I'm coming. I'm coming so hard that I see fucking stars. Hettie screams, her own desire evident all over my cock and between her thighs. She rides out her own orgasm, my name on her lips as she comes for me.

The base of my cock swells, and my knot forms, locking us together. Hettie gasps, grabbing on to my shoulders. "What is—"

"My knot, mate. Get used to it because you'll be taking it a lot."

"Rip, fuck, how big is it going to get? It's not going to fit; it's—"

I silence her with a searing kiss. The protests die on her lips, and she kisses me back. I distract her, making sure she receives the pleasure she deserves. It's been so damn long since I've knotted anyone. But none felt like this. Not even close.

"Feels...good..." she moans between kisses.

I smirk. "Good." Caressing the side of her face, I look down at the bite mark at the juncture of her neck. "How does this feel?"

"It hurts a little. But not too badly. I can...feel you. In a way I couldn't before," she says slowly.

"It's because we've completed our mating ritual. Our bond is finally intact. You're mine, Hettie." I can't keep the possessiveness out of my voice.

My mate smiles up at me lazily, running her hands along my body and stopping at my chest. "That also means you're mine. So, don't fucking try to hide your rut from me again."

Despite myself, I laugh. "Yes, mate. I'll steal you away for my next rut, but we aren't nearly done with this one."

Hettie's eyes widen. She wiggles underneath me, and I groan. My knot keeps her close, and even if it didn't, I wouldn't let her out of my sight.

"This didn't satisfy your rut?" She shakes her head. "Fuck, how high of a sex drive do you have?"

I lean closer, pressing our foreheads together. When I speak, my lips brush against hers. "I'm an alpha in rut, mate. This could last for days. I'm not nearly finished with you."

Fear and lust glint in her eyes. "My poor vagina," she mumbles. "You're going to have to carry me everywhere after this."

"Gladly." I pull her against my body. "Now hold on tight, mate. You're going to ride out this knot."

There are no complaints on her part. She's tired, but that doesn't diminish her eagerness for me. And I work again to draw out our next orgasm, pulling Hettie over the top with me each time.

Time stills.

There's only her.

CHAPTER 24

HETTIE

My body is sore in places I've never been sore before. The last few nights are a blur of bodies, sweat, and desire, desire so intense, neither Rip nor I could keep our hands off each other.

I naively thought I understood ruts from the brief explanation given by Thorne and Tallie. I quickly realized I knew shit about ruts, mating, and knotting. Fucking knotting. Never in my life had I felt so full and connected to another person. Literally.

There was pain at first, but Rip helped me through it, although I know holding back was hard for him. The pain didn't last long, though. My body grew accustomed to his size and soon craved him like an addict. I've never considered myself the submissive sort, but Rip has brought out a part of me that no one else has before.

I'm not sure exactly when our sex-induced haze ended, but it was sometime last night after my fifth—or was it sixth?—orgasm of the day. My body had finally had enough, and I vaguely remember passing out on Rip. We were gross. Covered in sweat and cum, but I didn't even have the energy to shower. Rip, though, somehow found the strength to carry me into the small bathroom and give me a bath.

Out of everything we did over the last couple of days, somehow that felt the most intimate. No words were said; nothing needed to be said with our bond in place. We could communicate in a new way now. The last thing I remember is taking his hand in mine before everything around us went dark, and I finally gave into sleep.

I've been asleep ever since then for what has felt like days. When I finally rejoin the living, I open my eyes to darkness. My vision takes time to adjust, fighting away the sleep fog. I expect to see sun filtering in through the window, but only moonlight shines through. Next to me, Rip snores softly, his arm stretched over my body.

He looks boyish as he sleeps, reminding me once again he holds great responsibility for his age. He's a good King Alpha, but even good kings need their rest from time to time.

I stay curled up in a thick woolen blanket next to him, watching him sleep. I feel only a little like a creeper, but considering the things this man did to my body, I think staring at him while he sleeps is the least of my concerns.

I stay in the warm comfort of the blankets and Rip's arms until my bladder threatens to explode. I don't want to disturb him and do my best to shimmy out of his embrace without doing so. Rip doesn't even budge from his spot, so I know he must be tired. The crash after a rut is intense.

I half hobble, half scoot to the bathroom, ignoring the aches in my body. Even sitting takes great effort. I nearly whoop in triumph when I manage to lower myself without angering any of my muscles.

Even though Rip bathed me not too long ago, I still feel

dirty. The warm bath water should also help to soothe my tired muscles. After I finish up on the toilet and wash my hands, I fill the tub with warm water. Steam fills the room, and I smile as I slowly submerge myself into the tub.

The tub is small, far smaller than the one back at the packhouse, but I bend my knees slightly to fit comfortably. I sink down the back until the water is up to my shoulders. My muscles scream their thanks as the heat helps soothe them.

And that's where I stay. I'm not sure for how long, but I doze off twice, fighting sleepiness a third time when I hear the door open. My head snaps in that direction just in time to see a messy-haired, glossy-eyed Rip stumble through the door. He's naked, and this is the first time I've really paid attention to his body since the start of his rut.

His chest looks as if he was put through a shredder. There's even slight bruising around his neck. Fuck...did I do that? And if I did that to him...what the hell do I look like right now?

Rip doesn't speak but makes a gesture I interpret as wanting to get in the tub with me. I scoot forward, and he steps in behind me. Water splashes over the top, but he doesn't seem to mind.

Rip settles his large body behind me and snakes one arm around my waist, pulling me back. My head rests on his chest, listening to the steady beat of his heart. *"Good evening, mate."* He speaks through our bond, and even in my mind, his voice is husky, tired. "Mate" takes on a new meaning now that we've completed the bond. It feels... permanent.

It feels right.

"It's evening?" His words slowly register in my head. "We only slept for an hour or two?" The sun was just setting when we went to bed last night, but I thought surely we had been asleep for longer.

I feel Rip's laugh from deep within his chest. "We've slept close to twenty-four hours, Dove."

"Twenty-four hours?" My eyes widen. Explains why I had to pee so badly. "I blame you for that."

"I accept the blame." He tightens his hold on me, bringing his chin down to rest on my shoulder, careful of my sensitive mating mark.

"You look stunning wearing my mark," he purrs into my ear.

"Possessive bastard," I hum, fighting back the smile. He nips at my neck gently, but I just laugh.

"We've come a long way since the first day we met," he says.

I'm inclined to agree. I never thought we would get to this point. I hadn't been keen on opening myself up to another relationship. I've had my heart broken too many times to want to go down that path again.

And now...

Rip changed it all.

As much as I want to stay in this blissful bubble for longer, a small, nagging voice tells me we are going to have to face reality. The real reason why I'm here.

"Now that we are mated fully, does this mean we can defeat Michael and the Nephilim he's working with?"

Rip takes a deep breath. The mood switches, reality creeping back into our sex-crazed cabin. "I'm not sure how this works. Ender isn't forthcoming with his information, but he seems to believe a strong bond between us will help change the tides of war."

Strong bond between us. Not love, but also not *not* love. We are both in unfamiliar territory here, and for as much as

Rip claims to have his emotions under lock and key, I know there's a part of him that's scared for things to end badly.

The bond creates no secrets between us. It's both overwhelming and refreshing. It makes me feel stronger, but more vulnerable too, because I now have a massive weakness. If anyone wanted to hurt me, they'd simply have to hurt Rip. And with the threat of the looming war, we don't have time to truly explore these new feelings. Not yet, at least.

"We have to get back to the real world soon, don't we?" I sigh, knowing the answer before he responds.

"We do. Our pack is still in danger and..." he trails off.

"We just spent the last few days fucking our brains out?"

"Yeah, something like that." He chuckles, though there is no real humor behind it.

Were we selfish in spending the last few days together and leaving the pack to fend for themselves? I refuse to feel bad for mating with my husband; I don't regret it at all. But I can admit the timing isn't great.

Wolves lie in their hospital beds, counting on us to find a cure.

Suddenly, the room feels all too cold.

"I need to find more wolfsbane," I say. "Like I did with Tallie and Thorne. It called me once; it can call me again."

Leaning my head back, I take in Rip, who seems to wrestle with this. "Yes, finding wolfsbane not locked up by Michael is important, but the woods are too dangerous right now with the wolves and Nephilim closing in. Promise me you won't go into the woods without me. Even if you hear the call, find me first."

"What if I'm with Thorne or Tallie?" Surely he would allow his best friend to escort me again.

But Rip shakes his head. "Not even them. Just me. I need your promise, Hettie."

I don't like it. It feels too much like control, but a part of me understands his concern. It's the only reason I nod, agreeing to his terms.

For now.

"Thank you, Dove." Rip leans down to kiss me, the final seal on our time together.

Because the moment we walk out of this cabin, the blissful oasis we created will disappear, and the true war will begin.

I'm not sure I'm ready.

CHAPTER 25

HETTIE

"This is the last of the wolfsbane you located, Luna. This last dose will cure a child. Perhaps even a small female wolf." Lucielle inspects the vial of lavender-colored liquid. The last medicine we have.

"How many cursed wolves do we have?" I probably should know this answer, but I haven't been able to stomach going back into the infirmary. It's fucked up on my part because I'm not the one dying, but seeing my packmates suffer brings an unexpected sadness that sits heavily on my chest.

It's been a week since Rip and I made our appearance back into pack life. A week of harmless jests and teases from Tallie about surviving my first rut. It's also been a week of constant work, pulling me one way and Rip another. The time spent at the cabin feels like so long ago.

"Upwards of thirty. Maybe forty." Lucielle sighs, placing the medicine back into the holder. "We would have had more, but with the wolfsbane you found, we were able to heal close to ten wolves."

"Forty?" Tallie speaks up from her perch in the corner,

ignoring what Lucielle said about healed wolves. Grass lies over her legs as she strokes his head. He's all but ditched me for Tallie, but I can't say I blame him. "That's the most we've had in a long time."

"Yes, well…" Lucielle shakes her head. "I fear it will only continue to get worse until we break this wicked curse or have enough wolfsbane to counteract it."

I feel the eyes of the other healers on me. I don't need to hear their thoughts to know they are waiting for me to play my part as their Luna. I found wolfsbane once, but haven't been able to do it a second time.

I haven't even tried. I've been busy enjoying my mate when I should have been helping my pack.

Guilt threatens to drown me. Is this what Rip feels all the time? If so, he shouldn't be carrying this burden alone.

Before I can dwell on my shortcomings as Luna, the door to the lab opens, and all heads swivel in that direction.

Thorne walks in, scanning the room until his attention falls on Tallie. His features soften, and he smiles in a way that's reserved for her. Then his gaze lands on me, and his smile dims some. "Luna, King Alpha Rip requests your presence in his meeting. I can escort you when you're ready."

I look back at Lucielle and Tallie. Both women nod at me, telling me it's okay that I go. "I promise to look for wolfsbane soon, Lucielle." Though I don't know how to keep that promise. I'm not sure how to make the plant sing for me—or whatever the hell Tallie said it did to call me. But I'll figure it out. Somehow.

I offer my companions a soft smile before turning to Thorne. "I'm ready to go. Take me to my mate, please."

I'm the last one to enter Rip's office. Thorne shuts the door behind us. The room feels austere, lacking the warmth I associate with Rip and our pack. Rip sits behind a mahogany desk. The corners of his lips twitch up when he sees me.

"Your Luna is here, King Alpha," Thorne says, keeping up the formality when in the presence of...someone.

There are two people seated on the opposite side of Rip's desk. They are large, like my mate, and possess the same aura of strength he does. Neither man looks at me as I cross their paths, moving to find my seat by Rip.

It's only when I'm next to him do I realize there's no chair for me. Does he expect me to stand like some intimidating bodyguard? I shift uncomfortably from foot to foot until Rip grabs my waist and pulls me into his lap.

"My mate, Luna Hettie," he introduces me.

My face heats in embarrassment, but I do my best to smile at the two men. Neither seems fazed by Rip deciding to be my chair, so I try not to think too much into it.

"Hettie, this is Alpha Grant and Alpha Maximus. Both serve as our army commanders," he explains.

Alpha Grant is the older of the two, with salt-and-pepper hair. He's shorter than Maximus, at least sitting down, but both men feel equally powerful. Maximus looks young, younger than even Rip. There's a certain hardness in his expression, hinting at a rough life.

"It's good to meet you, Alphas." I offer my hand in greeting, expecting one of them to take it. Maximus and

Grant simply stare at it until my cheeks flush red, and I drop my hand.

Rip rubs my back gently. "It's frowned upon for other alphas to touch mates who don't belong to them. Especially the Luna."

"That would have been good information to know five seconds ago," I murmur.

"Our humblest apologies, Luna. We mean no disrespect." Grant offers me a half smile. I awkwardly return it. Clearly there's plenty I still need to learn about shifter culture and customs.

"None taken," I assure.

"It's good to finally meet our King Alpha's Luna," Maximus says in a deep voice.

"We were just discussing Michael. I wanted you here to listen to the report," Rip explains. and I straighten my back, fully tuned into the conversation.

"Did something happen? Was there another attack?" I think of the poor wolves already in the infirmary at capacity and the healers with nowhere else to put them.

"Not yet." Something in the way Grant speaks doesn't reassure me. "But we believe it's only a matter of time."

"The wolves on morning patrol report seeing Michael speaking to a creature described as monstrous. We can only assume the witness spoke of a Nephilim, but there's been no confirmation yet," Maximus adds.

"More sightings of these monstrous creatures have come almost daily for the past week. If these creatures are Nephilim, and we have no reason to think otherwise, we believe the war for our kingdom isn't far off." Grant runs a hand through his buzz-cut hair, sighing.

"We believe it is time to call in for backup," he continues. I wait for him to explain, but he doesn't.

"What does he mean by backup?" I ask Rip.

Rip is deep in thought, and at first, I don't think he heard my question, but then he sighs. "He means Malix."

I don't need to ask why he hasn't reach out yet. Rip and his other alphas are proud. But surely he can see any outside help would benefit us, not make us weak. "Is he an actual dragon?" I feel like that's an important factor in our aid situation.

"When he wants to be, yes."

I blink. Once. Then twice, waiting for Rip to say he's kidding and of course he already sought help with an actual fucking dragon.

When he doesn't say that, I test my power here. "Alpha, I don't think we should turn away aid."

"Neither do we," Maximus speaks up. "We believe it's time to accept the dragon's help. I can compose a letter—"

"No letter," Rip interrupts, shaking his head. "We can't risk it getting intercepted. Grant, how many men would you need to take a team to Dragon's Keep requesting aid?"

The older alpha purses his lip, taking a moment to think. "We don't have the count of how many rogues Michael has, but we can assume it's over twenty from the last attack. We also don't know how many Nephilim are lurking in the forest. To be safe, King Alpha, I would want to take no fewer than twenty men."

"Twenty men?" I blurt, unable to help myself. "You want to take twenty of our alphas and leave us defenseless?"

To be fair, I don't think we would be completely defenseless, but I also don't think it's smart to lose that many alphas. It would be a prime time for rogues to attack, once they find out we are without half of our protectors.

Through our bond, I feel unease. I turn to Rip, but he's

not looking at me. He clenches his jaw, lost in thought. I know he doesn't like this any more than I do.

"Twenty alphas is a hefty number, Grant. With so many of our wolves cursed and our omegas more frightened by the day, I don't know if it's best to send so many. We may be able to spare a few betas," he says.

"Is it better to send a few to their slaughter?" Maximus asked. "Because we can expect the full force of the rogues and Nephilim if we're caught. This is not ideal; we won't pretend like it is. This journey is too strenuous for many of the betas. They will better serve you here as fighters. But it is of utmost importance that nothing stops us from reaching Dragon's Keep."

I've been in the pack for a little over a month, give or take a day or two. These men have been engaged in conflict a lot longer and know more than I do. Still, I can't help but feel like this isn't the best plan of action. Rip says this is my pack too, and as their Luna, I'm keeping their best interest at heart.

"I don't think it's wise to send so many wolves away when we have so many cursed lying in the infirmary," I say. Maximus tenses. I'm clearly not making the best impression with him. "I do think we need assistance, but I don't think we need to risk so many of our wolves."

I expect Rip to back me up. Not because we are mates, but because he sees the flaws in this plan. He clenches his hand on the table so hard, his knuckles turn white. His rigid posture doesn't ease the doubt creeping in.

"Can you promise me you can get there and back with twenty men at your disposal?" Rip asks, and it feels like hands wrap around my heart. It's not a good feeling.

Grant nods. "It's better to be safe, King Alpha. The

forest is a dangerous place. Too many enemies lurk in the darkness. We need to stay vigilant."

"We must remain vigilant here too, protecting those who can't protect themselves." My anger threatens to boil over, and I wait for Rip to say something. Anything. But he's still not fucking looking at me.

"Twenty men and twenty men only?" Rip asks, and the hands on my heart grow tighter.

"Yes, sir. Not a wolf more," Maximus assures.

"So be it. Pick your men, report to me in the morning, and plan to leave in two days' time," Rip says.

All the air from my lungs leaves my body as if he sucker-punched me.

"Of course, King Alpha. Thank you." Grant bows his head in respect. None of them are even looking at me. So why the hell am I here?

Wordlessly, I push off Rip. He reaches for my wrist, but I dodge his hand. "Dove—"

"Don't fucking *Dove* me," I growl, finally giving in to my anger. The other alphas in the room tense, but I ignore them.

"Why did you even want me here if you weren't going to listen to a damn thing I said?" I feel like a fool in front of these men. Two I don't know and Thorne, whom I consider a friend. Thorne has wisely stayed quiet, but I have a feeling he agrees with the majority. I hate this feeling. I've been here before. Asked by boyfriends to attend a meeting— usually of an illegal nature—and paraded around like a fucking object.

Rip's eyes narrow. Anger blooms in our bond, but I push mine back just as hard. "Next time, don't bother asking me to come." I spin on my heels and head straight to the door.

"Hettie, wait." If I were any other member of his pack,

his alpha command would make me obey. But I'm not just any member; I'm his mate. His command does little but piss me off more.

If Rip wants to run the pack and make decisions by himself, so be it. But I won't be the pretty plaything he keeps on his lap while he does it.

Rip calls my name again, but I'm already out the door, heading to the staircase. I don't turn back once, even though I feel his heated stare on my back the entire way. When I'm away from him, away from the other alphas in the room, I allow the first tear to drop.

I thought he'd be different.

CHAPTER 26

RIP

"We should go. We'll see you in the morning, King Alpha," Maximus says, but I barely hear him, far too focused on Hettie's abrupt departure. Maximus and Grant bow their heads in respect and file out the door, leaving Thorne and me alone.

I don't dare look over at my second, knowing I will only see disappointment written across his face. It will mirror my own. I truly believed inviting Hettie to the meeting would be in good faith. This should have showcased our unity and leadership, but I fear we only succeeded in showing a divided front.

"That could have gone better," Thorne says unhelpfully.

I perch on the edge of my desk, crossing my arms over my chest and scowl. "You don't say?" My voice drips with sarcasm. "You saw how it went. Now two commanders of our guard think we are an incompetent team."

Thorne rolls his eyes. "Hardly. What they saw was two passionate people disagreeing over the safety of our pack. These are unprecedented times, Rip. Tensions run high, even between our King Alpha and his Luna. It's normal."

"You call that normal?" I'm convinced Thorne wasn't in the same room as us. That or he's simply trying to be obtuse just to piss me off.

"Yeah, I do. There are learning curves in all new relationships. I imagine especially between a human woman and the King Alpha. You both are still learning how the other operates. May I offer advice?" He folds his hands into his lap.

"Yeah."

"Stop seeing Hettie as a meek omega. You didn't marry a submissive omega who will go along with your every wish. You married an opinionated human who has adapted shockingly well to pack life. Give her some credit."

"I take it back. I don't give a shit about your advice," I growl, not liking the implication that I treat my mate with less respect than what she deserves.

But, maybe...

Thorne laughs softly. "My apologies then. What do I, a happily mated wolf, know about relationships anyway?"

"Giving you my blessing to mate my cousin was the worst decision I've made thus far," I say with no real ire behind my words. Because as much as I don't want to hear what Thorne is saying, I can't deny that he is making me second-guess every interaction I've had with Hettie.

Not the physical moments. Those I'll never second-guess. Our bodies fit perfectly together, and there's no thinking about what the other one wants. We just know. And we are damn good at it.

But this? Making decisions for the pack? I have been operating as a single unit for so long, I've never learned how to answer and discuss with another person who holds the same amount of weight as me in the pack.

"I'm not saying your idea is wrong, and hers is right,"

Thorne says. "I'm saying it would be best for the pack and your relationship to find a middle ground."

This feels like a test in my relationship, and I've failed. Thorne gets up and affectionately claps me on the shoulder. "You're doing good, Alpha. You just don't have to carry the weight of the pack alone. Let Hettie help. She clearly wants to."

Thorne drops his hand and walks to the door. "Off to find my mate. Maybe you should do the same." He then leaves, and I'm alone once again.

Thorne has given me a lot to think about. I'm not too proud to admit to my stubbornness and take advice from those I respect. I can't change overnight though. It will take time for me to lean completely on another person, but I can try.

For Hettie.

Hell, for *me*. There's only so much I can take on without succumbing to the darkness that lingers just out of reach.

Fatigue sets in, and I know it's time to quit stalling. I push myself off the desk and leave my office. Hettie's scent still lingers in the air, the faint smell of lavender and honey. Just the smell of her has my body hard, eager to get my mate back in my arms. I'll apologize if that's what she wants. Or maybe I'll fuck my apology into her.

I taste her anger like vinegar on my tongue. I try to push my need for her and remorse for what I did through the bond, but she closes her mind to me. I didn't even know she knew how to do that.

I growl low in my chest as my cock strains painfully against my pants. I take the staircase two at a time and all but jog down the hallway to our bedroom door.

I hear sloshing water. Is she in the tub? Without me?

Of course she is. She's pissed at me.

I grab the doorknob and try to turn it, but it doesn't budge. She locked me out. Anger and desire battle within me. How dare she lock me out of my room. I could kick the door in and spank her ass red for locking me out...but that isn't what Hettie needs right now.

She needs...not me.

And that fucking hurts.

It's my fault, though.

Water sloshes again, and an image of Hettie naked in the tub plays through my mind. Her big tits with pointed nipples. The sweet cunt I want to bury my face in each time I see her. And that ass...so fucking perfect. I haven't taken her there yet, but I will.

I don't know why I'm punishing myself. I'm so damn hard, all my rational thinking leaves me as I unzip my jeans, pulling out my aching cock. I'm very aware I'm in a hallway where anyone could walk by and see me jacking off by my bedroom door, but I'm too gone to care.

What is she doing in there? Touching herself? Playing with that little clit I love to tease? I grip my cock harder around the base and drag my hand up with a groan. It's not the same, not nearly enough, but this is my penance.

My balls are heavy, desperate for release. I jerk my cock again and stroke it just how I like it. A little pain. A lot of pleasure. I picture Hettie on her knees in front of me, mouth open, her tits heaving as she comes down from her orgasm.

I imagine coming all over her sexy face, marking every inch of her body. The way we would moan together, sated in our release.

My breath hitches, and soon I'm coming. But instead of painting my mate, I paint the door. Despite the circumstances, I can't hide my smirk. I couldn't physically mark her like I wanted to, but I still claimed her in a different way. This room and all who occupy it are mine.

For now and until my last breath.

I tuck myself back into my pants, doing my best to slow my rapidly beating heart. It takes all my strength to turn away from the door and walk back down the dimly lit hallway.

She wants to be left alone. So I leave her alone.

But only for tonight.

Tomorrow, Hettie is mine.

CHAPTER 27

HETTIE

I wake up alone the following morning. Rip's side of the bed is cold and empty. Not even Grass is here, since he spent his night with Tallie. I feel so small and insignificant in this large bed.

A bed my alpha should be in.

I glance at the door. It's still closed because of course it is. I locked it last night out of anger. I was—and still am—angry with Rip. I hate how easily he disregarded my concern. He didn't even consider a different option. He went with his plan, and I was left looking like a fool.

A locked door wouldn't have stopped an alpha, let alone *my* alpha. I locked it just to annoy Rip, because a part of me expected him to knock down the door to get to me. I would have still been pissed, but I might have softened a little knowing he wanted me that badly.

And now I'm mad all over again.

I groan and roll out of bed. The cold air assaults me instantly, and I shiver. "Fucking cold. Fucking wolves," I mutter, glancing over at the fireplace. No one came in to start the fire this morning.

Because the door is locked.

I already hate today.

My mood doesn't get better as I get ready for the day, putting on several layers of clothing to keep out the bone-deep chill. I'm not exactly sure what I plan on doing when I unlock and open the door, but it's not going to find Rip. I can ignore him just as easily as he can ignore me.

I'm about to walk down the hall when I see an odd stain on the door. It's like someone took icing and sprayed it across the middle of the door and—

That's *not* icing.

"Is that...?" I trail off, and upon closer inspection, it only confirms it.

It's sperm.

Fucking gross.

Is it Rip's? Of course it is. I felt him approach last night. Felt his desire but tried to cut off my mind and emotions from his. I just don't understand his angle? What message was he trying to send me by coming on the fucking door?

And why do I feel jealous of an inanimate object?

Pushing the cum-stained door aside—I *will* be addressing this later—I continue down the hallway and stairs until I reach the front doors of the packhouse. Not wanting to be alone right now, and not particularly wanting to face my mate yet, I walk the short distance to Tallie's house.

Although Tallie told me once that I didn't need to knock, I could simply walk in, I feel too awkward barging in and knock anyway. There's a scrape of chairs and—was that a sniffle?—before the doors open, exposing a red-eyed Tallie.

"Hettie," she sobs and flings herself into my arms.

I stumble back, catching myself just in time, and slowly

wrap my arms around her. "Uhm, are you okay?" Dumb question. If she were okay, she wouldn't be crying in my arms right now. I'm not good with this whole friend thing, but I'm trying because I love Tallie.

"Let's walk." She wipes her eyes and loops her arm through mine. I've no choice but to follow.

"Sorry, I just needed some air." She sighs. "You probably think I'm an emotional mess."

"Of course I don't, but do you want to tell me what's going on?" I ask.

"Thorne told me about the meeting yesterday. I heard it didn't go well."

I try to hide my scoff but fail.

Tallie gives me a sympathetic look. "Well, Thorne is leading the group of wolves leaving tomorrow night, and we haven't been apart from each other since we mated. Knowing he's leaving the safety of our borders and traveling into rogue and Nephilim territory is terrifying. I know he's capable of taking care of himself, but we are up against an unknown enemy. Anything could happen."

My heart hurts for Tallie. I can't even fathom the emotional roller coaster she's on. Even though Rip and I are fighting, if he were to leave for an undetermined amount of time, facing who knows what dangers, I don't think I would be as composed as Tallie. The terror of losing him would be too consuming.

"You should be with him right now," I urge.

Tallie shakes her head. "He's going over logistics with Rip and the others joining him. I'll see him tonight."

"Well, is there any way I can help you keep your mind off it?" The distraction would be for me just as much as it would be for her.

We pass the residential houses, moving closer to the

town's center. The wind has picked up, blowing my hair out of my face. Soft chattering from shopping residents rings in my ear, louder than I would think possible this far away.

"It's frightening to see our town so empty," Tallie interrupts my thoughts. "I guess people are choosing to remain in their houses today, knowing a change is coming."

I frown. "Empty? It doesn't sound empty. I hear—" I break off, looking at the shops. There isn't the usual crowd moving around. In fact, I barely see any movement at all, save for a few people shuffling down the road.

"You hear what?" Tallie stops walking, pulling me to a stop as well.

"I hear..." I pause, waiting for the sound to come back. Nothing...nothing...

There!

The noise gets louder, but now it's impossible to mistake it as chatter. It's a call, just like before. Back when I found wolfsbane for the first time. Now that I know what it is, the same almost painful feeling of last time resurfaces, demanding I follow.

"It's calling you, isn't it? Wolfsbane?" Tallie bounces from foot to foot, hiding her excitement as well as a black panther in snow, which is to say, not at all.

"It is. It's more intense this time. Tallie, we need to follow it." I am already following the sound, pulling me toward it. I don't get far though when a hand grips my arm, yanking me to a stop.

"We can't. Rip doesn't want anyone going out in the forest alone, especially not his mate."

"He doesn't seem to care what I think, only that I obey him like the perfect little wife he wants me to be." Even as I say it, I regret the words immediately. I'm bitter. Hurt. And, frankly, a little embarrassed.

"I'm sorry," I murmur. "He's your cousin, and I shouldn't—"

"Let's make one thing perfectly clear. Yes, he's my cousin, but I know he's not perfect. You are allowed to vent to me. What he did was shitty. I will not make any excuses for him. He needs to apologize. I don't think he expects you to be an obedient little wife, though. He just needs to be put in his place." She smirks.

I try to nod, but the sound is getting incessant. My head thrums, and the start of the headache creeps in. "Trust me, I'll give him an earful."

"And you can tell him about the wolfsbane. Make a plan to track it down together."

I don't like waiting. Not when the urge to find the only known cure is literally calling me. I think about the sick souls lying in bed. How many of those wolves can I help? How long do they have?

We can't gamble our time when lives are at stake.

But I don't think Tallie would let me go. She'd drag my ass back to Rip and I don't need to give him more reasons not to trust my judgment.

So I relent. For now.

The call is still there, still ringing in my mind. But it's a little easier to ignore.

"Fine," I sigh. "Let's go back to your house. I need to drag Grass back home, and then I suppose I'll face my mate."

And make sure he knows just how pissed I am.

CHAPTER 28

HETTIE

I don't go straight home after wrestling Grass from Tallie's house. The big grump is pissed at me for taking him away from his new best friend, and I don't have the heart to keep him against his will for long. I take a walk with him, hoping it will help me clear my head. The faint call of the wolfsbane is getting easier to ignore, but I'm not sure for how long.

Part of me wants to say fuck it and follow the call. After all, that's what I'm here for. To help save the pack by counteracting their curse. If I went alone, though, I'm risking my safety and the wrath of my husband. I want to do this the right way, and I just have to trust I'm doing the right thing.

I trudge ahead through the thick snow and chilling winds. Besides that, it's beautiful. Our town looks picturesque, like one of those paintings by Thomas Kincade my mother loves so much. Smoke burns from chimneys, and snow covers the roofs of houses.

After making my lap around town, I let Grass run back to Tallie. Better he's there while I talk to Rip. I make it back to the packhouse and up to our room in record time, only to find the room empty.

Disappointment sinks in.

I tell myself I don't care. I tell myself it's better that he's not here, so I can spend a few hours by myself, relaxing. I tell myself it's better this way.

It's all a lie, of course.

With a sigh, I strip, taking off the layers of clothes I put on this morning until I'm down to my bra and panties. To kill some time, I decide a good soak in the tub will do me some good. Taking a walk with Grass hadn't helped clear my mind, but maybe this will.

I head into the bathroom, turning the water on and waiting for it to get hot. My preferred temperature is molten-lava hot and not a degree below. Once the water is to my liking, I take off my panties and bra and ease myself in.

The hot water hits my skin, a shocking contrast to the coldness of my body. I moan, sinking into the tub until I'm submerged from the neck down. My eyes flutter closed, and I lean my head back, trying to turn off my overactive brain.

It works for approximately ten seconds, until I hear the door creak. My eyes pop open. Movement from the other side of the wall keeps me still. Footsteps grow louder but finally stop just right outside the door.

I know it's Rip. I can feel him. Sense him.

I'm not sure if I want him to come in or walk away.

The handle turns, and I suck in a breath as Rip pushes it open, strolling in.

"The door is shut for a reason, asshole!" I glare, trying to hide how much his presence is really affecting me.

Rip only smirks, looking far too smug. Bastard.

He's shirtless, because of course he is, with his pants

hanging low on his waist. I can see the patch of dark hair on his lower abdomen, leading down and disappearing inside of his pants. My eyes roam down, stopping at his crotch. Images of his rut flood my mind. Him fucking my mouth like I was little more than a whore. It had been fucking hot as hell.

Rip's smirk only grows, reading my wayward thoughts as I quickly look anywhere but *there*.

"What do you want?"

"Tallie told me you heard the call today." He crosses his arms over his chest. It wasn't what I expected him to say, and I'm a little peeved Tallie would disclose that to him, but I know she did it out of care for me.

"I did. And, unlike you, I didn't run into the woods because I actually listen to what you say." Not completely the truth, but Rip doesn't need to know it took Tallie to talk me out of doing just that.

"You were a dick, Rip," I continue. I've never been one to beat around the bush. He needs to see he's upset me, but more importantly, he needs to know I deserve better. "You embarrassed me in front of your commanders. I felt like a pretty object you wanted to show off but not hear. Do you understand how awful that feels?"

His cocky smirk finally vanishes. His shoulders sag as he crosses his arms over his chest again. He almost looks... embarrassed? Remorseful?

Good.

"I never meant to make you feel that way, Hettie."

"Well, your intentions mean shit. That's how I felt. I'm not sure what you expect from me, but if it's to keep my mouth shut and go along with everything you say, you are in for a rude awakening."

"No, no, that's not what I want." Rip runs a hand

through his disheveled hair. He has dark circles under his eyes, making me wonder if he got any sleep last night.

"Then you need to figure that out, because I need us to be on the same page." I grab the soap. If he's going to stay here, then he's going to watch me clean myself.

I rub the bar of soap on my arms, up to my shoulders. I feel Rip's eyes on me, and it sends a thrilling tingle down my spine. Although I'm mad at him, I also can't help but tease him. Just a little.

I bring the bar of soap to my chest, rubbing it across my breasts. I pay extra attention to my nipples, rubbing and pinching the sensitive nubs between my fingers. An involuntary moan leaves my lips.

"Are you punishing me, Dove?" Rip's voice is low, almost a growl. I wasn't planning on punishing him, but I think I'm rather enjoying it now.

I ignore his question. "What do you want, Alpha? A meek wife who will blindly follow your rule? Or one who will challenge you without fear?"

When he doesn't answer, I move the bar of soap down between my breasts. I draw a slow, tantalizing line down my stomach, inching closer to my pussy.

But my hand never makes it there. Faster than I thought him capable, Rip is on me, hauling me out of the tub.

I scream, "Rip! What the fuck?"

The bastard doesn't listen. *Again.* And carries me, dripping wet, to the counter. When my ass hits the dark granite countertop, Rip pushes his way between my legs, forcing me to open for him. I'm stuck between the hard wall and my large alpha.

"What I want is you. Your sass, attitude, and opinions. I want to make decisions *with* you, and I want you to put me in my place when I fuck up. I want everything you are willing to give me, Dove.

"I shouldn't have dismissed your concerns like I did," he continues.

"No, you shouldn't have." My voice goes breathy because Rip cups my pussy, his thumb rubbing against my seam. It makes being mad at him incredibly difficult.

"I'm sorry, Dove. Will you accept my apology and end this torture?"

I scoff. "I hardly tortured you. I just didn't let you into the room last night."

"I beg to differ," he growls. "Knowing you were in here, naked and bathing alone, doing goddess only knows what to yourself drove me positively feral. I was so hard thinking about you, Hettie. So fucking hard."

Moisture pools between my legs, and I bite my lip. "That wasn't my fault."

"But it was. It was very much your fault." He moves his thumb to my clit, and I suck in a breath as he moves in slow circles. "Like an untrained dog, I had to relieve myself outside the door."

I take a moment for his words to register, and when they do, my eyes widen. "I knew that was fucking cum on the door! You're so damn gross."

Though, thinking of Rip outside the door, working himself up to an orgasm for me is so fucking hot. I shouldn't be into it, but I am.

He applies more pressure to my clit, and I moan, wiggling against him. "Say you forgive me."

"I forgive you," I say in one breath, arching into his touch.

"Good girl." He hums like he won. Honestly, he probably did, but a girl can only think so hard when a sexy man is playing with her clit.

"I will do better. Make sure I listen to you and your reasonings. And you will continue to stay out of the woods. We will find wolfsbane together once our men come back from their journey to Dragon's Keep." He marks his words by pushing two fingers inside of me, curling them.

I gasp, reaching out to steady myself on his shoulders. He's got me so needy; I'm going to agree to anything he says just so he can fuck me.

"I'll stay out of the woods. We'll search for wolfsbane together. Only if you give me your cock, Alpha."

A cocky grin spreads across his features. "If that's what my mate wants."

It's agony watching him reach for his pants, slowly pulling them down. He's teasing me, seeing just how far he can push me, but two can play this game.

I knock his hand away, pulling down his pants until his big cock springs free. There's already a small bead of cum on his mushroom tip. I use my thumb, spreading the moisture around.

He eyes me curiously. Despite him letting me take the lead, I can see how badly he wants to lose control. The tension he's holding in his shoulders, waiting to be inside of me.

For the first time, I feel like a damn queen.

I run his tip through my fold, teasing us both. My neediness is evident in my glistening pussy and my juices on his cock. I can't keep either of us waiting any longer as I line him up and guide his cock inside of me.

We moan together, and the little control Rip has shatters. His hand comes to my neck, pinning me in place and adding the faintest bit of pressure. I gasp, trusting him completely.

"Accept my apology, mate." He punctuates each word with a thrust, my whole body moving on impact.

I already accepted his apology once, but I will again and again if that's what he wants. Anything to make him keep going. "Yes, Rip. Yes."

"Alpha," he growls. "I'm your fucking Alpha right now."

"Yes, Alpha, fuck. I forgive you."

I barely get the words out before his lips are on mine, burning me from the inside out. He doesn't just kiss me. No, this man claims me. My mouth. My pussy. My body. Everything. It all calls to him.

But it's so much more than that. So much more than a simple claiming. I feel safe around him. Like my existence matters to him. He's branded himself on my heart, making himself a part of me.

It's scary. It's thrilling. It's...everything.

Of their own accord, my legs wrap around his torso, heels digging into the top of Rip's sculpted ass. Seriously, it's unfair how perfect it is.

I'm close. I just need... "There!" I gasp when Rip moves deep inside me, speeding up his thumb on my clit. It's too much. The pleasure builds inside of me, my whole body trembling with unleashed passion.

"Come with me, Dove." The need and desire in Rip's voice is the final straw that pushes me over the edge. I'm coming hard all over his cock. He explodes inside me, making me a complete and utter mess.

Rip pants, leaning forward to rest his forehead against mine. It's a small act, but one that fills me with warmth.

"I've been leading the pack myself for so long, I don't know what it means to have a partner to share it with. But I can't think of a better person to share this pack with than you. I never want you to feel like that again, Hettie. I'll work on it." Rip's voice is soft and so sincere. I think this is the first time I've ever heard a genuine apology.

"Thank you," I whisper. Emotions I can't quite describe fill my chest. My words aren't enough, but they're going to have to be. It's all I'm capable of right now.

Rip pulls out of me and goes to grab a towel to clean me off. I happily let him, suddenly feeling extremely fatigued.

"Rest," Rip says, picking me up from the counter and carrying me back into our room. He places me down on my side of the bed and then climbs over to his side. His arms wrap around me, pulling me to his chest.

My eyelids droop, seconds away from giving in to sleep. "Goodnight," I murmur, hardly aware of what I'm saying. "Love you."

The last thing I remember is Rip tensing behind me, and then everything goes dark.

CHAPTER 29

HETTIE

The team of alphas hand-selected by Maximus and Grant gather by the packhouse, saying their final goodbyes to their families. This should be a simple trip, one many people wouldn't think twice about, but the dangers lurking in the woods have everyone on edge.

Rip is consoling an omega by the name of Zora. Her mate will accompany Thorne to Dragon's Keep, and she's not taking it well. I've heard how attached omegas can get to their alphas, but I have yet to see it in person.

I try to put myself in her shoes. How I would feel if Rip was the one leaving today. Images of last night flood my brain. How he made me come undone on the counter and carried me to bed after. I remember being slightly delirious from lack of good sleep and amazing fucking, and I may or may not have said the "L" word to him. I hope it was a dream. He's said nothing about it, and neither have I.

But if he were leaving today like Zora's mate, would I say it again? I don't know. But I don't think I'd be handling myself any better than her.

I search through the group of wolves saying goodbye, but I don't see the one person I'm looking for. "Excuse me —sorry—" I push my way through people to get to Thorne.

Thorne is rarely without a smile or a teasing gleam in his eyes. The man I see before me is one of military caliber, dishing out orders and providing comforting words to family members. His face brightens marginally when he finally notices I'm here and excuses himself from his conversation.

"Luna, it's good to see you here," he greets formally. I know it's for the benefit of others, but I still don't like it.

"Where's Tallie?"

Thorne sighs. "Back at home. We said our goodbyes already. We didn't want to prolong it anymore."

I nod, feeling partially responsible for this, even though that's not the truth. I just think if I did more to find wolfsbane, or could magically defeat the rogues and Nephilim, no one would be teary-eyed right now.

It's irrational, but guilt usually is.

"I have no right to ask you this, but while I'm gone, could you look after—"

"Of course," I say before he can finish asking. "I'll watch over Tallie and keep her company. She has Grass too, and he is the best cuddle bug."

That earns me a smile, and I reach out to squeeze his arm. "Bring back help. Let's end these bastards."

Finally, the silly, wolfish grin I've come to associate with Thorne makes its appearance. "I like your spirit, Luna. It's going to take our pack far."

I only hope he's right.

I hang around a little while longer, waiting until Rip needs to go over the final details with Thorne before I leave.

It takes me only five minutes to get to Tallie's, and I let myself in for once.

"Tallie?" I call but get no response, so I push my way inside.

As always, the house is immaculate and cozy. A roaring fire burns in the fireplace, and a woolen blanket is draped over the blue couch. Breakfast still lingers in the air. The doors leading to the backyard from the main room are open, and I see a flash of golden fur.

"Tallie?" I call again, and this time Grass picks his head up. When he notices me, his tail wags in excitement. "Hey, boy," I smile. "Where's Tallie, sweet boy?"

"I'm right here," she calls from the porch. I don't see her until I exit the cabin. Tallie is curled up on the wooden rocking chair, a blanket wrapped around her shoulders. She smiles at me, and I'm relieved to see it's genuine. "Hey."

"Just came by to check on you." I take a seat next to her. Grass, who thinks he's a lap dog, crawls up to situate himself on me.

"Honestly, I just want this all to end. I'm so tired of living in fear. So tired of not knowing if I'll get the sickness or if someone I love will. I would rather have Thorne with me, but if this means ending this cursed war, then it's a small sacrifice." She takes a sip from her mug.

Tallie and the rest of the pack have dealt with the rogues, Nephilim, and sickness longer than I've been here. I can only sympathize with a fraction of their pain.

"It needs to end." Tallie puts her mug down on the table before turning to me. "If we had more able-bodied wolves to fight, we could defend our kingdom better. But the cursed sickness is wiping us out rapidly."

"I know, we need to help the sick wolves—"

"We should find the wolfsbane calling for you."

I blink, uncertain I hear her correctly. When she doesn't laugh or say she's kidding, I snort. "Weren't you the one who told me to wait yesterday?"

"Yeah, well—"

"And that it would be dangerous for us to go?" I add.

"Yeah, but—"

"Tallie, if Rip knew I left, especially now, and with you... I think he might actually kill me." We had somewhat of a breakthrough last night, building trust. Not only within each other, but also as a couple. I don't want to jeopardize that.

"I know what I said yesterday, but seeing Thorne leave and feeling completely helpless...it's a horrible feeling, Hettie. I don't want to feel useless. I want to help in any way I can," Tallie explains.

I understand her need to help and feeling useless. Rip is shouldering too much and not being able to act on my ability hurts. It feels like he still doesn't completely trust me. Rationally, I know it's because he just wants to make sure it's safe to go exploring. But even now I hear the call. Ever since yesterday. Calling me toward a cure that could help so many of my people. Doing nothing feels wrong, but so does betraying Rip's trust.

Either choice I make will hurt someone. Rip or the sick people on their deathbed. I didn't have the chance to save my father while he was dying in the hospital, but maybe now I'll have the chance to save someone else's parents.

Maybe Rip would understand. He'd have to.

"I think I should go tonight," I say at last.

Tallie beams, punching the air in triumph. "Great, I'll—"

"Me, Tallie. Not you. I'm not pulling you into this shit."

"Well, consider me pulled in, because I'm going. You

think I would let our pack Luna do this by herself? Absolutely not."

"Rip is going to be so pissed," I groan. I should ask him to come, but he's stretched thin with so many alphas gone. He said we would look for wolfsbane when the alphas returned. But can we realistically wait that long? I know I can do this, and I don't want to add another thing on his plate, especially when it's something I could do alone. If we're lucky, he won't even notice I'm gone.

I sigh, hoping I don't come to regret this later. "Fine. Tonight. I need to go home and get a few things, but I'll meet you back here at nightfall."

Tallie looks far too excited, seeing as we are about to directly defy her cousin. Still, Rip can't be mad once he sees the risk is worth the reward at the end.

I just hope he sees it that way when he finds out.

CHAPTER 30

HETTIE

The crisp air carries the faint smell of pine and needles. Darkness covers the forest, making visibility difficult but not impossible. It's quiet, save for Grass's soft footfalls and woodland creatures scurrying about, trying to find safety for the night.

I pull my red coat tighter around me, reaching down to double-check the ax at my hip is secure and clamp down on the guilt that threatens to take hold of me. Guilt about dragging Tallie into this, even though she was the one to suggest we go, and guilt over going behind Rip's back.

Getting away from Rip proved to be surprisingly easy. He was summoned to a meeting with members of his patrol, needing to discuss logistics now that a good chunk of their patrol is away.

I had smiled, telling him I just wanted to get some sleep. The worst thing is that Rip believed me. I prayed he didn't poke around in our bond because then my plan would come undone.

But he didn't. He trusted me. Gave me a kiss and left.

Now here I am, outside, waiting for Tallie. As guilty as I

feel, it's not enough to make me tuck tail and head back home. I need to do this, even if I can't quite put into words the reasons why. It simply feels like an inevitability.

The soft crunch of snow has me turning my head to see Tallie approaching. She wears a determined expression as she closes the gap between us. "You ready?" No prelude, just straight to the point.

"As ready as I can be," I murmur, wanting to get this over with. The faster I get the wolfsbane in my hands, the quicker I can get home and hand off the cure.

"I'm going to travel as a wolf. I'll be able to hear and see better. I'll follow your lead, but warn you if something is amiss." Tallie strips, and I turn my head to give her privacy. The wolves aren't fazed by nudity, but it's going to take me more time to warm up to the idea. The sound of broken bones and ripping flesh makes me cringe.

When I turn back around, a large gray wolf stands where Tallie was only moments ago. She's just as beautiful in this form as she is in her human one. Grass rubs against her flank, wagging his tail excitedly.

At least one of us is excited.

Before I begin our journey, I take a moment to listen to the sounds of the forest. The call for wolfsbane starts again, almost as if it knows I'm ready to find it. It's a low, gradual sound and pulls me forward. "Let's go."

Grass and Tallie fall in line behind me. I'm led by an invisible string, just like the last time. My body is a vessel, and I allow myself to be pulled. The uneven terrain of the forest floor causes me to stumble, and I have to catch myself before I fall on my face. I swear I hear Tallie's wolf laugh at me.

Unlike the first time, we are pulled deeper into the forest. My hand hovers just above my ax handle. I hope I don't need it, but I'm not willing to take the chance. It helps me to not feel completely defenseless.

About fifteen minutes into our journey, we come to a drop-off point. I hear running water and make my way to the edge. A steady river flows about six feet below us. Large rocks and fallen tree trunks wedge themselves between the water and the bank. Few things grow on the rocky floor, and I nearly dismiss it.

Except when I try to turn away, the sound grows louder, and I clamp my hands over my ears to drown out the noise. Tallie whimpers, coming to my side and rubbing against me. Except the noise doesn't stop. It pounds in my head until my vision becomes blurry.

I want it to stop.

My body shakes as I turn back to the river. Finally, mercifully, the noise lowers to a low thrum. "It's here," I croak, waiting for my ears to stop ringing and for my eyes to focus. "I'm certain of it. You and Grass stay up, watch our surroundings. I'm going to climb down—"

Tallie growls. I can't communicate with her like this, but I know it's her way of showing her dissatisfaction with my plan.

"I'll be careful," I assure. "I'm not completely uncoordinated." Besides, the pull is too strong to ignore. I'm not sure I could ignore it, even if I tried.

Tallie grunts, and I take it as acquiescence. "I'll work fast," I promise and slowly start my descent. It's not a long climb down, but I'm still careful. Falling six feet wouldn't cause much pain, but it would hurt my pride.

I let out a triumphant whoop when my feet hit the ground, which is answered by a howl from Grass. The journey back up won't be much better, but I concentrate my efforts on my task at hand. Finding wolfsbane.

It's darker here, and I desperately wish I thought to bring something to light my way. If I hadn't been so worried Rip would find out what I'm doing, I would have thought this plan out better.

I'm careful to keep some distance between myself and the water. Half of the river is frozen, but it's a light layer. Not enough to hold my weight. I crouch low, trying to get a better view of the floor. Debris and the occasional weed are the only things I see.

"Where is it?" I growl to no one in particular, growing frustrated with my lack of progress. Tallie howls, and it feels a lot like she's telling me to hurry.

Growing desperate, I move faster, hands out in front of me, searching for the plant. I feel like Velma from one of the old Scooby Doo shows, looking for her glasses.

Focusing on what is directly in front of me, I miss the log peeking out of the water. My right foot snags on the wood, and I go down hard with an *oof*. Small rocks get stuck in my hands and knees.

"Fuck," I growl, picking myself up. In a moment of anger, I kick the log, only to have my entire boot go through the wood.

This is karma. Fucking karma for lying to my damn mate and going on this fruitless quest.

Disappointment settles in, knowing I will go home empty-handed. Knowing the wolves I could have saved will grow sicker. Angry tears blur my vision as I turn to climb back up.

In the midst of turning around, something catches my attention. A flash of purple and green stands out in an otherwise colorless area. I take a tentative step forward, noticing that, when I kicked the log, I moved it back a few inches, uncovering something growing underneath.

Wolfsbane.

Not as much as last time, but still enough. "Tallie, it's here!"

She doesn't respond, but I hear Grass. He's barking, but it takes me a moment to realize his barks aren't playful or happy. "Grass?" I call, but his barking only grows more incessant.

And then I hear it. Growls. And not from Grass.

Heart racing, I grab up the wolfsbane, shoving everything I can into my pocket. "Tallie!" I scream for her again, but she doesn't make herself known. What the fuck is going on?

I climb back up the steep hill on all fours, moving as fast as I can. Growls and what sounds like bodies colliding filter down to me, and my stomach drops. When I finally reach the top, my body freezes at the scene before me.

A gray wolf is locked in combat with an unfamiliar brown wolf. A rogue—it has to be. Grass bites at the heel of the brown wolf, trying his best to keep him away from Tallie. One rough push from the brown wolf's hind legs sends Grass flying back. He lands in a heap on the ground, whimpering.

Someone screams. It might be me.

But it's the wrong thing to do. Tallie loses her focus, snapping her attention in my direction. The brief distraction is all the brown wolf needs to make his next move. He lunges, his canines sinking deep into Tallie's neck.

Tallie growls, tries to break free, but the brown wolf's hold is too strong. I watch, almost as if I'm watching the scene play out in slow motion. He clamps down hard on Tallie and then tosses her to the side as if she weighs nothing at all. The sickening sound of her body hitting the tree sends me into a full-blown panic.

"Tallie!" I scream again, this time getting the attention of the brown wolf.

He stares at me, tilting his head to the side, studying me. I fumble to get the ax at my side, trying to remember the training Rip made me do. I charge at him. Desperation, fear, and anger mix like a deadly cocktail.

The brown wolf narrowly dodges my ax as it sticks in the ground where he was only moments ago. I struggle to free it, and that's when I hear the mocking male laughter.

"You must be Red," the strange voice says.

I dislodge my ax and stare down a massive man. Not Michael, but not any less frightening.

This man stands at least six feet tall. His mop of brown hair is buzzed short. He has a large hook nose and soulless eyes. He's naked, of course, exposing every tight muscle of his body.

I raise my ax again, but the man tsks. "You really don't want to do that, Red. Michael won't be happy."

"Fuck Michael," I spit. I charge at him again, putting all of my strength behind it.

Once again, he dodges it, but not before I nick his arm. A steady stream of blood flows freely.

"You little bitch!" he snarls and comes after me.

I hold the ax tighter, just as he gets his hand on it. "It's only going to get worse the longer you stay away from Michael," he hisses, finally grabbing my wrist and twisting to get me to loosen my hold.

"No!" I scream, but the man pries the ax from my hands and throws it to the side. I move to run after it, but his hold on me tightens.

"Let me go!" I kick out, trying to hit any part of his body I can reach. I'm no fighter, but it doesn't mean I'm going to simply lie down and take it.

The strange man wrestles me to the ground. I thrash, screaming. My leg finally connects with the sensitive part of him because he grunts in pain but doesn't let me go. Bastard.

"I don't know why the fuck Michael wants you alive. Killing you would be so much easier," he says just as my elbow connects with his jaw. His head snaps back, and he curses.

My victory is short-lived, however, because he yanks my arms above my head, pinning me in place. I try not to think about his naked body straddling me or the fact that Tallie and Grass haven't gotten up.

They are okay. They have to be okay.

"Things are about to get a whole lot worse, Red, if you keep Michael waiting. Want your little pack to suffer? Because they will. The attacks will only grow more frequent, and it's only a matter of time before the Nephilim become impatient enough to intervene."

My mind spins with the details he's freely divulging. "If Michael wants me, then why did he send a dumbass in his place?"

I shouldn't be antagonizing the man on top of me, but I'm trying to buy time. Time for...I don't know exactly. For Tallie to get better? For someone—anyone—to find us?

The man growls, narrowing his eyes. He is hatred personified, clearly not used to being spoken to this way.

"I gave you Michael's warning. Come to him or let your pack suffer. My agreement with him is finished." He licks his lips, looking down at my body. A predator playing with his prey. "I'm certain he'll forgive me if you come to him with a few marks and bruises."

The evil gleam in his eyes shoots cold fear through my

body. I have no time to move. No time to call for help or fight him off.

The man on top of me shifts, and the brown wolf from before stands in his place.

His snarl shows off a row of sharp teeth. Before I even have a chance to scream, the brown wolf lunges for my throat.

I'm going to die here, and Rip will never know.

CHAPTER 31
RIP

I don't know where Hettie is.

I've spent my day seeing my men off, making sure their departure went according to plan. It feels like the first act of war, probably because it is. We need the dragons' numbers and strength. I need King Malix's knowledge of defeating Nephilim. All of these things I stressed to Thorne repeatedly until he grabbed my shoulders and told me he understood.

Then I watched the group of alphas leave, praying to the Goddess each one of them will return home safely. The beds in the infirmary are already full of sick wolves. I have no space for injured ones.

After consoling a few omegas and setting them up in the packhouse together and then checking in with patrol, I go in search of my mate. I search in her usual spots—the dining room, the bathroom, and our bedroom. I search our bond, but it's fuzzy at best. A faint light flickers, catching glimpses of her emotions, but I'm not truly able to feel her.

I wonder if she remembers what she said to me the other night. *Love you.* Two simple words that hit hard. Is that the reason she's ignoring me? Because she's embarrassed? My wolf growls, letting me know he wants us to tell Hettie our feelings for her.

I check Tallie and Thorne's house, but it's empty. So I go to the last place I can think of: Aunt Imelda's house. I barge through the door, keeping down my rising panic. My aunt jumps off her couch in alarm at my abrupt entrance.

"Rip, goodness, child. You scared me," Imelda gasps, holding a worn book in her hand. When she reads, Imelda completely immerses herself in her books, forgetting the world around her.

"Sorry. Have you seen Tallie and Hettie?" My tone is far too brisk, worry slipping through.

Imelda tilts her head to the side. My stomach drops when she shakes her head. "No, I'm sorry, Rip. I haven't seen them. Have you—"

I'm not one to turn my back on my aunt. She's the closest thing I have to a mother, and I show her nothing but the respect she deserves, but my mate and cousin are missing. I'm out the door before she can stop me.

My mind fills with the worst possible scenarios. Did someone come for them? Steal them under our noses? That seems unlikely, even with our smaller patrol units—which means they probably left of their own accord to follow the call. Without me.

Even after she promised me she wouldn't.

The moment I'm outside, I shift. My clothes rip, falling to the ground in shreds. My wolf is angry and scared. A deadly combination for an alpha. I can smell and see better in this form. Hints of my cousin and Hettie linger in the air. I also smell Grass. Should have known the dog would follow those two anywhere.

I don't think. I run. Push my legs as hard as they can go.

A new layer of snow covers any tracks the three of them may have left, but their scent hasn't completely gone away. It's muted, but the farther into the woods I go, the clearer my bond comes with Hettie.

And she's fucking terrified.

I push myself harder. Branches and twigs scrape at my fur, but I ignore it. Hettie is close. I feel her. Can taste her fear like poison on my tongue. I hear the sounds of a struggle and a scream, and it's the last push I need to get to Hettie.

"Hettie, I'm coming," I roar into our bond.

"Rip!"

I break through another thicket of trees, and the scene before me sends me into a murderous rage. Tallie's crumpled body lies next to a tree. Grass crawls over to her, whimpering and nuzzling her flank.

Then I see Hettie. A brown wolf, twice her size, pins her to the snowy ground. He exposes his teeth and lunges for her, and that's when I attack.

My body crashes against the brown wolf, claws and teeth sinking into his flank and neck. The wolf howls in equal parts surprise and pain. Hettie whimpers. I'm not sure what the brown wolf did to her, but I don't need to know.

I've seen enough.

My cousin is down.

Grass is hiding.

Hettie's hurt and scared.

The wolf deserves no mercy from me. The brown wolf wrestles his way out from under me, limping slightly. He lunges for me, but he's sloppy and untrained. I swipe my paw out, claws scratching down his chest. The air blooms with a coppery smell. Red wells up, dampening his fur.

It only proves to piss him off. He throws himself at me, attempting to bite down on my leg. His fangs don't get me, but his claws do. It hurts like hell but gives me perfect access to his neck.

The easiest way to kill a wolf.

With him distracted, I growl and clamp my jaw around his neck. Instantly, the wolf stills.

Normally, this would be the part where I would give him the chance to submit to me. Allow him a choice on whether he will follow me or die. But I don't feel particularly merciful tonight. Not when he's hurt my family.

I bite down harder on his neck, feeling his body tense. He tries to pull away from me, but my grip on his neck is too hard. Blood fills my mouth, and I jerk my head to the side roughly.

He howls, body spasming.

Then everything goes quiet, and he goes limp.

Dead. With his throat ripped out.

Red stains the snowy white ground. His life bleeds into the earth. But I feel no remorse.

I shift. Blood still coats my mouth down to my chest. My calf has claw marks on it and hurts like hell. It's the only place I'm bleeding, though. My first instinct is to look over Hettie. Her hair is a mess, and she hugs her arms around her chest. Her lithe body looks even smaller now.

But physically she's fine.

I tear my eyes away from her and go to my cousin. Tallie doesn't stir. Her body is far too still.

I lean down, reaching out my hand to rest on her back. For a moment, I feel nothing. No intake of breath. No beating of her heart.

For a moment, I think Tallie is dead.

For a moment, I'm broken.

Then I feel the slightest rise of her chest, and the tension in my body leaves immediately. "Tallie." My voice cracks, seeing my strong, capable cousin reduced to this. Blood coats her fur, and I brush my hand through it.

That's when I feel the bite. Not something I would normally be too concerned about, but the last time rogues attacked and bit my pack, they instantly fell ill with the cursed sickness.

No. Not Tallie. Never Tallie. I'm supposed to protect my family, but I've never felt so helpless.

"Is she okay?" I hear a small voice behind me.

I spare Hettie a glance. She's picked herself up off the ground. She's holding her bloody ax at her side and looking at me with a mixture of concern and dread.

"No," I snap. "She's not, thanks to your actions."

Hettie flinches, and I almost feel bad. Almost feel the need to apologize, but I can't find it in me. I'm too mad. My cousin is hurt because of Hettie. She promised me just the other night that she would not go into the woods without me. If she would have just fucking listened, none of this would have happened.

I'm gentle as I pick Tallie up. She hasn't shifted back, but I know it's only a matter of time before she loses the connection with her wolf.

"Grab Grass and follow me. Don't fucking wander."

Again, she flinches, and again I feel like an asshole, just not enough of one to change my tone or apologize. From the corner of my eye, I see Hettie nudge Grass. The dog is a little shaky on his feet, but otherwise looks unharmed. He stays by Hettie's side, whimpering.

I carry Tallie close to my chest, listening to the soft footfalls of Hettie and Grass behind me. I'm on full alert, making sure no one else will appear from the darkness.

"Rip, I'm..." Hettie starts, but I glare. Her words die on her tongue.

I'm not ready to talk to her. I'm not ready to hear her excuses.

"I need you quiet unless you want to get attacked again," I say, not kindly.

She sniffles but nods.

So we walk in silence all the way back to the infirmary as the future I once saw with Hettie starts to crumble.

CHAPTER 32

RIP

Aunt Imelda brings Tallie's hand up to her lips, pressing a soft kiss to it. Somewhere between the woods and the infirmary, my cousin lost her hold on her wolf and shifted back to her human body. It happened so quickly.

As soon as I placed her in the last available bed in the infirmary, I went to find my aunt. Her face of abject horror when I told her about Tallie will stay with me for the rest of my life.

She places another thick blanket on top of Tallie, the color stark against Tallie's too pale skin, before scooting her chair closer to her bedside. It's late, and my aunt should sleep, but I don't dare suggest she leave her daughter. Even if I insist, Imelda won't leave. I know my stubborn aunt too well.

"Can I get you anything?" I feel so fucking helpless, watching my cousin just lie there unconscious. I need to do something, not just sit around here while Tallie gets progressively worse.

Imelda shakes her head, like I suspected she would.

"I'm fine. Let the healers know to check in on her when they are able."

It's a kind dismissal, but a dismissal nonetheless. I lean down and kiss her temple before showing myself out. I pass rooms of families all gathered around their loved ones. Their attention is on me as I pass. I see nothing but pain and sadness in their expressions, and it only serves to drive the knife deeper into my chest.

The cursed sickness. The rogues. Michael. The Nephilim are all tests of my ability as King Alpha. So far, I have failed my pack around every corner.

I round the hallway that opens to a waiting room. Grass and Hettie are curled up on a small couch, huddled close together. Hettie's red-rimmed eyes stare off at nothing. Grass lifts his head when he notices me.

It takes Hettie longer to notice I'm here, but when it finally registers, she jumps off the couch and hurries over to me. At first, it looks like she's going to hug me, and my body stiffens. She notices, and her face falls, stopping a few feet in front of me.

"How is she?" she asks softly.

A part of me wants to scream and tell her she has no right to ask such questions. To yell and demand what would even possess her to bring Tallie into her plan. We're walking a fine line right now because I can't control my anger. I don't want to say something I might regret later.

So I keep my answers brief. "Sick. She won't wake up."

The worry on her face only amplifies. "Not at all? Have you tried—?

"Why were you out tonight?" The harshness in my voice silences Hettie. She retreats into herself, and our bond feels empty. Desolate.

"I thought I could help," she whispers.

"Help? You thought you could help?" I bark out a bitter laugh. "No, Hettie, this wasn't help. Not only did you put yourself in danger, but you involved my cousin and Grass too. All of you could be dead right now. Do you understand how idiotic your actions were?"

"I didn't mean for it to go this way."

"But it did!" I don't realize I've raised my voice until a healer peeks around the corner to see what the commotion is. "Your actions and choices have consequences."

"I didn't know. I really—I'm so sorry." Hettie chokes back a sob, tears welling in her eyes. She searches my face for understanding, something I just can't give her right now.

"You're our pack Luna. You came here to help us, not to put the pack in more danger."

"I know. I know that. Rip, I'm so sorry."

"Sorry isn't going to fix this, Hettie!" I don't mean to blow up. It pains me to see her retreat into herself and cry harder. I want to console her, but I also want my space. She lied to me. Broke her promise. And now people are hurt because of it.

I sigh, doing my best to calm down and lower my voice. It's late, and I don't want to disturb the patients. "Just...go. Go back to the packhouse. I'm staying here for the night." I need the space. Time to think properly. "I'll send guards to escort you back." I turn to leave, but Hettie reaches out for my hand.

"Wait," she pleads.

I don't speak, but I stop walking, allowing her a moment. She rummages through her coat pockets before producing a handful of weeds. I don't see the purple flowers at first until Hettie hands them over. "Wolfsbane. We found some. It's not enough to cure everyone, but it's something."

No, it's hardly enough to cure a handful of people. Anger flares to life again inside me. She risked her life and that of my cousin for this?

I snatch the wolfsbane from her hands. "I'll give it to Lucielle." And hope she can make the cure before Tallie gets any worse. I try not to dwell on the fact that she's taking the cure from someone who has been in this condition longer, and, because of that, we may have more deaths on our hands.

I leave Hettie crying behind me. I've said enough for the night. I motion for the guard standing watch in the hallway to escort her home.

Hettie doesn't argue. She accepts her fate, giving me one last longing look. It breaks my heart. Breaks my fucking spirit, but I do and say nothing. Betrayal cuts too deep.

"I'm sorry," she mouths one last time before following her escort back to the packhouse, leaving me alone to clean up the mess she's created.

CHAPTER 33
HETTIE

The door shuts behind me with a resounding thud, leaving me and Grass alone in a dark room. Rip's hurt and disapproval stays with me, long after I leave him. The hurt and pain I caused not only Tallie, but everyone who loves her.

I fucked up.

I fucked up bad.

And the worst part? Thorne has no clue his mate lies cursed in the infirmary bed. He left thinking she would be safe, and in a few short hours, I completely ruined that. He asked me to watch over her, and I ended up being the reason she's cursed.

He's never going to forgive me. Rip is never going to forgive me. I don't think I have any more tears inside me, but they fall freely down my face again.

My body gives out, sinking down the wall and onto the floor. I pull my legs to my chest, hugging my arms tightly around them. Shuddering sobs rack my body, and I can't stop. Grass whimpers and nudges my arm as if saying, *I'm here, and I'm not leaving.*

Coming to Mescos was supposed to be my new start. For years, I dragged my family through the pits of hell. It only got worse when my father died because, instead of processing the guilt and grief that comes with losing a loved one, I acted out even more than I did while he was alive. I partied, drank, fucked around to outrun the grief.

It destroyed my family. My beautiful mother turned into a mere ghost of her former self. She did her best to keep me in line, but I've always been impulsive. I don't mean to hurt people, but no matter how good my intentions are, someone always seems to get burned because of me.

I saw this time and time again with my sweet sister. She's just a kid but had to grow up before her time and be the big sister I wasn't capable of being.

Leaving is the best thing I have ever done for my family. I gave them the ability to start over. To not have to worry constantly about money, where our next meal would come from, or if I'd make it home that night without winding up in a jail cell.

Basically, I'm used to being the fuck-up.

But I thought things would be different here. I thought *I* would be different.

Except I hurt people I love once again. And I do love Rip. I'm not sure when that happened, but I have fallen for him completely. He makes me feel safe. Like I can bring some good to the pack.

I guess we were both wrong.

I'm not sure how long I sit on the floor crying. I cry until I finally run out of tears and Grass has fallen asleep at my side. I feel numb, which is a small reprieve from the anxiety and loathing that came in waves before.

I weigh my options on what to do next. I could simply waste away in our bedroom, hoping Rip can fix my mistakes and our enemies won't attack. Or I can think of someone else other than myself. Fix the mistakes and make sure no more harm comes to my pack.

The answer is easy, and yet there's nothing easy about what I'm going to do.

I do my best not to wake Grass as I get up and search the room for something to write with. I find a pad of paper and a pencil hidden away in a drawer. For the longest time, I stare down at the blank canvas, willing the words to come. I have so much to say, but I don't have the words.

Each time I put pen to paper and start writing, I rip it up and try again. My words are that of a desperate woman, sometimes legible and sometimes nothing more than harsh lines of aggression.

After another ten minutes of arguing with myself, I finally settle on my message. It's short and sweet. Conveys what needs to be conveyed with no excuses. Carefully, I fold it up and scroll Rip's name on the front of the note. I tuck it away for now before climbing into my empty bed.

It smells like Rip. His piney scent reminds me of home. I steal his pillow and cradle it to my chest. I try not to think that this might be the last time I'm ever this close to him again. I want to imprint his smell on my memory. The way he smiles and his deep laugh.

My heart breaks into a thousand tiny pieces, but my mind is made up. I will atone for my mistakes. I will prove to Rip that Ender was right when he chose me as Rip's mate. Even if it hurts so damn much.

But right now, I allow myself a couple more hours in my home, pretending Tallie isn't cursed. Pretending my mate isn't mad at me. That I don't have to leave.

And then I fall asleep, dreaming of the life I could have had with Rip.

CHAPTER 34

RIP

Two healers and Lucielle come in throughout the night. None of them can wake Tallie up. There's also no wolfsbane ready to cure her yet. The bite she received from the rogue expedited the cursed sickness, meaning Michael and his people are getting stronger.

Neither Imelda nor I leave the infirmary that night. I left the room twice. Once to speak with Hettie and another time to bring my aunt tea and buttered bread. The buttered bread is left untouched on the nightstand, but Imelda clasps the tea in her hands, absentmindedly sipping from it every so often.

My mind isn't my own. I'm plagued with images of my cousin lying lifeless in bed. What hurts the most is Hettie's face when I sent her away. Out of everything she admitted to me tonight, the one thing I truly believe is that she's sorry. That was evident in the pain on her face and the plea in her voice.

I'm a mate torn. I'm so fucking mad at her. Mad that she took this risk and lied to me. Mad that Tallie got hurt. Despite all of that, though, I want to take Hettie into my arms and console her. I was rough on her—for good reason —but it didn't make looking at her broken and sad any easier.

I grapple with my decision to send her away for hours, crammed in a small, uncomfortable chair. Darkness soon gives way to daylight as the sun peeks in through the curtain. It illuminates Imelda's face. She stares at Tallie, unmoving. Since we've been here, Imelda took her daughter's hand in hers and hasn't let go since. Not even when the healers came to check on Tallie.

I don't think we could pry her away from her daughter even if we tried.

I feel so fucking useless right now, and my body hums with pent-up energy. I need to move. Need to run. Need to do something other than sit here and feel bad for myself.

I push out of the chair with more force than necessary. Imelda jumps at my abrupt movement, giving me a strange look. "We should eat. Do you need food?"

I don't wait for her response or give her time to refuse as I leave the room. My body works on autopilot, walking down the hall. I pass a few familiar faces but don't have the energy to attempt conversation. When I pass the waiting room where Hettie and Grass were last night, my stride slows.

I don't know why I'm disappointed to see no one there. I made Hettie go home, sending guards to take her directly to our room like a damn criminal. Of course she won't be waiting out here for me.

I don't know if that makes me relieved or angry.

Pushing all thoughts of Hettie aside for the time being, I head to the infirmary's cafeteria. There are only a few people manning the back, and they all greet me when I walk in. I manage a simple smile I hope doesn't look more like a grimace as I go through the food. I settle on apple cinnamon oatmeal and milk for Imelda. Nothing here looks appetizing for me, but I can hardly demand Imelda eat if I don't plan on doing the same.

After a moment of thought, I grab another oatmeal and pay for our meals. My walk back to Tallie's room is slower; fatigue is finally catching up with me. I enter the room, half hoping Tallie would be up and smiling.

She's not, of course.

But Imelda has moved. She sits at the small round table by the window, letting the sunlight warm her skin. She barely glances my way when I walk in and place our food down on the table. "I hope oatmeal is okay." I slide over her breakfast.

"Thank you." It's the first thing she has said to me in hours. Imelda reaches for the milk, ignoring the oatmeal, and takes a sip.

That's how we sit for some time. Not saying anything, but finding comfort in each other's presence. Imelda manages a few bites of her oatmeal. I would have liked to see her eating more, but it's better than nothing.

"We'll get her better. I promise," I reassure her just as much as I hope to reassure myself. I can't think any other way. Can't believe in a future without Tallie.

"I know you'll do all you can." Her words do little to absolve my guilt. In fact, they only make me feel worse because it's almost as if she believes Tallie won't make it.

"I'm sorry, Imelda. What Hettie did is unforgivable—"

"No, my boy, I do not blame your mate," Imelda stops me cold. "Tallie is a grown woman who can make her own choices. She made the choice to go and suffered the consequences. I do not blame Hettie. I don't blame anyone but the rogue responsible."

Imelda reaches across the table and grabs my hand. Her touch is warm, filling me in a way only a mother could. "I know you're angry," she starts.

"She lied to me, Imelda. She promised me she wouldn't venture into the woods."

"I know, and I'm not excusing any of that. But I also don't believe she defied you out of malice. I believe she wanted to help you so badly that she was willing to risk her own safety for this pack. And do you know why I think she did it?"

I shake my head, afraid of what she'll say. Afraid because, deep down, I think I already know the answer, and I yelled at her for it.

"I think she did it because she loves you and this pack. She's working as a Luna and, sometimes, no matter how good the intentions are, people get hurt. The jobs of a Luna and her Pack Alpha will never be easy. But it seems to me that Hettie will fight for her pack. Are you willing to fight for her?"

My aunt's words replay in my head throughout the rest of my day. Am I willing to fight for her? This is the question I think about the rest of the day, long since leaving my aunt and cousin.

Still needing time to clear my mind, I head to the lab, checking in on Lucielle. She's in the middle of crushing up the wolfsbane Hettie found when I walk in.

"King Alpha! So glad you're here." There's a slightly frenzied look in her expression, but I imagine that has to do with not sleeping much these days. Lucielle is a dedicated healer and often forgets to take care of herself.

Seems to be a theme of my pack.

"Do you have news for me?" I walk over to her station, careful not to mess anything up.

A mortar and pestle sit atop the table with various vials, all filled with different substances. Papers are strewn about, and a pile of books is stacked precariously close to the edge. It's chaos, but I've learned over the years that Lucielle works best in chaos.

"Yes, that last batch of wolfsbane you supplied me is our most potent to date. I've already made twice the number of cures, and I've only used about half the supply," she says excitedly, a wide grin on her face. It's contagious, and I can't help but return it.

"My team can administer cures as early as tomorrow evening, as soon as the solution settles." She goes into the science of the resting period, but it makes little sense to me. What I hear instead is that Hettie, once again, saved our pack.

And I treated her like a traitor.

I feel like the world's biggest asshole. She deserved so much more from me, and I chose anger. Much like the rest of the men in her life did.

Lucielle rattles on about her cure, and I nod, interrupting her, "You have my full support. Do what needs to be done."

I can't stay here anymore. I need to find Hettie. Lucielle looks taken aback but nods. "Of course, King Alpha. We will inform you if we have any updates."

I nod before heading out. The distance between the lab and the packhouse isn't long, but it feels like an eternity before I reach home. Two guards are stationed at the door. I turn to the one on the left and ask, "Where's my mate?"

The guards share a look before the one I spoke to finally answers, "We haven't seen her, King Alpha. Perhaps the dining room?"

I thank him before heading to the dining room. Even before I enter, I know she's not there. I can't feel her. It's possible she's shut down the bond between us, but I don't think that's it. It's more likely that my mate isn't here at all. Hoping I'm wrong, I search the rest of the packhouse.

I check my study, the library, and the courtyard. Hettie is in none of those places. Worry and doubt creep in. This is an all-too-familiar feeling, but there's still one place I haven't checked yet.

Taking the stairs two at a time, I reach the second floor of the house in seconds. I dig deep into our bond, but don't feel Hettie. I tell myself it's because she's upset and has blocked me from feeling her. But I know the truth.

When I reach our bedroom, I test the knob. Not locked, so I open it. I prepare myself for Grass's excited greeting, but the golden-haired dog never comes. It's dark in our bedroom. The curtains are closed, and the fire has long ago died out in the fireplace. It's cold here, and though the temperature rarely affects me, I can't help but shudder. Hettie doesn't like it this cold.

The door to the bathroom is slightly ajar. I check in here, but it's empty. There's no condensation on the mirror or water droplets leftover in the tub. I check the closet next, but Hettie isn't in there either. Panic threatens to overtake me, and I have no one to blame but myself.

I try one last effort to reach her through our bond, spreading it as far as it can go. I don't sense her anywhere on this estate. Her scent, which usually overtakes the room, is faint. Almost as if she hasn't been here in a while.

She's not fucking here. Out of anger, I grab the blanket atop my hastily made bed and rip it off. It's irrational, but part of me hoped Hettie was hiding under the blanket, ready to pop out. It's empty, though.

In my fit of anger, a piece of folded paper floats off the bed and falls to the floor. I almost ignore it until I see my name written across the front. I snatch it up, body shaking as I open it. It's from Hettie, and her words make me feel true, tangible fear. The words are few, but they have me running through the house like I'm chasing her ghost.

Might as well be.

I'll fix this. I'm sorry, and I love you.

Hettie

CHAPTER 35
HETTIE

I've never considered myself brave. Reckless and impulsive, sure, but brave? Brave are the heroes like Hercules and Achilles. Brave are the fictional characters like Rapunzel and Merida. Brave is something we strive for, but very few of us are placed in situations where bravery means lives are on the line.

I can't fuck up another family. The Guardian brought me here to make a difference, and I think I finally know what he means. It's not magic that's going to save the pack. It's me. My choice to leave and give Rip and the others a fighting chance. I'll walk into this knowing I made a difference, to hell with what happens to me.

I just wish Grass hadn't come along.

He doesn't need to die because of my choices. I tried to make him stay. Tried locking him in the bedroom, but he kept escaping before I could. Leaving the packhouse undetected was easy, considering so few guards were left. Leaving during shift change also helped us escape without anyone noticing.

So now Grass and I navigate a forest that is still very much a stranger to me.

I've always considered myself good with direction and getting around, but it's different when everything looks the same. I'm not a damn Girl Scout. I don't know how to read fucking moss on trees to tell me if I'm going in the right direction.

I'm not sure where I'm going, if I'm being honest. I'm going off the assumption that Michael wants me. I'm moving farther away from safety, alone and defenseless, an easy target for the rogue alpha. Eventually, he's going to notice, and I'm banking on the fact that he wants me alive to keep me safe.

Safe-ish.

I pull my red coat tighter around me. In a field of white, I stand out harshly. There's no disguising the blood-red color. It's a deliberate choice to make spotting me that much easier.

I didn't leave the pack totally defenseless, though. Strapped to my hip is my ax. It's heavy and makes me lean to the right, but I feel more secure with it on me. It's like a weird comfort blanket for me. You know, if axes could be that.

After a few strenuous hours of walking, my feet cramp, making each step painful. "We need to rest, Grass. Just for a moment," I pant, leaning against a tree.

Grass looks around our surroundings. He has made little noise since we started, and I take that as a good thing.

I sink to the ground, ignoring the cold sting on my ass. My head drops into my hands, and I try to even out my breathing. Thinking of what I left behind makes me want to crawl back like a coward. But I can't. I need to save Tallie and my pack. I need to show Rip that I'm not a total screw-up.

I lift my head when Grass growls beside me. He's crouched in a defensive position, looking off between trees. I see nothing at first, but Grass doesn't let up. He barks, getting more agitated.

"What is it?" I ask like my dog could answer, but I don't sense the danger he does. I try to strain my ears to pick up on any sound, but nothing stands out. In fact, there's no sound at all. Has it always been that way? Or is this just recent?

I call for Grass. I'm about to tell him to follow when he spins around and barks more loudly and frantically than before. I don't get the chance to turn and see the danger though because, at that moment, something hard strikes the side of my head. Pain blooms in my skull, and the world goes dark.

A CRACKLING fire draws me out of the darkness. I come awake with an ear-splitting headache and sore muscles. I groan, trying to move my body, but I realize something is hindering my movement. When my eyes finally adjust and I'm not seeing a blurry world, I notice the rope tied tightly around my torso. My hands are bound in front of me.

Rough bark digs into my back, and I realize I'm tied to a damn tree. A soft whimper off to my left has me snapping my head so fast, my vision blurs. When it finally rights itself, I see my dog tied up about ten feet away. Judging from the markings in the snow, Grass put up quite a fight until he tired himself out.

He doesn't look hurt otherwise. A small miracle.

"Ah, she's awake," a familiar voice says, and ice-cold fear fills my body.

A man appears from behind the fire as if born from the ash itself. Soulless black eyes stare back at me. The jagged cut across his face is more pronounced today, reminding me of the dangers this man is capable of.

Michael's smile is all predator and does little to quell the growing panic inside me. Light catches on something attached to his hip. The unmistakable metal of an ax protrudes from the small gap in his jacket. My eyes dart to my hip, and I curse.

My ax, my only defense against threats, is gone. Now on the hip of my enemy.

"I knew you'd see reason, Red." Michael smiles. "I'll admit, there was some doubt on whether you'd show up for me, but I knew in the end you'd do what was right."

"Fuck you, Michael." My words are slurred. I feel dizzy and disoriented. Clearly, the hit to my head was harder than I realized. It's like I'm stuck in sludge, trying to navigate my way through it.

"Such a way with words, Red," Michael chuckles and crouches down before me. This is the first time I've seen him in clothes. He dresses exactly as I thought he would. Cargo pants and a tight black shirt. His brown duster coat is open, allowing me to see he's weaponless except for my ax. The ax is nothing compared to him, though. His wolf is his weapon.

"So, here's how this is going to work." Michael grabs my chin, forcing me to look up. I try to fight his hold, but it's useless. "The Nephilim think I'm going to hand you over to them like a good wolf. They want you dead. But don't worry, Red. I won't let them kill you."

Michael pauses like he expects me to thank him. I knew I probably wouldn't be getting out of this alive, but it doesn't make the fear any less real. "Why do they want me dead?"

"To take your magic for themselves, of course."

"I have no magic."

"All humans possess magic. Why else do you think you're here? You didn't actually believe Rip loves you, did you?" Michael's smile turns cruel.

My face heats; whether from embarrassment or regret, I'm not sure. Rip did love me...didn't he? He never said it, but it was in the way he acted and the adoration he sent me in our bond. The smiles and touches. I was the one who broke his heart, not the other way around. I lied and went behind his back.

"You did. How pathetic." Michael rolls his eyes. "Unfortunately, Rip is going to have to die."

"No!" I scream, throwing myself against my restraints. They don't budge at all.

Grass picks himself off the ground and starts to bark. He's desperate to get over to me, but Michael stares Grass down. Something in his stare has Grass backing down and whimpering.

Michael's dark eyes find mine again. I see nothing but evil within them. "But, yes, how else will I stake my claim as their new King Alpha? If the pack is lucky, only Rip will need to die. Anyone else who challenges my rule will join him. I don't particularly want to kill any more wolves, but I will."

"Why are you doing this? Why are you working with the Nephilim just so you can take over as king?" It doesn't make sense. Why would he go through all the trouble with the Nephilim only to betray them in the end? According to Rip and Thorne, they aren't an easy enemy.

"The Nephilim were coming whether or not I agreed to work with them. I saw my opportunity to use them to gain access to Lycan Forest. I cut off their access to wolfsbane, knowing it would make them desperate. And it has. Some of Rip's pack have joined mine, and now many of his alphas are in Dragon's Keep, leaving Lycan Forest vulnerable to attack. It's the perfect opportunity to strike.

"You are my ticket to defeating the Nephilim, Red. That's why you are so important." Michael finally lets go of my face, and I jerk away. "You claim you don't have magic, but I can feel it inside of you, just begging to be used. You make wolves stronger, Red. Imagine the power I can have if you agree to be mine."

Michael's delusional, but that much was evident the first time I ran into him. I can't make anyone stronger. I was brought here for Rip and Rip alone, and that's who I make stronger. Or, rather, I did, but I've managed to fuck that up.

True fear takes over as I scream, "You said you would leave the pack alone if I came to you. You lied!"

"Hardly," Michael scoffs. "I'll leave them alone in the sense that I won't attack them or expose them to the curse. I'll cure them all. Those who wish to follow me, that is."

"You can't harm any of them." I have nothing to bargain with, but I will not let him hurt my pack. I will protect them with everything I am. "I won't agree if you kill any of them. You need me, don't you? To defeat the Nephilim?"

"It would be a lot easier, yes." Michael narrows his eyes. "But not entirely impossible to do without you. As long as the Nephilim don't have you. I would hate to kill you, Red. You're growing on me. I think we could become...well, not friends, but partners.

"But let me sweeten the deal, Red." Michael smirks, getting in my face. He's so close, I can see the stubble on his face and the fine lines around his eyes. "I heard a friend of yours got sick. She got bitten by one of my wolves, did she not?"

I don't answer. I don't have to because he clearly knows.

"She will not get better. At least not without a lot of wolfsbane. More than you could find. See, working with the Nephilim comes with many great perks. Like a lethal bite." His lips turn up into a sinister smile.

The rogues' bites expedited the curse. Lucielle had theories, and Michael all but confirmed it. None of us realized just how strong the rogues were getting. And with the Nephilim fighting alongside them...we don't stand a chance.

"Agree to be mine, and I'll make sure your friend lives," Michael continues.

"How can I trust you? All you've done is lie."

"No, all you've done is misunderstand," Michael growls. "So I'm putting it plainly, Red. Agree to be mine, and your friend lives. Don't, and she dies. And so will you and everyone you love."

It's not a choice at all. I'm backed into a corner, and he knows it. But what did I think would happen? At least this way, I can help save my pack. And, eventually, I can bring down Michael—maybe. I won't stop. If he thinks I'll cooperate, he has another thing coming.

"Fine. You keep her and my pack alive, and I will join you."

"That's what I hoped you'd say." Michael picks himself up and disappears behind the tree. My restraints loosen, and finally fall free. I let out a sigh of relief.

That is until he ties the rope to my bound hands and drags me up.

"Let's go, Red. There are people waiting to meet you." I don't have time to respond before Michael pulls on my restraints and tugs me forward. He grabs Grass's makeshift leash and pulls us deeper into the forest.

Farther away from Rip.

I hope he knows just how sorry I am.

CHAPTER 36

HETTIE

I don't know how far we walk. There were several times I swore Michael led us around in circles just to throw me off in case I tried to escape. Admittedly, I thought about it a few times, but there is no way I can navigate my way back. Even if I could somehow magically find my way home, Michael and his rogues would attack.

More blood on my hands.

I'm not willing to risk that.

Eventually, our wandering brings us to a campsite. A few dozen makeshift tents are sporadically placed throughout the area, and a huge bonfire blazes in the middle of the shelters. A few men sit around the fire, laughing and drinking a pale liquid.

A hush falls over the men when they notice Michael. Something akin to fear sparks in their eyes. They might follow Michael, but it's clear they are uneasy in his presence. "Morning, men," Michael all but purrs. He reaches behind himself to grab my arm and pull me forward, placing me on display. "Look who decided to join our cause."

The fear they hold for Michael is replaced with smirks and delighted hollers. "About damn time," a brown-haired wolf says. He is on the smaller side with scars coloring part of his face. It only adds to his rogue persona.

Grass lets out a warning growl, moving to stand in front of me. He stares down the five men, but Grass isn't built to intimidate. He doesn't fill the rogues with fear.

One rogue reaches for Grass, and, on instinct, I kick my leg out, catching him in his knee. "Don't touch him," I sneer.

"Or what, human?" The man's eyes narrow. "You're going to hurt me?"

"Yes."

My response is greeted by laughter. My face flames red because they know I can't stop them from doing anything to Grass if they really wanted to.

"Enough. No one touches Red or her dog," Michael speaks up, catching me off guard. But he ruins it when he adds, "Unless Red acts out. Then we may need to encourage her to do as we ask."

Michael reaches down to scratch Grass behind his ears, but Grass barks at him, snapping at his hand. "Your dog could stand to learn some manners." He frowns.

I don't respond, only move closer to Grass.

Michael quickly loses interest in us and turns back to his men. "Where are they?" he asks no one in particular. I wonder if *they* are the Nephilim.

"Last we heard, they were about two miles from us, heading in our direction," the scar-faced man says. "We got our boys following them."

"Gives us about twenty minutes before they get here, give or take. I assume you are prepared to join them, since you have time to sit and gossip around the fire like old women. How many of them are there?" Michael asks.

My head swims with new information as I desperately try to keep up.

"About ten, I think?"

Michael curses under his breath. "I hoped for less, but we'll work with what we have."

Suddenly, Michael pulls me forward until our chests are touching. His hot breath hits my face. Hygiene is clearly not a main concern out here because his breath is horrific. It takes everything in me not to gag.

"We have visitors coming, Red." His hand tightens around me to the point of pain.

A whimper escapes my throat, and I struggle against him, but Michael is a damn rock and refuses to move. "You're fucking hurting me."

Michael only smirks. His hold doesn't loosen, though. "Don't you want to know who is coming to see us? They are coming for you, after all."

My face pales, and I tense in his grip. Michael just laughs at my discomfort, like it's a joke. Just like every other man in my life has done. All except Rip.

I don't want to know who's coming, but I also don't *don't* want to know. "Who?" I finally ask, voice a mere whisper.

"The Nephilim. They are coming to collect what they think is theirs."

The Nephilim. The creatures of nightmares. Coming for me.

I knew this was a possibility. I knew going into this that I might not make it out alive. Their name alone evokes a fear in me so strong, I don't want to know what it will feel like when I see them in person.

"Don't worry, Red. Remember when I said you're mine, and I'll protect you? I meant it." Michael pushes a stray lock of my hair behind my ears, and I'm too frozen in fear to do anything other than let it happen.

"How will you protect me?" I hold no delusions that Michael will actually protect me if it comes down to it. He says he wants me for the magic I possess, but I also don't see him hesitating to discard me if it means he would live.

Michael's gaze falls to my neck. I take a moment to realize what he's staring at until he brings two rough fingers up to trace along my skin, right where Rip's mark is. My whole body goes cold and rigid in his grip.

"I can't have you wearing another man's bite when you're mine now, Hettie. There's only one way I can truly protect you and gain access to your magic." Michael grips the back of my neck hard, and I cry out in pain.

"Please don't do this. Please..." Tears flood my eyes. The mark is the only thing I have connecting me to Rip. Losing it will be like leaving him all over again. I selfishly want to keep his mark with me so I can carry a small piece of him always.

Now Michael wants to take that away from me.

"Please..." I beg again. I'm once again transported back to the girl on the streets, begging men to not leave her high and dry. I never wanted to be this girl again, but perhaps it's the only life I deserve.

"It won't hurt...much." Michael grins before barking orders to the men behind us. "Grab the damn dog. If she tries to resist, kill him."

"NO!" My scream is lost in the cacophony of sounds.

Two men get up and go grab Grass. Grass barks, trying to fight his way out of their hold. He bites one of them on the hand, and the rogue curses.

"Fucking mutt," he growls, taking him by the neck while the other rogue clamps his hands around Grass's muzzle.

"Please don't hurt him!" I scream, begging for someone to listen.

Michael gently strokes my cheek. It doesn't soothe me like Rip's touch does. It makes me feel dirty. "No one wants to hurt the mutt. Just do as I say, and no one will get hurt. You can do that, can't you?"

What choice do I have? Either let Michael bite me and erase Rip's bond, or refuse and have him hurt Grass and then bite me anyway.

Tears for myself and those I'm hurting and leaving behind fall freely down my cheeks. I don't think I'm capable of speech anymore and just nod to Michael. He notes my acquiescence.

"Pull away and your mutt dies," he threatens one last time.

Then Michael strikes. His fangs dig into my neck, and pain like razor blades carves into my skin.

I scream and pray for it to end.

CHAPTER 37

RIP

The forest is ripe with Hettie's scent. Unfortunately, it is also a labyrinth with no clear path to the finish line. I've been running for hours, trying to use her scent and our bond to bring me to her. Except our bond is foggy at best, growing bleaker with each moment that passes. Which means she's hurt. I can't allow myself to think of the worse alternative.

I'm so fucking angry at myself.

If I would have just calmed down long enough to actually understand why she did it, maybe we wouldn't be in this situation right now. Thinking about all the what-ifs will not help me, though. Hettie needs me, and who knows what Michael is doing to her? I swear I'm going to rip his fucking head off if he touches even a hair on my mate's head.

I've always known the type of wolf Michael is, and yet I still underestimated him. He sank his claws into Hettie, appealing to her bleeding heart. My woman is so self-sacrificing, quick to offer herself up if it saves others. As a Luna, these are the qualities a pack wants. But as a mate? They're fucking infuriating.

Michael's smart. He lives in the woods but never stays in one place for too long. His pack is nomadic, constantly moving to keep my pack in the dark. That's not to say we haven't found them in the past. We've just never initiated an attack unless it was imperative. I don't enjoy killing for the sake of killing.

Hettie is somewhere in these woods, and I'm going to find her.

I continue, following her scent. There are tracks left over in the snow—two sets of feet and four paws. Grass is with her. That does little to quell the nerves inside me, but at least she's not alone.

Seconds turn into minutes; minutes turn into hours. Michael expects me to come looking for her, and he's done a hell of a job making the trail difficult to follow. But the farther I explore, the more her scent blooms around me. *My mate.*

Despite that, I'm getting discouraged. If I haven't found her yet, am I not going to find her?

Just as the thought crosses my mind, a loud, ear-piercing scream rings out. A group of birds squawks before flying away.

It's the sign my body needs to push myself faster, straining all my muscles to get to her. Because that scream came from Hettie. She's hurt or worse. *I'm coming, Dove. Just hold on a little longer,* I send through our bond, hoping she hears it. It's answered with her pain and fear.

Poorly constructed tents come into view. Several tents have large gashes on the side, doing little to protect the occupants from outside weather. A group of men huddles around a roaring bonfire, smirking and laughing at something. A few feet away from them are two more rogues, holding down an animal. I take a moment to realize it's Grass. He's not making their jobs any easier either, by thrashing and attempting to bite them.

The screaming starts up again, and the coppery smell of blood permeates the air. Michael stands with his back to me, head ducked down and arms around a smaller frame. I notice her curves, the way her body tries to fight him off but goes slack in his arms.

He's biting her. Biting over the mark I claimed Hettie with. *Mine.*

I see red.

There's no plan or thought process. My wolf wants blood, and that's exactly what I'm going to give him. I growl before charging full speed at Michael. The man has just enough time to pull back from Hettie. Michael's blood-red lips are slightly parted, and his eyes are blown wide before I crash into him.

Michael and I roll to the ground, and I claw at his chest. Deep red gashes appear in an instant, welling up with blood. My wolf is blood-thirsty. He wants more. Needs more. My canines rip into his shoulder, and my mouth fills with the vile taste of his blood. I don't think; I just rip. Hard.

Michael bellows, screaming curses at me. The next moment, he shifts. His wolf is big, but not nearly as big as my dire wolf. I have strength over him, but Michael has speed. He slips out from under me and snarls before hurling himself forward. His claws catch the side of my face, digging deep. It burns like a bitch.

Someone screams. I think it's Hettie, but checking would be a distraction. Michael growls, wrestling me down. I use my hind legs to kick him off, and he goes flying, landing on the ground a few feet away. He desperately gasps for air.

From the corner of my eye, I see Hettie try to run for me, but the two bastards who held down Grass now have a hold on her arms. She's bleeding badly from the bite on her neck. Her movements are sluggish, but they don't appear to be life-threatening.

Michael is back up, teetering from side to side. Three more wolves flank him. I don't like the odds, but I lunge anyway to make the first attack. I swipe at a black wolf who barely dodges me. Another one leaps out from behind him and jumps on me. I grunt as he collides, but then quickly bite down on the soft part of his underbelly.

The wolf yelps and falls off me. He's down. For now.

But he was just a distraction. I realize that too late as Michael sneaks up from behind and clamps his jaw around my back foot. I howl in pain but kick back hard with my non-injured hind leg. I hear a sickening crunch, and the pressure around my foot lessens. I don't allow myself to dwell on the fact that I've just become infected. Not when Hettie needs me.

Still more come. I didn't assess the area to see how many rogues Michael has. I'm running on pure adrenaline, but fatigue is setting in. Michael snarls. More wolves flank him and, as one, they descend upon me.

I've always considered myself a skilled fighter. As King Alpha, I have to be. Wolves have challenged me for my spot as King Alpha, and many times I've had to defend my pack. However, I'm not invincible. I have limits.

And this is my limit.

Michael and four other wolves ascend upon me. Biting, tearing, scratching at any available service they can reach. I stand my ground, getting in as many bites as I can, but it's not enough. Pain erupts in my side when a black wolf charges me and something snaps inside of me. A bone? My ribs?

It hurts. My movements are jerky and ill-timed. Blackness blurs my vision.

Hettie is going to see me die.

Run, Dove, run.

My death doesn't have to be for nothing. She can escape; she can...

Something hard hits me across the face, and I crumble to the ground. The disease spreads through me, and I'm not able to hold my wolf any longer. I shift back, my body broken. Blood fills my mouth, and it takes me a moment to see clearly. Michael stands above me, no longer a wolf, holding an ax. Hettie's ax.

"Now that I got your fucking attention," Michael growls and slams the end of the wooden handle into my stomach. I groan...maybe scream?

My body feels like it's been dragged behind a horse. My ribs are broken, and I'm sure other parts of my body are too.

I'm losing so much blood. Consciousness is an effort.

"Rip!" Hettie's sobs reach me. I turn my head slightly. What a sight I must be. I can feel my eyes swelling shut. My lip is busted, and blood trickles down my nose. I've been in bad shape before, but none of that compares to the current state of my body.

I smile, but I think it's more of a grimace. "Dove," I whisper, my voice hoarse and rough.

"Do not die on me, Alpha. Don't fucking die. You were supposed to stay with the pack. You were supposed to..." Hettie breaks off in a sob. Grass is with her. He's such a good boy. The perfect pet. Hopefully, he'll be able to see Hettie through this.

"You can run, Dove, but I'll find you. I'll always find you." My words end up in a cough. Blood fills my mouth.

"No..." Hettie sobs.

I'm the one dying, but I want to wrap her in my arms and promise her everything will be okay. It's absurd to feel happy, but right now all I feel is joy. Joy for knowing and loving Hettie. For experiencing love for the first time.

"I love you, Rip. I'm so sorry. This is all my fault. Please don't die. Live. I need you to live," she begs, and I want to tell her nothing hurts. I don't feel anything, but words don't come to me.

"Alpha Michael, they're here," a voice says above me. All their faces mix into one, and I can't decipher who is talking or who they are talking about. "Should we kill him?"

"Don't touch him!" Hettie screams, but her pleas are greeted with cruel laughs.

"Leave him," a voice I recognize as Michael's says. "He'll be dead soon, anyway. We have the Nephilim to deal with. Let the girl say her goodbye. Don't say I never did anything for you, Red."

Nephilim. Seems like they are finally going to show their faces. The group of wolves all grunt and walk over me to join Michael in...whatever he has planned with the Nephilim.

Hettie is by my side the moment the others leave me to die. Apparently, I'm no longer of concern to them. I'm as good as dead.

Soft hands cradle my face gently, so as not to cause me any more harm. "Rip, you silly, foolish man. You were supposed to stay with the pack. They need you. I...need you." Hettie leans down, her forehead pressed against mine.

I think this might be paradise.

"I love you, Hettie." The words don't accurately convey how I feel about her. I just wish I had more time to tell her. She deserves to hear it every day.

"Don't you dare, Alpha," she snarls. "Don't say that because you think you're going to die. If you love me, you're going to live. Do you hear me, Rip? Live."

I smile, though it's painful. I wish she knew how much I wanted to live. How much I wanted to spend every waking second with her. But I don't think that's in the stars for us. At least not anymore.

We would need a miracle. But that's not what we get.

Instead, we get fire that lights up the whole forest.

CHAPTER 38
HETTIE

The world is on fire, and I watch it burn right in front of me. I don't move, resigned to my fate. Maybe this is hell. My mate is dying, and I can't do anything about it. I wanted to make things better, but I'm cursed to only make things worse.

Rip is fighting consciousness. His eyes are swollen shut. His busted lip is still bleeding from the cut, but he wears a smile. Or what I interpret to be a smile, at least.

His face is bad, but it's the rest of his body that scares me. Long, deep gashes cover every inch of him, exposing red tissue. Most are still bleeding profusely. I don't know how he hasn't passed out from loss of blood. The strange hitch to his breathing also tells me his ribs might be broken.

Smoke fills the area, making it harder to breathe. Where is the fire coming from? Did Michael decide to torch the area? My mind desperately tries to come up with a plausible reason when the sky darkens above us.

I lift my head and gasp. I don't know what I'm expecting, but it isn't the black-scaled dragon hovering fifty feet above us. It's massive, probably the size of a commercial airplane. A terrible sound, almost like a growl, emits from the dragon, followed by red flames. Heat from the flames warms my body to an uncomfortable level.

A soft, feminine voice makes me jump. "Luna Hettie?"

I protectively angle myself over Rip's body. A wet nose presses against my forearm, and I sigh in relief that Grass is here.

I take a moment to allow my brain to process the woman standing before me. She's beautiful. Reddish-brown hair with pale skin. Her choice of clothes is interesting. She wears a full black leather dress that looks tailored perfectly to her skin. The sleeves extend to her wrists, where she wears black gloves. Her kind eyes stare at me before dropping to Rip on the forest floor. He's gone unusually still. If it wasn't for the faint rise and fall of his chest, I would think he's dead.

Despite her lovely appearance, she's a stranger, which makes her dangerous. "How do you know my name?"

"A friend sent me." She smiles.

"A friend? Who?"

"Hettie, it's okay," a new voice sounds behind her. I squint to see past the smoke, but soon I catch sight of a familiar face.

"Thorne," I sob, never so thankful to see a friendly face. "How are you here?"

Thorne kneels down next to me, gently taking my hand. I didn't know how much I needed comfort until it's freely given. My relief only lasts a moment until I realize Thorne doesn't know his mate is sick. Cursed because of me.

My smile fades instantly. "Thorne, I need to tell you something."

"Later," he says. I know this isn't the time to bring it up, but it still bothers me that he doesn't know.

"This is Queen Rose," he explains, gesturing to the pretty red-headed woman. "She's married to King Malix, the dragon king."

My lips part in a surprised O. "You're the one from Grym Hollow. You're like me."

The woman—Rose—smiles. "I am, and I sensed you needed me."

"You did?"

"She did," Thorne answers on her behalf. "Rose and Malix were already halfway to Lycan Forest when we found them. Said she knew we needed their help. We've been on our way back since last night when we caught sight of Nephilim movement."

"Nephilim? They're here now?" I expect one to appear in front of me. The smoke and flames make visibility near impossible, so even if one stood near, I probably wouldn't see it until the last possible second.

"They are. Not many, but enough to be a problem. My dragons and your wolves are in battle now," Rose says.

"Then we should help them. We...we should—"

"Hettie, I need you to take a breath for me, okay?" Thorne moves out of the way so Rose can crouch down next to me. It's silly, but I want to tell her not to get her dress dirty on my account.

"Go help your people, Alpha. Hettie and I will be okay," Rose assures Thorne.

The man hesitates, not sure if he should stay or join in the fight happening around us.

"It's okay, Thorne. We'll be fine," I say, though I'm not sure if I'm telling the truth. It seems to calm Thorne, though. He nods once and shifts before running off to join the others, but not before he casts a pained expression to his fallen friend.

"Now, let's heal your mate, shall we?" Rose smiles, reaching for my hands. Under different circumstances, I think Rose could be my friend. I instantly like her. She has a warm, calming presence to her.

"I hear you were able to cure your people. Is that correct?" she asks.

Realization is slow to dawn, but when it does, I shake my head. "Not really. I just found the cure to help them. It wasn't actually me."

"Sounds like it was you. Has Ender talked to you about your magic?"

It was the same thing Michael said. Rose thinks I have magic, when I only have weird little voices in my head telling me where to find wolfsbane.

"No...but I don't have magic," I admit.

Rose purses her lips, and then drags my hands to Rip's chest. "Can we try something? I'll guide you through it, but you'll need to trust me and yourself."

My confusion only deepens, but what other choice do I have? Rip will definitely die if I don't do something. If this is even a chance to save him... "Yeah, okay."

"Close your eyes."

I do and wait for my next instructions.

"I want you to picture Rip and the memories you have of him. Channel the love you have for your mate and the need to make him feel better. Just feel."

I don't know how this is going to help Rip, but I do as she asks. I think back to the first time I saw Rip. How handsome I thought he was. I remember our first kiss at our mating ceremony. I didn't know then that the kiss would change my entire life, but it was the catalyst for love. Every moment after was like trying to feel that way again without giving in to our feelings.

Falling in love had never been so easy or surprising. The comfort I feel with Rip is like nothing I've ever experienced before. I'm not ready to lose that. I don't think I'll ever feel like I've had enough time with him. I want many more days with him. To show him I can be the mate he needs.

I push love into our bond. His connection to me is faint, but he's still there. Michael didn't erase us completely. I fill the bond with warmth and devotion. With strength and healing. But will that be enough to bring him back from the gates of death?

I don't know.

I'm not sure how long my eyes are closed or how long I keep my hands on Rip's chest, but soon I feel a gentle hand on my back. "Open your eyes, Hettie," Rose says. Something in her tone gives me pause.

Did I fail?

Slowly, afraid of what I'll see, I open my eyes. A wishful part of me hopes I'll see Rip without a scratch on his body. But when I stare down at the man I love, nothing has changed. He's still bloody and bruised.

I failed.

"No, you haven't," Rose says, and I don't realize I've said the words out loud. "Look at him, Hettie. *Really* look at him."

And so I do.

Through my helplessness, I didn't see the changes in him right away. I scan his body and stop at his lip. Moments ago, it was busted and bleeding. Although the blood is still there, it no longer is puffy or bruised. His eyes, though still a little swollen, aren't blackened or swollen shut any longer.

His body is still covered in blood, but the deep gashes are now scabbed over. Some are faint pink lines. He's not breathing strangely anymore. His chest rises and falls normally.

I blink once in case I'm imagining what I'm seeing. Rip isn't completely healed, but he *is* healed. His wounds look days, if not weeks, old now.

I'm crying again, but this time for a new reason. "What just happened? How is this possible?" I sob. Rip's eyes flutter, which only makes me sob harder.

"You've healed him. Mostly." She laughs softly. "Ender isn't the most forthcoming with information, so I'm left to figure out why he chose us and discovered our magic. I woke up the cursed dragons in my kingdom. When Thorne told me you led him straight to the cure for your wolves, it made me wonder what else you could do.

"You see, I think our powers are all centered on healing. I didn't know that for certain until I watched you heal your mate," Rose says. "I think if we work on that magic—or whatever you want to call it—we'll get stronger."

Her words are slow to process. Magic. Healing. Mate. Soon I'll be able to wonder if her theory is correct, but right now I'm more concerned with the man moving underneath me.

"Rip?" I move my hands from his chest, only to stare down into two deep brown eyes.

"You healed me, Dove." He grins and goes to move. I don't miss the wince he tries to hide as he sits up. "I'm fine. Just a little sore, but you took away the worst of it."

"Never scare me like that again," I growl, flinging myself into his arms.

Rip lets out a pained gasp, and I curse, trying to pull away. But his hold on me tightens, so I stay firm against his chest.

"Thank you," he says, and I realize he isn't talking to me. He's looking at Rose.

The Dragon Queen smiles. "Told you we could be friends."

A loud howl interrupts our moment. I turn and see a large wolf charge for us. Michael. He's still alive amidst the chaos. He's a wolf who knows he's losing and plans on taking down anyone he can before they take him down.

I go to push Rip out of the way, but he doesn't budge. He pushes me behind him, and I yell in protest. I just healed him; he's nowhere near ready to fight. Michael lunges, and I can do nothing but close my eyes and wait for the pain of his jaws.

Except it never comes. A loud thud followed by a crunching noise makes me blink in surprise. A purple dragon sits in front of Rip with a wolf dangling from their mouth. The wolf howls and desperately tries to claw itself free, but the powerful dragon clamps down.

And then Michaels falls.

In two pieces.

"That was very dramatic, Vivia." Rose rolls her eyes but smiles.

"Friend of yours?" Rip asks, hiding his shock better than me.

"One of my best friends," she says before addressing the dragon. "Can you tell us what is going on?"

The dragon shifts and, in her place, is a petite but muscular woman. Her black hair is cropped short, and blood runs down the sides of her lips. She's not pretty per se, but there is a certain attractiveness about her.

"King Alpha. Queen Luna," she greets with an elaborate bow. For anyone else, it might seem as if she's mocking us. But she's able to make it look sincere.

"Six Nephilim are down. The wolves are taking care of the last few. The rogues," she looks at Michael's dead body in two on the ground, "are now dead. No casualties on our side, but a few injuries. Should we burn the bodies of the Nephilim?"

"Hettie," Rose says gently, "would you like the dragons to dispose of Nephilim bodies?"

The question is so absurd, I choke out a laugh. These are not the questions I would have ever thought I'd be asked.

"Oh, there goes another one," Vivia says, staring at something behind me.

I turn just in time to see a giant creature with shredded wings. I didn't expect the Nephilim to be so tall, and it makes me feel smaller than an ant next to them. Their large, skinny bodies are blackened, almost charred-looking. Where their eyes should be, white orbs stare hauntingly at me.

These horrific creatures were what Michael believed he could take down on his own? I'm almost sad that Michael's dead because I would have loved watching him fight these monsters—and fail.

The Nephilim falls, shaking the ground on impact. Wolves howl as they jump on top of the creature, tearing viciously at its body. I have to turn my head because the sight is too gruesome to watch.

"Yes, burn them," I say, because what else is there to do with creatures of that size? "And the rogues too." I look over at Rip to make sure he's okay with that, and he's smiling at me with pride in his eyes. It feels...good.

Vivia gives a curt nod and shifts back to her dragon form. "She's off to let the others know," Rose explains. "You did amazing, Hettie, but Rip still needs to see a healer. I don't think your alpha will take kindly to riding a dragon?"

The disapproving growl from Rip tells us exactly how he feels about that. "Yeah, I didn't think so. In which case, let's load him up on a horse. Have you ever ridden before?"

I just stare at her before she bursts out in giggles. "Right. Grym Hollow resident. Not exactly the best place to learn how to ride a horse."

"I know how. I'm well enough to navigate us home," Rip says, though he doesn't sound overly pleased with the idea. I'm just glad he's not being difficult about it. "Send your injured my way. Our home is closer, and they'll receive immediate care."

"Thank you. That's very kind of you," she says as a black dragon lands beside her. His dark scales are a stark contrast to the white scenery. Horns protrude from the top of his head, looking just as deadly as his piercing teeth. The dragon huffs and wraps its tail around Rose. "My husband, Malix," she says. "He's ready to get me home."

"Wait." I untangle myself from Rip and stand. "Thank you. Both of you. I don't want to think about what would have happened if you all didn't show up." Rip wouldn't be sitting, talking, and smiling like he is now. That I know for certain.

"Of course. The fight might not have been on our land, but it doesn't make it any less ours. We can't stop until they're no longer a threat," she says.

"So, I'll see you again?" I love the friends I made in my pack, but Rose is from Grym Hollow and knows how it feels to come to a strange new world and marry a man you know nothing about. The thought of not seeing her again makes me feel empty.

Rose smiles with her whole face. It's contagious, and I can't help but return it. "Of course. Our kingdoms are so close, and we can write."

"I would like that. A lot." I close the distance between us and hug her. Rose returns the embrace. We stay like that for a minute. Just two women who came from Grym Hollow and now have kingdoms to run.

When we finally break apart, Rose gives me one last wave before climbing atop her dragon husband. Malix nods once and then pushes off the ground, stretching his powerful wings. And then they are airborne.

"Hettie." Rip's voice pulls my attention away from the ascending dragon. Our eyes meet, and love floods the bond. "Let's find Grass and go home, mate."

Home. Together.

HETTIE

I t takes us nearly three hours to get home. Multiple times throughout the trip, Rip's complexion grew too pale for my liking, and I forced him to take a break. The stubborn man didn't appreciate that, but I didn't appreciate him nearly dying.

When we finally make it back, I usher him straight to the infirmary. The healers are waiting for us. A friendly healer offers to watch over Grass while we get tended to. Half of our group arrived before us, letting them know about the injured. By some miracle, enough beds and supplies are scrounged together.

Rip is given a private room. He all but collapses on the bed, and the healers are on him in an instant. A few bandage my wounds, but I'm quick to shoo them away so they can tend to my husband.

Two hours.

That's how long they spend with Rip. My healing saved Rip from death, and the wolfsbane coursing through his system saved him from the curse, but his body went through a great ordeal. Lucielle sees to him personally, making sure he receives the proper care. I get the feeling I'm not supposed to be in the room while they work on him, but each time I try to leave, Rip growls and pulls me back to him. I give up trying to leave after that.

Soon, the room is blissfully empty, and Rip sleeps peacefully. My brain is still too wired to do more than stare at him and make sure he's not in any pain.

"I know you're watching me," Rip says, causing me to jump. The bastard is supposed to be sleeping.

"Can you blame me?" I try to tease, but my words come out slightly hysterical.

Rip's eyes flutter open, and he reaches for me, but I shake my head. "I shouldn't…"

"Your mate needs you. Get into the damn bed, Dove."

"You're bossy when you're near death," I mumble, but I'm all too happy to climb into bed next to him. Truthfully, not being close or able to touch him is difficult. I fear losing him still and wonder if this feeling will ever go away.

"Hey," he says gently, pulling me against his chest. I should chastise him because he doesn't need my weight on him, but I have a feeling he wouldn't listen.

"I'm okay," he assures. "Because of you."

"Because of Lucielle and the rest of the healers."

"No. Because of you," Rip repeats, voice firm. "You were the one to save me long enough to get me back here."

"I still don't know how I did it. Not really. Rose said to feel, and I did, but…nothing felt different. Shouldn't you feel something when you use magic?"

Rip shrugs. "Not always. Sometimes it's natural, and you won't feel any changes. Everyone is different. We can look into it once I'm healed."

Honestly, I'm not in a rush. There are more pressing issues than studying what magic I may or may not have.

Like making sure we get the wolfsbane for the sick wolves now that we have access to the rogues' stash.

Silence stretches between us. I think Rip has fallen back asleep until his arms tighten around me, and he says, "I'm sorry."

He's...sorry? "I don't understand. Sorry for what?" I raise my head so I can look him in the eyes. He's so damn handsome, even pale and roughed up like he is.

"For not listening to you or letting you explain why you left with Tallie. I was scared for my cousin and for your safety, but I shouldn't have dismissed you like I did. And even after I was such an asshole to you, you still wanted to save this pack. You were willing to sacrifice yourself if that meant our safety."

"You make me sound so brave." Being brave was the last thing on my mind when I left. I just wanted to fix my mistakes. Give the pack a chance to survive.

Rip's hand comes up to rest on my cheek. I lean into his touch. A touch I didn't think I'd ever feel again. "You are brave, Hettie. The bravest woman I know. The pack owes you a life debt."

"No, they don't. We're their leaders, aren't we?" Rip nods slowly. "They trust us with their safety. I would do it again if it meant I could save them and you. I'm sorry too. I didn't mean to break your trust or put Tallie in danger."

"Let's make a deal, Dove. No more running around sacrificing yourself or my cousin, and I'll make sure I never shut you out again. Deal?"

"Deal." I smile, and Rip brings his lips to mine. I sink into him and kiss him back. It only lasts a minute, though, before there's a knock on the door.

"No fucking privacy in this damn infirmary." Rip

frowns. He looks so much like a little kid pouting that I can't help but laugh.

"Come in!" I call, just as Rip says, "Go away."

I playfully smack his chest and quickly regret it when I see him wince. "Sorry," I murmur.

The door opens, and Thorne sticks his head in. He grins when he sees we are awake. "Care for some visitors?"

"No."

"Rip, be nice," I scold before addressing Thorne. "We would love a visitor."

"Two, actually." Thorne disappears behind the door again, and a moment later, it opens wide. Thorne reaches for someone, and then Tallie walks into the room. Well, "walks" is putting it kindly. It's more like a sluggish shuffle. Still, I gasp and roll out of bed.

"Tallie!" I cry happily, stopping a few feet in front of her. I want to wrap my arms around my friend, but she's as pale as her cousin and seems to struggle with standing.

Thorne notices this too and takes her hand. "Sit, my Star." He helps her into a chair.

She squeezes his hand and leans against him. "Thorne told me what happened. I don't know if I want to be mad at you or congratulate you," Tallie finally says.

"Both. Both is the appropriate response," Rip pipes up from behind me.

I ignore him because I'm still stunned Tallie is even awake. "How?" That is the only the word I can say.

Luckily, Tallie understands my question. "Lucielle used the wolfsbane you found to cure me. I needed most of it, but a few others have also received treatment. You did that, Hettie. You saved us, and I'm so honored to call you my Luna and dearest friend."

Tears sting my eyes, and I'm moments away from ugly crying in front of these people I love. Tallie said I'm her best friend. I don't think I've ever been anyone's best friend before.

"And more wolves will in the next few days," Thorne adds. "With the rogues and the Nephilim no longer on our land, we now have access to the wolfsbane growing in the rogue territory. A group of guards, along with two healers, are already en route to gather it. Enough to cure every sick wolf here."

"That is...amazing." This is exactly what I had hoped for when I left to find Michael. I just didn't think I would be here to enjoy the after-effects.

"All thanks to you, Hettie." Tallie smiles.

It wasn't me. At least it wasn't only me. Rip played a part in this. Rose and her dragons played a huge part in helping our wolves take down the rogues and Nephilim. So many people worked and fought for a cure and the safety of our pack.

And we succeeded.

"We won't stay long. Tallie just wanted to see you both," Thorne says. "She shouldn't even be out of bed, but..." He shrugs. Clearly he was coerced into letting her come here.

"I just wanted to make sure my best friend and my cousin are okay. You're okay, aren't you?" Tallie directs her questions to Rip.

"I'm okay, Tallie. You'll need to wish harder for me to disappear next time."

"Oh, hush. You are infuriating, even injured." Tallie rolls her eyes, but there's relief in her features too.

Thorne picks Tallie up, holding her bridal style. "We'll check on you in the morning. Goodnight, Luna." He bows his head and then turns to his best friend. "Glad you're still with us, brother."

"You and me both. Take care of her." He inclines his head toward Tallie, who's fighting sleep in Thorne's arms.

"I will." He carries her out of the room.

I'm grateful for Thorne and relieved that Tallie looks like she's going to be okay. I still feel guilty for being the reason she's in the hospital in the first place though. I don't think that will ever change.

I don't realize I'm swaying on my feet until Rip reaches out to steady me. "Come to bed, Hettie. It's been a long few days."

I don't even remember the last time I slept. The adrenaline that has fueled me during all of this is finally fading, and sleep is calling, which is why I don't protest getting back into the small bed.

Rip pulls the threadbare covers over us. It's a far cry from our bed back home, but it'll do for the night. He wraps me up in his arms, providing all the warmth I need. My eyes grow heavy, knowing I can't fight sleep for much longer.

"Hettie?"

"Hmm?"

Even though I'm moments away from sleep, I hear the words Rip says clearly, "I love you, mate."

He said it once before, but that's when I thought he was dying. It's different this time.

With the last bit of consciousness I possess, I say, "I love you too, Alpha." And then I let sleep overtake me.

CHAPTER 40
RIP

3 Weeks Later

There was once a time I fooled myself into thinking I didn't need love. I didn't need a partner I could wake up and go to sleep next to. If I was desperate enough, I could always take a lover to bed for the night. But that was all it would ever be. Just one night.

Until Hettie.

My mate writhes under my tongue, soft sounds of pleasure leaving those plump lips. The same lips that were around my cock only moments ago. Hettie reaches down, running her hands through my hair. She pulls, and we both groan. I fucking love it when she pulls my hair. It means she's close.

I suck her clit into my mouth, my tongue teasing the sensitive bud. "Rip!" she gasps. Her thighs are shaking for me, even as she tries to close her legs.

"Open," I growl, forcing her legs back apart. This pussy is too good and pretty to be hidden away from me. Her cunt needs to be worshiped.

And it has been. Nearly every day since leaving the infirmary.

I plunge my fingers deeper inside of her. She's so fucking wet, and they slide into her easily. I curl them, and she arches her back off the bed. She's so close. I can feel it.

In no time, she's coming hard for me. I lap at her sweet taste, greedily devouring her. I don't stop until she goes limp and whimpers. Only then do I pull away, wiping my chin. "Fucking delicious."

"You made us late," she pants, head tilted back. It gives me a good view of her claiming mark on her neck, one I have bitten over again to erase any and all signs of Michael, fully restoring our bond.

"Me?" I smirk. "If I recall correctly, I woke up to your lips around my cock."

My mate only smirks. "Didn't mean you had to reciprocate."

I always reciprocate, and she knows it.

Gently, I push myself up, crawling up her body until I can kiss her lips. Our combined pleasure mixes, and she moans into my mouth. I want more. So much more, but it'll have to wait. Hettie's right. We are late.

With great reluctance, I break the kiss. "I suppose we should be in attendance for the pack celebration."

"Well, we do have a lot to celebrate." Hettie smiles, pushing herself off the bed. This gives me the perfect look at her body. That beautiful ass I want to sink my cock deep into.

Later.

Right now, it's time for the celebration.

It's been three weeks since my near death experience and the death of the rogues and Nephilim. Three weeks since we have gathered enough wolfsbane to cure every sick wolf in the infirmary. No new cases have appeared either. As much as I scoffed at the idea before, I truly believe our love for one another is the reason our pack is thriving.

We were told that we got off easy with the few Nephilim roaming our area. According to Malix's intel, they have spread out amongst the other kingdoms, but there's still no sign of Gadreel, the King of the Nephilim.

Although Lycan Forest is safe for now, we are still vigilant. The threat isn't completely gone, just moved on. Our pack will continue to work with King Malix and the other kingdoms until every last Nephilim is eradicated from this earth.

But that can wait a day. Today my mate and I celebrate.

Hettie returns from the bathroom wearing a long-sleeved dress. "You look beautiful," I tell her.

"You would say that if I was wearing a potato sack." She giggles.

"I doubt I'd be able to keep my hands off you in one of those."

"You're so weird." She smiles. "Get dressed! Tallie is going to kill me if I'm late helping her run the games for the pups. We've been planning hard these last few weeks."

I love her dedication to our pack, but more importantly, her love for the pups. I would be lying if I didn't admit it makes me want to start a family with her sooner rather than later.

"You're great with the pups," I try to say casually, reaching for my pants.

"They are so fun. I wish I had half their energy though," she says. "Will our future kids have that much energy?"

And there it is. Proof she wants the same future I do. My chest swells, knowing my mate wants to have pups with me. If I think about her plump with our babies for too long, I will not let her leave this room.

"They'll be the children of a human and an alpha. I'm afraid they will have more energy," I break the news.

"Figures." She finishes up her hair. "Ready to go?"

I pull on my shirt and reach for her hand. "Yeah, Dove. I'm ready. You lead."

A cute smile plays on her lips. "I lead? I like the sound of that." She leans in for a quick kiss. She doesn't know that I will follow her lead to the ends of the earth. Wherever she goes, I won't be far behind.

"I love you, Alpha," she says and pulls away. "Don't say it back. I want you to show me you love me once the celebration is over."

We're celebrating our victory and the end to our curse. It's time my pack experienced joy and laughter once again. For the first time, I feel like I've succeeded as my pack's King Alpha, which I couldn't have done without my queen by my side.

With one last smile, Hettie tugs on my hand, leading us out to join our pack. Our family.

This isn't the life I expected, but maybe it's the one I deserve.

EPILOGUE

The Guardian

The rain is unforgiving. All those with a shred of self-preservation would know to stay in their homes, escaping the worst of the flood coming to Grym Hollow. Flood is perhaps dramatic, but it's more than we've seen in years. Mother Nature is punishing us for our sins.

Or maybe she's just punishing me.

I deserve the ire.

Visions of bloody greed and corrupt power play in my mind like my personal hell. I've built my prison within Grym Hollow, and the humans here are none the wiser. How quickly they allow themselves to trust me is frightening when I don't even trust myself.

My prison grows weaker with each mate I deliver to the Kings of Mescos. Seeing others find their happily ever after is torture, but one I hope will pay off in the end. Besides, I owe Malix, Rip, and the other four kings everything, cleaning up the mess I've made and left behind.

Only once the wrongs have been righted will I be able to find *her* again.

My mate.

My love.

My enemy.

Redemption is why I'm out in the pouring rain, looking at the cozy duplex in front of me. At first glance, it appears like every other duplex on this street. Small porch, with a planter box of coneflowers decorating the concrete slab. The brown door leaves much to be desired, with peeling paint and uneven coats. A single tree grows in the yard.

However, this is where the similarities stop. If one cared to pay attention, they would notice the grass hasn't been mowed in months, and the white mailbox is near bursting with untouched letters. There's also a rather impressive dent in the middle of their garage door. One the size of a fist.

The front door suddenly slams open, revealing a stumbling man dressed in old denim and a faded black shirt. He holds a beer in one hand, bringing it to his lips to sip every last drop. Judging by the way he's stumbling and cursing, this isn't the first beer he's had this evening. Maybe not even the third.

"You fucking bitch!" he screams, though thunder drowns out most of his words. "You'll never find a man that loves you. Fucking slut, sleeping with any man that looks in your direction."

There's no reply, only soft crying coming from inside. If I had a heart, it would break at the helplessness and pain that encompasses this house. It's haunted by the living, though an existence like this one would lead anyone to an early grave.

The man spews more hate and curses, promising the

occupant of the house that she'll never find anyone who will take care of her like he does. He fumbles and kicks at the garage like it insulted him. It's painful to watch him attempt to open it, and when he finally does, he slips and lands on all fours.

Another vile insult, and then he's searching for the keys to his truck. This man is in no condition to drive, and perhaps if there were people on the road, I would stop him. But it's midnight in the middle of a horrendous thunderstorm. The roads in our small town are deserted. The only life this monster is putting in danger in his own.

The world won't mourn the loss of a corrupt soul.

In his desperation to get into his truck, he never notices me standing in his front yard, shrouded in shadows.

The tires squeal as he pulls out of the garage. He turns his truck too soon out of the driveway, narrowly missing their mailbox but hitting the garbage can instead. Trash goes flying, picked up by the wind. The heavy items float down the water pooling on the side streets.

And then he's gone. Almost as if he had never been there. Except, like me, he left despair in his wake.

I was called upon by Erin, the newest woman who approached me for a deal. Many came before her, but only Erin stood out. There is something...special about her. So, I gave her the contract.

That was nearly a week ago, and I haven't heard from her since. Both Rose and Hettie answered me within three days. Her lack of response was unusual and, admittedly, disappointing, but I can't force mates to take their places with their kings. Their consent must be freely given.

However, a feeling so troubling came over me, one I couldn't ignore. I walked through the rain and in the dark, and it led me here.

I cross the lawn, making my way to the porch. The front door is wide open, slamming against the side of the house. I step over the threshold and am instantly hit with the vile scent of cigarettes and the pungent smell of alcohol. The walls are stained with smoke, once white, now a worn, yellow color.

The rest of the house isn't much better. Furniture is overturned. Glass broken. Holes in the walls. The room, which I presume to be the main room, is cluttered with broken picture frames and empty beer cans. The TV plays the news on low in the background, warning citizens of Grym Hollow to stay safe in their homes.

At first I didn't see her tucked behind the overturned couch. Only the silent sobs racking her body catch my attention.

"Erin?" I don't want to startle the poor woman, but my voice has her jerking back anyway. She tries to make herself appear smaller, putting her arms over her head, shielding herself the only way she knows how.

Like a frightened animal, I approach her with caution. I can't change my large, nonhuman appearance, but I can at least show her I'm not a threat. Not to her, anyway.

"Erin," I speak again, only gentler this time. "It's The Guardian." I try not to wince at the title I once held dear but made a mockery of. But it's how people know me, and I'm not keen on changing their perception. Call it cowardly, but I don't want to divulge my story to anyone yet.

Erin lifts her head up cautiously. Her bloodshot eyes take me in. I don't get a good look at her until she sits up straighter, and what I see turns my blood to ice.

What I thought was merely a shadow around her right eye is a dark purplish-blue bruise. Her bottom lip is bleeding, and her neck...dear gods, her neck.

Much like her eye, angry purple and blue bruises have formed, showing off handprints. He didn't just strangle her —he tortured her over a prolonged period, continuously wrapping his hands around her neck to cut off her breathing.

Erin has lived through hell and survived it, but healing will take time. No one goes through what she has just experienced unscathed.

"He's gone now, Erin, and he won't be coming back." I don't know if that's true. If, by some miracle, he doesn't kill himself by driving drunk in a storm, he will come back. He might apologize and promise it will never happen again, or he might say she deserved it and continue where he left off.

However, if she agrees, I can take her out of here and deliver her to her true mate. The Kraken King. He's expecting her but knows her arrival depends on her willingness and consent to be taken to Mescos.

"I can take you out of here. All you need to do is sign the contract," I say.

Erin just stares at me, lifeless eyes boring into mine. Allarick will not have an easy time with her, but she deserves someone's love and patience.

Just as I think she will not respond, Erin extends a shaky arm and points toward the kitchen. I maneuver my way through the mess on the floor and into the kitchen.

This room is mostly unscathed by the man's terror, but a few broken glasses litter the floor. On the table is a familiar stack of papers. I wander over, my eyes scanning the documents. I flipped to the last page, the most important page in the document.

My eyes dart down to where the signatures should be. Mine and hers. I let out a sigh of relief when I see her handwriting, neatly rounded letters, spelling out her name.

The permission I need to get her out of here.

I fold up the contract, tucking it away in my jacket pocket, before heading back over to her. "Can you walk?"

Erin opens her mouth to speak, but then winces. Judging by the bruises around her neck, her vocal cords must be compromised. Instead, she simply shakes her head.

"Then I shall carry you." I take a step closer, but Erin flinches away. I pause, not wanting to alarm her more.

"It's the only way I can get you out of here and to safety. I'll be gentle. You have my word." I'm virtually a stranger, but I'm her only hope at the moment.

After a moment of consideration, Erin nods at last. She is still shaking when I go to pick her up. I see the extent of her injuries. The bruises don't stop at her neck. They go down to her arms and legs, and if I were a betting man, I would bet they cover her torso too.

She's so small. Frail.

I can't wait to see her blossom into a queen.

"Come, sweet girl. Allarick is waiting." With that, I open the portal and carry the future Kraken Queen to her husband.

To be continued...

WANT MORE?

Want to read about Rip chasing Hettie through the woods as a fun and sexy game of cat and mouse? Make sure to join my newsletter to read all about their night together.

Sign up for my newsletter here or head to Instagram and click the link in my bio.

Also By Tati B. Alvarez

<u>Dawn Of Dasos</u>

1. The Ambrosia Throne

2. The Ambrosia Deception

<u>Grym Hollow</u>

1. The Dragon's Rose

1.5 Tallie's Secret

2. The Wolf's Mate

3. The Kraken's Queen

4. The Demon's Beauty - Coming Soon

THANK YOU FOR READING!

I can't thank you enough for picking up my book. I hope you enjoyed it as much as I enjoyed writing it! If you did and are willing please consider leaving a review on your favorite book sites. This helps out small authors like me so much. Thank you for your continued support!

ABOUT THE AUTHOR

Tati B. Alvarez lives in Austin, Texas with her family. She spends most days lost in her own head, creating stories. When she is not writing, you can find her vacationing at Disney World.